Assessor

Iain Gately was born in 1963 and spent most of his childhood in the Far East. He studied law at Cambridge and has since been occupied in a number of professions ranging from brewing beer to banking. *The Assessor* is his first novel.

GW00888653

IAIN GATELY

The
Assessor

Mandarin

Published in the United Kingdom in 1997 by
Mandarin Paperbacks

1 3 5 7 9 10 8 6 4 2

Copyright © 1996 by Iain Gately

The right of Iain Gately to be identified as the author
of this work has been asserted by him in accordance
with the Copyright, Designs and Patents Act, 1988

This book is sold subject to the condition that it shall not,
by way of trade or otherwise, be lent, resold, hired out,
or otherwise circulated without the publisher's prior consent
in any form of binding or cover other than that in which it is
published and without a similar condition including this
condition being imposed on the subsequent purchaser

First published in the United Kingdom in 1996
by Sinclair-Stevenson

Mandarin Paperbacks
Random House UK Ltd
20 Vauxhall Bridge Road, London SW1V 2SA

Random House Australia (Pty) Limited
20 Alfred Street, Milsons Point, Sydney
New South Wales 2061, Australia

Random House New Zealand Limited
18 Poland Road, Glenfield, Auckland 10, New Zealand

Random House South Africa (Pty) Limited
Endulini, 5a Jubilee Road, Parktown 2193, South Africa

Random House UK Limited Reg. No. 954009

A CIP catalogue record for this book
is available from the British Library

Papers used by Random House UK Limited
are natural, recyclable products made from wood grown in
sustainable forests. The manufacturing processes conform to
the environmental regulations of the country of origin

Printed and bound in Great Britain by
Cox & Wyman Ltd, Reading, Berkshire

ISBN 0 7493 2028 1

Do not despair: one of the thieves was saved.
Do not presume: one of the thieves was damned.

1 The Anatomy Lesson

1 I have lived through the most dangerous century in history. I have observed violence, inhumanity and destruction on a titanic scale; I have seen the birth, and assisted in the overthrow, of repulsive political creeds. I have encountered much in mankind's behaviour that alarms or offends me, but nothing so vile as the pervasive cowardice of late-twentieth-century existence. The concepts of inherent Good and Bad have given way to a latter-day religion of blamelessness. Society has become afraid to judge. People treat their fellow citizens as victims of choice instead of creatures of circumstance. They search for motives to enable them to forgive the actions they should condemn. I am different. I am the founding father of a unique system of character analysis – the discipline of Assessor – and its existence is a direct result of the human need to avoid the truth.

An assessor possesses an unusual status. I am not a lawyer, yet my assessments of an individual's character are accorded the same weight in criminal proceedings as the testimonial of an expert witness. Similarly, I am not a doctor: I do not make appointments with the sick, but my diagnostic methods parallel those used in conventional medical analysis, and my knowledge of anatomy, neurology and reflexes far exceeds that required by the common-or-garden general practitioner. I achieved official recognition for my work as an assessor in 1958, but to explain further I must regress in time:

I was enrolled as a medical student in Guy's Hospital at the outbreak of the Second World War, and interrupted my training to enlist in the RAF. Enough documentation exists of that troubled period to render superfluous an account of my part in the struggle. My place in the conflict was insig-

3

nificant, and carried out at a great distance from the comfortably upholstered seats of power. I flew as a reconnaissance pilot, first in Lysanders, then Mosquitoes, delivering agents and goods, usually by moonlight. I enjoyed a detached view of the battles, drifting above a flesh-and-blood apocalypse in the chill isolation of the night air, until an event occurred which confirmed my bond to my fellow combatants: I was shot down over the Ruhr, and spent the next two years in operating theatres and convalescent homes – not, as I had intended when a student, in the role of healer.

The damage I sustained in my vertebrae and legs was not capable of being cured. I had advanced far enough in my prewar studies to realise that total paralysis was one day inevitable. However, when I was discharged, with pension, at the age of twenty-four, I elected to complete my medical training, a strong sense of gratitude now enforcing my original vocation. Knowing I had only a few years of co-ordination in me, I worked with obsessive speed to qualify as a surgeon. I specialised in the ailments which inflict that most sensitive organ – the brain. Great advances had been made during the 1940s in the treatment of physical wounds. Modern warfare provided a range of injuries capable of satisfying the most blasé surgeon. There were, however, many casualties deemed beyond treatment: the combatants who were physically intact but whose identity had perished. Both soldiers and civilians had been exposed to unforgettable horrors that rendered them incapable of functioning as efficient citizens. Collectively, their afflictions constituted a dark continent – the *terra incognita* of the medical atlas – an area I resolved to explore.

I set my sights high. I realised that the key to healing lay in the establishment of an anatomical explanation for consciousness. Not only was this region unexplored, it was protected by numerous and powerful taboos. After all, consciousness is the key to human existence – the intellectual's Holy Grail. Life itself is no secret; that we are aware is the greater mystery. I wanted to extend the charted science of neurosurgery – that is, the analysis of the brain as a concentration of nerve cells, an organic junction box to receive and direct sensations – to cover an area previously reserved for the mystic babble of psychiatry. Contemporary medicine considered this an impossible aspiration.

When I began my research I was treated with understandable scepticism. However, my peers soon realised I was no ridiculous Frankenstein figure stitching together the severed limbs of strangers in vain attempts at reanimation and I was given the resources to work alone. In addition, and, I admit, to my advantage, the sheer number of humans whose lives had been displaced by the war gave me access to individuals on whom to test my theories. As those needing treatment exceeded the capacity of existing medical facilities, I was granted a freedom to evolve my methods which could not have occurred in any other time. Indeed, it would be impossible to repeat my experiments today, and modern biologists are only now creeping towards the confirmation of my theories as to the structure and function of the brain. On occasions I envy them for their super-computers and electromagnetic scanners. Had I had access to such technologies in the late 1940s, I could have gone so much further. I could have mapped the cortex, documented consciousness, perhaps produced an exact key to all mental functions. I could have been the greatest healer since Jenner, Pasteur, or Alexander Fleming. Even the few experiments I succeeded in concluding broke new ground. Every day, I trembled with the thrill of discovery. It was as if I had been placed alone in an Eden – a fertile garden of supernatural abundance. I felt I was storming heaven with a scalpel blade.

I loved my work. I became obsessed with the rich diversity of tissues contained in the human brain. With care, with affection even, I unfolded cortexes, made tender incisions into the cerebellum. Most of my research was carried out on live patients. It seemed impossible, yet wonderful, to trespass in the chamber of reason of an anaesthetised subject. However, like all temporal idylls, this creative period could

5

not last. At the end of the 1940s my access to live subjects ended abruptly. Almost simultaneously, my co-ordination deteriorated at an accelerating rate, and it was impossible for me to operate within acceptable safety limits. The magic world of tissue became a forbidden kingdom. I was forced to change my methods.

I adjusted my research to focus on the external manifestations of the processes going on within the cranium. It was a period of frustration. Behaviour is a greatly diluted expression of brain function. Hours of patient analysis are required to determine what could be revealed by a single glance through a powerful microscope. Nevertheless, I persisted. You see, in the course of my surgical research, I had chanced upon a discovery in the arrangement of certain neural groups linked to the cerebral cortex. These were invariably arrayed in one of two basic sequences and the specific sequence present in any particular individual had a direct correlation to behaviour. I further discovered that, by applying a series of unusual and powerful stimuli, coupled with exhaustive cross-referencing and rigid controls. I could identify this 'polarity' without recourse to surgery, and that this factor determined whether an individual was good or bad. The discipline of Assessor was born.

I presented the conclusions of my research to the Royal College of Surgeons on 26 January 1953. They were badly received, but no one could refute them. Fortunately, I was indifferent to the ill-informed criticism of my peers and, undeterred, established an independent practice. I was regarded as a maverick throughout the remainder of that decade, but gradually, as the conclusions of my assessments became known – and proved to be accurate – official recognition was bestowed. In one of the myriad law reforms of the 1960s my profession was granted legal status: a qualified assessor's analysis of a criminal may be presented in court, after the jury have reached a verdict, as a 'relevant factor' to be taken into account by the judge when determining sentence. It serves as a statistical measure of the probability of recidivism. A number of statutory safeguards were instituted to ensure that the assessment delivered is objective, free from bias, and has been made without regard to the circumstances under consideration. This is a further aspect in which my profession is unique – an assessment must be undertaken without attaching any weight to the misdemeanour the accused is alleged to have committed. An assessor exists to judge character and character alone. His opinion whether an individual has transgressed, or could be capable of doing so, is not solicited. He is required to determine whether a man is good or bad.

The disciplines I have developed over nearly four decades of practice are intended to ensure that it is impossible for an assessor to reach anything but an objective decision. If the methods are applied stringently, they will dictate the conclusion. That is why a person requires unique talents to become an assessor. Assessors must learn to reduce themselves to mere passive vessels – binary machines who conduct exclusive tests until the foundation of an individual's character is revealed. They cannot allow themselves to take a personal interest in any client – moral, amorous or otherwise. They cannot be swayed by attraction or repulsion, cannot allow themselves to regard their subject as an amiable or distasteful sort of fellow, someone whose company they might welcome, relish, detest, avoid or encourage, let alone question him or her with interest about the state of family or affairs. In short, an assessor is required to see each patient as a machine, just as a surgeon should, and to forget that the part of the machine he is required to analyse is the control mechanism which dictates the actions of the rest.

All my initial subjects were convicted criminals. During the 1960s, this country's apparatus for the administration of justice underwent the greatest revolution since its inception: a move from the punitive approach to the rehabilitative. It was supposed that a tendency to crime was a disease, curable as any other. This was, I presume, an imaginative extension of the great advances that were occurring contemporaneously in medicine: if typhoid can be prevented, why not petty theft? Although the discriminatory nature of my assessments was at odds with the underlying supposition that drove the revolution – namely that no one is born bad – my methods were applied to the mind – the general area of curiosity – and I was right so often that I could not be swept aside as some mad empiricist relic.

My profession's usefulness grew to be widely recognised in the 1970s, when the insurance industry discovered a commercial value for assessments. At that time, it was beginning to be understood that companies are not the 'happy worker' collectives which figure so alluringly in capitalist tracts; rather they are fiefdoms of powerful individuals who use them as tools to compete with each other in the contest rings of the world's financial markets. If such an individual perished, the company would suffer in consequence, so insurance was sought against this eventuality. It is now customary and is known as 'Key Man Insurance'. These days it is industry practice to carry out a preliminary assessment of the insured before underwriting such policies.

When an insurer wishes an executive to be investigated, the assessment is usually disguised as a test for epilepsy. This affliction is acknowledged to be commonplace, hereditary, and difficult to detect, which is why it is necessary to conduct lengthy and rigorous examinations in order to achieve an accurate assessment. In forty years, I have assessed a total of 5,002 individuals, not one of whom has been aware of the precise nature of the tests to which he or she is being subjected. Some of the more intuitive – usually criminals – have come close; the business executives rarely suspect, and, if they do, their vanity is so complete they assume that the rigorous methods employed are a tribute to their individual importance, or result from uncontainable and spontaneous admiration on the Assessor's part.

Six years ago I moved my practice from Harley Street to my house in Elgin Crescent, close to Holland Park. The vicissitudes of the property market had ennobled my home address, and my infirmity had increased to the extent that I was forced to choose either retirement or an alteration in my manner of business. I carry out few assessments now – perhaps one a month of a commercial nature, plus occasional examinations of malefactors, usually on direct request from the Court of Appeal. My methods have not changed: I continue to apply those that were perfected in the early 1950s, although advances in technology, particularly the ones provided by the computer, have simplified the exhaustive cross-referencing processes required. An assessment takes two weeks to complete. It comprises three recorded interviews, a written statement and several applications of unusual stimuli. Each Friday I collate the material gathered in the course of the preceding week, ensure that all control procedures have been observed, then reduce each element to the binary reasoning required to feed the neural networks in the master assessment model on my computer. Once more than 1,000 factors have been cross-referenced, tested and forced to compete, I will know, with absolute certainty, a single truth about the character of my subject.

2 This week I have one patient: Simon N—.

Simon is an interesting subject, or rather, I should say, he is a difficult assessment. The adjective 'interesting' implies a curiosity on the part of the Assessor, which is unacceptable. Assessors are required to be objective at all times, but since they, too, are only human the nature of the examination is structured to remove any residual involvement.

Simon was recruited six months ago as financial director of Mardon Packaging Corporation and Key Man Insurance has been requested. His first interview was held yesterday – a Thursday, as it happens – and, according to my custom, I am collating the results with his statement. The statement is the first formal step in an assessment and resembles an extended curriculum vitae. It is completed by the individual to be assessed, follows a standard pattern, and provides an outline of that person's life from birth to the present day. Its primary function is to enable the Assessor to disregard all circumstantial factors that may have contributed to the formation of the subject's character. For example, if an individual has led a peripatetic life, this could be assumed to have exposed him or her to a variety of conditions, occurrences and opinions in excess of those experienced by a sedentary patient. Such influences must be identified and disregarded. Assumptions are dangerous. The wandering may have been accidental – the result, perhaps, of career moves made by the subject's parents (a father in the armed forces, that sort of thing). In many such cases, the seemingly active patient will have been exposed to a far more limited world than the stay-at-home born to liberal parents. The statement includes a medical report; this serves as a placebo, a device that diverts the subject from the true purposes of the assessment.

Simon N— is five foot ten tall, twelve stone in weight, with heart rate and blood pressure so close to the mean as to be unworthy of comment. From birth until the age of twenty-one, he lived with his parents in Cheam, Surrey. His father was an accountant, his mother a teacher. The years 1976–1979 were spent at Bristol University, where Simon gained an honours degree in economics, class 2.1. He represented his university at golf and tennis – a continuation of his success in these sports at his public school, where he was head prefect. In 1979 Simon joined the accountancy firm of Spicer Pegler. The same year he married Vivienne S— and they bought a flat together in Clapham. He qualified in 1984 and joined the merchant banking firm of Pendle & Co., where he remained for four years, two of which were spent in Tokyo. Simon left the City in 1988 for an appointment in the treasury department of one of the newly privatised industries. In June 1989 he resigned and took up his present position at Mardon Packaging Corporation. After a series of domestic moves he now lives in a detached house near Teddington.

The statement requires the subject to catalogue his current diversions and Simon's are stated as cycling, golf and 'family life'. He has two young children – Hannah (9) and Jennifer (6). The statement concludes with two blank pages on which the subject is invited to write a summary of achievements in the course of his life to date. It carries the caveat that the individual should give equal weight to occurrences in early years; this is intended to prevent repetition of matters covered in the questionnaire portion, and to pinpoint factors which the Assessor will be required to disregard. Simon's handwriting is neat, consistent and legible. He has used an expensive ballpoint pen – Mont Blanc, I think – the two pages are free from blotches. The statement is clear of emendations. It is a fair copy. Margins are regular and the writing ends an inch from the bottom of the second page, leaving space for a signature which is not required. His statement reads as follows:

I am requested to provide a summary of my achievements to date. As some are still ongoing, I have taken the liberty of including these as well, even though I am aware I might be tempting fate. I understand 'achievements' to be things that I have done of which I can be proud. Obviously, some won't seem exceptional.

The first is reading. I have always loved literature, and learnt to read books when I was five. My mother was a teacher, and I owe most of this achievement to her encouragement. Being able to read with ease motivated me in my studies. I think it was this factor that enabled me to keep going through ten years of public exams!

The next was learning golf. Sport is important to me for relaxation. My father gave me lessons when I was ten. It was two years before I played a single hole to par, but I can never forget the feeling of achievement when I bent down to pick up my ball. I think it was on the eighth hole at Sunningdale. My game improved over the years. I had the fortune to represent my school and university. But the first success was undoubtedly the most satisfying.

When I was eighteen I took a year off between leaving school and starting university. I spent six months of it doing VSO in Ghana. Conditions there were, literally, very poor. We lived in tents among the Ghanese and shared their lifestyle. I was responsible for boring wells and controlled a team of ten locals. This experience taught me the importance of co-operation and teamwork. Also, of understanding others, whatever their background. In the next six months I travelled round the world, covering 24,000 miles. I regard this as an achievement as well. I applied the self-discipline I learned at school and managed to get a taste of all the civilisations I had always wanted to see.

12

I have spent the last ten years working in the finance industry. Most of my achievements have occurred in this time. I became computer literate, an important step, I believe, as computers give access to information and information is the currency of the future. I learnt to manage other men. Good management is a combination of encouragement and judgment. I pride myself on never having avoided difficult decisions, even when they have seemed controversial.

Finally, I own my own home, which provides security for the achievement of which I am most proud – my family.

Indeed.

Simon has displayed thought and care in drawing up his achievements. These will be processed and then entered into the master assessment model.

Before the statement is analysed, it is usual to review the video of the subject's first interview. I conduct all interviews in a specially equipped consultation suite on the ground floor of my house. It comprises two rooms, formerly the drawing room and sitting room of a Georgian residence. I have kept the cornicing and fireplaces to promote a formal air. The remainder of the decoration is austere, intended to convey an impression of efficiency – the feel of a laboratory. The video camera begins to record five minutes before each interview is scheduled to commence. Technology allows me to have a timing display in the upper corner of the recording. In the past, I kept a clock on the wall facing the camera. The speed with which an individual responds to interrogation forms a vital part of each assessment.

Simon's first interview took place at four o'clock yesterday afternoon. The video tape of his performance is loaded, my study curtains are drawn: it is time to begin. I lock my wheelchair, face the large-format, high-resolution screen and press PLAY.

Simon N— appears to be a punctual man; just as the

13

timer shows the five-minute test period has elapsed, he is ushered into the room by my receptionist, Miss Younghusband. She is a large, heavy-boned, county woman, with a passion for organisation and a dictatorial air. She has worked in my employ for ten years. She has no real understanding of the exact nature of my profession, but is convinced of the value of her own opinion on each person I assess. She usually attempts to make this known through gestures when she leads them in for their appointment. This is a common, and often vexing, consequence of my occupation: friends and acquaintances – indeed, all of mankind – are forever judging each other and invariably solicit my opinion in the belief that the voice of a professional will assist them in reaching a conclusion as to another's merit. No one is above this sort of behaviour. On every occasion I visit my club it is inevitable that someone of my acquaintance will find time to slip the question 'What do you think of such and such a fellow?' into seemingly casual conversation. It is impossible to escape. I find this obsession with certainty – the need *to know* – perplexing. After all, as modern physics tells us, the world is a random place. Reduce the scale and even matter itself is uncertain – the question 'What was that?' can be parried with 'What was what?' . . .

I digress.

I have not revealed the conclusion of an assessment to any person other than the body by whom it was commissioned. Evasion of the many crude attempts to elicit such information is now a matter of course, and, I must add, effortlessly simple after so many years of practice. In truth, people are such hasty and impatient judges of each other that the significance of an assessment would be of little use to them. They find it impossible to be consistent, frequently damning one man with the same criteria they use to praise another. The key to judgment is objectivity. As I am required to identify then disregard every facet of an individual's character, I learn very quickly, from apparently inconsequential

14

matters and mannerisms, the nature of each subject I examine. Even so, I resist passing judgment.

Back to Simon N—:

The video screen is divided into a grid within which each facial expression displayed by the patient may be isolated, enlarged and analysed. The video camera is in a fixed position, so that the layout of the consultation room is the same in every tape. My desk is situated in the foreground of the picture. Each piece of furniture in the room is clearly spaced to ensure an easy passage for my wheelchair. My head and shoulders are just visible in the centre, at the bottom of the screen – white hair, dark suit jacket. All interviews are recorded in black-and-white to emphasise facial gestures.

Time to concentrate. I press REWIND and the machine spins the tape back to Simon N—'s grand entrance. Black-and-white figures dance together in retrograde motion towards the door, freeze, shimmering, on the screen when I press PAUSE, then recommence human activity on the prompt of the PLAY button.

Thursday, 12 February 1990. Time: 16.00.55.

Mrs Younghusband holds open the door for Simon, beams approvingly over his shoulder in my direction, lingers until she is sure I have acknowledged her, then vanishes as Simon crosses the floor. He wears a two-piece, charcoal suit, a striped shirt and spotted tie. His shoes are American-style loafers. Otherwise the impression is solid, conventional. His broad face is clear of wrinkles and his skin is fresh, which aspects lend a certain boyishness to his appearance – as if he were in his twenties, not his thirties. This is often an indication of retarded emotional capacities. There are thirty-two muscles in the human face, used in complex combinations to register and communicate feelings. Eighteen are needed to create a frown; almost all are involved in the manufacture of a smile. Individuals prone to an excess of emotion usually display this trait through the advanced development of the muscles in their face. That is why seamed and wrinkled faces incite interest. It is a curious paradox that insipid, flawless visages are chosen to adorn modern magazine covers and advertisements. These would have been disturbing to our ancestors, who associated such images with fools. A serene face in a common man was considered proof of subnormal intellect.

Simon N— frowns at the camera when he notices my wheelchair. He collects himself quickly, however, smiles easily, we exchange introductory pleasantries and Simon extends his hand across my desk towards the camera. I remember its touch: light, dry and quite powerful for an individual in a sedentary occupation. It was a tactile confirmation of the first impression his appearance created – an agreeable, self-confident young man. On film, I motion for him to be seated and he unbuttons his suit jacket before drawing up a chair.

Interview procedures are perhaps the most difficult assessment techniques to master. The subject must be directed into certain standard behavioural patterns in order that his reflexiveness (a technical term) can be measured. Reflexiveness is the speed and strength of an individual's instinctive responses to a predetermined set of criteria. You see, a person's behaviour is the sum of two forces: Nature and Nurture, which is to say instinct and conditioning. By 'instinct', I mean hereditary patterns of conduct; by 'conditioning', those mannerisms a person has acquired. It is necessary for an assessor to be able to identify which is master when an individual acts. This is a complicated process. In some men, instinct is weak and manners govern all their actions. In others, instinct speaks through even their most formal conduct. For instance: the behavioural pattern known as 'generosity', or 'altruism', is absent in approximately 60 per cent of mankind. Far from being innate, it is a manner of behaviour which might need to be studied and mastered. Altruism originated, and I apologise for the colloquialism, as 'herd instinct' – a survival mechanism that dictated the sacrifice of the individual for the good of his kin group. It is the cornerstone of co-operative existence; hence those in

16

whom the genetic characteristic is absent learn to imitate – to manufacture the responses associated with the emotion. It is the Assessor's duty to uncover such artifices.

I usually begin each interview with an explanation of the course of examinations the subject is to undergo. Simon believes he is being tested for epilepsy, and his image smiles as he makes an allusion to the dangers of a seizure at the conference table. Our *Doppelgängers* play with the idea together for a few sentences:

'I hate to make fun of it, but a fit could have passed unnoticed at one of my previous employers',' Simon says.

'Indeed? I understood dignified self-restraint was *de rigueur* in the world of corporate finance.'

'It was until Big Bang.'

'Big bang?'

'Deregulation, in 1986. Merchant banks bought out the stockbrokers, then the Americans stepped in and bought out the merchant banks.'

'Who bought the Americans?'

'The Japanese. They're at the top of every corporate food chain.'

'I'm pleased to hear that this country's financial institutions are in such capable hands.'

'Capable?' Simon repeats my word and frowns. 'Capable, I'm not so sure, but they're certainly careful, especially with their employees.'

'You must be expensive toys.'

Miss Younghusband has prepared a transcript of our conversation, and I correct it as I view the video. She has an irritating habit of placing punctuation marks in brackets – such as (!) or (??) – after certain statements. She cannot play chess, so I presume these are intended to convey her own feelings as to the character of the subject.

The initial interrogation of any patient includes a standard set of questions which generate data for the primary string in the master assessment model. These questions relate to animals. It is accepted wisdom that innate fear of predators

17

can trigger involuntary responses of panic which are the basis of epileptic fits. The true purpose of the questions is to detect whether the subject is an instinctive or conditioned altruist. Collectively, the questions comprise a test, which measures the subject's humanity. The test is based on the following reasoning. Those who are born with compassion reserve the emotion for humans. They will respond to human needs subjectively, and those of any other species objectively. They are attentive to animals' physical welfare but, unlike individuals who are born without altruism, will not cloak their actions with appeals to sentiment. The defectives, however, since they are applying a set of responses that results from conditioning, will attribute virtues to animals which are clearly nonexistent – they lock into compassion mode just as if a button has been pressed to set the machine rolling, and the counterfeit emotion is thus exposed.

Simon is relaxed and confident when he speaks. He crosses his legs, leans back in his chair, and answers all my questions fluently. He rarely hesitates before he replies.

An impressive young man.

He displays the self-possession typical of an only child. We are chatting about his medical history, when a control string is triggered. I stop the video, rewind and observe again:

'You seem to be blessed with a remarkably healthy constitution.' (My voice sounds curiously expressionless when recorded. In the past I attributed this to the quality of the equipment.)

'It runs in the family, Sir Charles.' Simon laughs off the compliment. 'If anything, it's been diluted. I'm a weakling in comparison with my parents. My father's the sort of man who never even catches a cold.'

'What about sports injuries? Your statement proves you to be a keen competitor.'

'The usual list [he smiles again], but nothing serious. A few broken fingers on the hockey pitch. Side strain from too much tennis. You know how it is.' He checks himself and looks embarrassed. He has remembered my evident physical limitations.

'War wounds,' I tell him and he frowns, briefly, then the habitual polite smile reappears. I think he is angry with himself for appearing insensitive. I am used to it. After an appropriate silence, I ask him: 'What about allergies?'

Simon hesitates before he replies. His voice is awkward when he speaks. 'It seems ridiculous, Sir Charles, but in fact I do have one – horses.'

I wave my hand to put him at ease. 'No need to feel embarrassed. It's very common. Some were born to ride, others to walk.'

Freeze frame. Square F2. The corner of his mouth. I feed commands into my computer and expand that area of the screen. There it is: plainly visible. A slight compression of the lips. A gesture which originated as an imitation of a sour taste, used by *Homo sapiens* to communicate displeasure. Simon did not enjoy the discriminatory implications of my last statement. The knowledge that others may ride while he must walk puts him at a disadvantage. He is not content to allow them a pleasure he cannot share.

Play.

'Thank God for Henry Ford,' he says.

'Or, at very least, George Stephenson,' I riposte, and we laugh together.

It is easy to discover the matters that each individual considers amusing. What is known as a sense of humour follows one of three basic patterns: cruel, ribald or surreal. It is vital that the Assessor can demonstrate empathy and so put his subject at ease. The most effective method to achieve this aim is by identifying the dominant element in their 'sense of humour' and playing to it.

'How are you finding your new employers? I'm sure it must be quite a challenge.'

'It is. I was privileged to be chosen as part of a new management team and I'm fighting to get hands-on experience. Mardon is larger than anything I'm used to and it's

19

growing all the time. Our capital expenditure programme alone is nearly two hundred million, and as for the capital markets programme . . .' He waves a hand. Perhaps Simon thinks he is blinding me with science. 'You see, Sir Charles, in the past I've always been on the other side of the fence, and it's interesting to be a client for a change.'

'I know what you mean. I feel the same each time I visit the doctor.'

'Of course!' – he smiles, pleased with the analogy – 'but I enjoy the work. Industry is quite formal – people want to know you, want to trust you, before they'll do business – which, I admit, I like. It's so much less ephemeral when you're working with people who really make things, like biscuits or tractors, than it was in the City, where they get their money in a sort of glorified game of pass-the-parcel. Besides, Mardon is famous for its strong sense of identity – its *esprit de corps*. The company is nearly a hundred years old and traditions and loyalties run strong. This is my first opportunity to run my team and I have to be sure I'm speaking the right language to everyone on it.'

'I'll buy some shares for my pension account.'

'Don't take my advice,' Simon replies, pleased that I appear to have a high opinion of his employer.

'Your headquarters are in Berkeley Square, aren't they?' I ask him.

'That's right. It's one of the benefits of a move into commuting. As well as the easier hours. The City was such a hike. Nowadays, I get an extra hour in bed. Sadly, it doesn't translate into extra sleep. My daughters are at that age when their greatest delight in the world is chasing parents.'

'That's a pleasure, Simon, I've never shared – though at my age, and with my temper, I think it would be hard to tolerate, at least before breakfast.'

'Nonsense! I can't believe I'd ever tire of them! Sometimes it seems a shame they have to grow up at all. But then, each year I love them more. My children are just fabulous – my life's greatest blessing. When Hannah was born it added an extra dimension, which I never knew might exist.'

There is an edge in Simon's voice which betrays the genuine emotion behind this statement. It is a common obsession. I was injured before I had the chance to marry, and in such a way as to preclude any progenitive opportunities. Like Simon, I was an only child, so lack the consolation of proxies – nephews and nieces on whom to lavish attention and gifts. My experience of offspring is therefore very limited. However, paternal affection is a dangerous obsession. Children, like animals, are used by their parents either as rubbing posts on which to discharge frustration or as blameless causes to defend. Adults advance the interests of their offspring as a Trojan horse in which their own fears are hidden – 'It's not me I'm worried about, it's little James/Juliet,' et cetera, et cetera, *ad nauseam*.

'I suppose you're already considering schools?'

'We've talked about it. But the idea of sending Hannah off, even though it's one or two years away, is quite distressing. I'm not sure I believe in the value of boarding school any more. I went, of course, as did Vivienne. In those days everyone did. I think that then the road to becoming an adult was so well defined, so leisurely, that the separation involved wasn't seen as a bad thing. But now that children become aware so much more quickly, a sacrifice to convention of those few short years of youth seems unfair. In the end it'll depend on them – on what they want.'

Something in Simon's expression catches my attention and I depress the FREEZE-FRAME button. I expand the section of the screen that contains his face until I detect the anomaly. There it is: in his eyes. Instructions are fed to my computer and their focal point is determined to be five yards distant – in other words, beyond me, the individual whom Simon is addressing. This trance-like state indicates that the subject has relaxed his natural vigilance. It is associated with love, an emotion prompted by recollection of his children. This is unusual. Obsession is a common emotion – think of magpies – but love itself is rare. I encounter it, at best, in 12 per cent of adult subjects.

I take notes, then depress the PLAY button.

'Simon, I'm going to show you some pictures of animals.'

'I suppose you want me to identify with one of them?'

'No. I'm not a psychologist. Why do you ask?'

Simon hesitates, unsure, then his training catches up with him and words rush out to fill the silence he has created. 'They used to form part of the interview process at Pendle's. We tried to recruit proactive trainees. Our American parent company believed that that sort always chose predators. I didn't hold any faith in it. Everyone I interviewed chose the wolf or hawk. No one wanted to be the cow.'

'Feel free to identify, if you please. I recommend the tiger. The one I'm going to show you looks particularly fierce.'

Simon is smiling at me, arms folded across his chest. He is enjoying himself, and as one accustomed to good health and a quick intellect he is willing to indulge the quirks of a 'specialist' searching for something he knows he doesn't have.

The pictures are kept in a folder in my third drawer. I remove the folder and place it, unopened, on the table between us. I indicate a small steel plate on the edge of the desk. 'Simon, this is a reflex test, which requires me to monitor your heartbeat. You see the plate by your left hand?'

'Here?'

'Yes. I need you to place your wrist on it while I complete the test. It measures pulse rates.'

Some subjects are nervous when I explain the purpose of the plate: they think that I'm trying to electrocute them, or else they are afraid that their heart might race out of control and divulge dark secrets they have dedicated their existence towards concealing. Simon doesn't care. He removes a cuff link, rolls up his sleeve, and places his wrist across the plate. As he does so, a column display appears in the right-hand corner of my VDU: sixty-eight beats per minute – quite low

22

for an executive in his position – a welcome sight to any doctor's eyes.

I unclip the wallet and hand him the first picture – a twelve-by-eight photograph of two white kittens on a red satin background. The soft texture of their fur and the liquid trust in their shining eyes dominate the composition.

Simon shrugs his shoulders and hands it back. 'Not my taste,' he says: 'too sentimental. The sort of thing maiden aunts send to nieces with one of those silly poems inside. Mardon has a subsidiary that makes them – quite a profitable line.'

Good. His pulse is consistent with his words. He's right, of course. The photograph is a hideous mess of sentiment.

'What about this?'

The next is a pack of hounds in full cry on a fine November morning. There is light mist on the ground among them. Their intent and concentration are evident.

'The picture appeals, but I don't approve of hunting.'

Simon is very quick. His instinctive response is immediately qualified by the rational – kittens and his employer's interests, predators at work and a moral judgment.

The tiger comes next, photographed in the verdant forest, in the act of disembowelling a water buffalo.

Simon studies intently, then raises his head. 'That's a great photograph. Is it Bailey?'

His pulse reading has remained alarmingly flat.

'I should think so,' I reply. 'It helps to justify my fees.'

The final picture is of an old horse, tethered and unsteady.

'That won't win the Derby,' he says, and laughs, pleased with his pedestrian wit. He's wrong – it did. The horse is Starlight Dancer, twenty-one years old and blind. Two handfuls of his semen are worth a million pounds. I don't expect my subjects to recognise the aged champion. This picture exists as a control. Alone in the series it is a combination test, which assists in determining the balance between instinct and conditioning. The remainder measure instinct only, as follows:

23

Kittens provoke curiosity – What is it? Can I eat it? – although, occasionally, they inspire protective leanings.

The hounds stimulate exhilaration – trigger the hunting instinct, also friendship, stemming from symbiosis.

The tiger generates fear and torpor – fear because it is an enemy, torpor because it feeds, and therefore, for the present, the observer is safe.

There have been so many years, so many generations, since the animals in the test presented real danger or challenge to *Homo sapiens* that the reactions they provoke are generally very mild – vestigial reflexes that require amplification. This area was a weak point in early assessments. Available equipment was insensitive, and I was forced to resort to cruder methods involving complex surgery. The tests are nevertheless vital to the success of an assessment. The access point to an individual's true psyche lies upon the dividing line between conditioning and instinct – sea and shore, if you like – conscious and unconscious behaviour.

My screen identity is stacking the cards to return them to their wallet. The edges quiver, exaggerating the shake in my fingertips. Simon notices this: his eyes rest briefly on my hands before flicking back to my face. A smile plays at the corner of his mouth. It appears he is pleased to have detected an indication of human frailty.

I stop the tape and turn up the lights in my study. Nowadays I seldom work past six o'clock. It requires intense concentration to observe and manipulate another human without suffering some emotional response. The Assessor needs empathy to draw his subject forth, but simultaneously he must hold his rational faculties aloof – in particular when analysing the results of interviews, where his role changes from *provocateur* to processor. Fortunately, the profession is no longer as physically demanding as it was in its infancy. The computer does the legwork. Time to load up the muscle-structure programme and retire. When I recommence tomorrow morning, perhaps a hundred sheets of paper will fill the printer tray: a catalogue of the movements of individual muscles in Simon's face on a frame-by-frame basis – from the contraction of each iris to the vertical, lateral and oblique movements of both lips – coupled, where appropriate, with pulse readings. It will constitute a comprehensive record of his reflexes in response to chosen stimuli. The assessment will proceed further, but it is a relief to know that I have already penetrated beneath his skin.

3 Winter is a season of vigilance – a sequence of three predator months which feed on the elderly. The chill air exposes weaknesses in our faltering metabolism. It reaches out a dry, dead hand to desiccate marrow within plaster-of-Paris brittle bones. Under its malign aspect, the crowd of microscopic scavengers – the host of human-specific diseases – grows closer and more daring.

Last year, when I diagnosed the shocks of pain in my skeleton as cancer, the despair resulting from the discovery of yet another flaw in my wretched body led me to contemplate suicide. This is not an unusual sentiment among the elderly; however, like so many of our thoughts and actions, it is effected without melodrama. We do not seek destruction but release. This is why most people choose their death, the day, the hour; it becomes the irresistible compromise: the performance is over. The theatre lights come up and it is time to leave, perhaps still dazed by the excess of emotions enacted on-stage. All that remains is to take the quiet exit on to an empty street.

I have been old for nearly fifty years. My wartime injuries terminated natural passion. At medical college in the 1930s I was considered very strong. I belonged to the hospital boxing team, and stroked the Vespa First Eight. It astonishes me to recall how quickly that vitality was extinguished. On 14 January 1943, I was six foot one, weighed twelve stone, and could run a mile in four and a half minutes. Two years later, when I emerged from a final rehabilitation clinic, I had lost three inches in height, and it was a struggle to limp to the kerbside to hail a taxi. There were compensations. I was born a fatalist. I knew at once there was no way to roll back the years. Besides, my handicap gave me a professional advantage: I had been through the devastation caused by a collapse in physical capacity, seen the commonplace pleasures of average health placed beyond my reach, so I recognised the frustration of the stupid, physical criminal subjects I assessed and condemned to incarceration. At times I was driven to sympathy. I had rejoined humanity as a different class of citizen, and for the first time in my life I understood the weak instead of hating them. Paralysis made me objective. I discovered the bogus values society employs to elevate its favourites.

It amused me then; it amuses me still. There is a wonderful pathos in the persistence of worship of physical appearance. Surely, in an age when the armed pygmy can vanquish a naked Hercules, intelligence should be the only genetic trait to attract respect? After all, intelligence is a physical attribute, as simple to determine (to the intelligent) as height or girth or pigmentation. Regrettably, it is not revered. Beauty wins regardless. The population continues to select and does so by the most nebulous criteria imaginable.

Never mind. Perhaps, as millenniums roll by, *Homo sapiens* will divide into two new species: one beautiful, to be adored, one intelligent, to understand and to forgive.

I digress.

It is my custom to begin work each day with research. This exercise occupies a significant proportion of my professional hours. It is an assessor's paramount duty to disregard the character of each subject. Paradoxically, in order to fulfil this requirement, the character first must be identified and comprehended, so that it may be discarded entire. Therefore an assessor must keep up with the times. He needs to study demographics, to be *au fait* (as the Europhiles in the ruling class might say) with the *Zeitgeist* – the spirit of the age. Consequently, an assessor's research is general. It seeks out race movements instead of hemlines. Humanity changes at a speed that would astonish its individual members. A behavioural pattern that has existed unaltered for a thousand years can vanish overnight – taboo become *de rigueur*. An assessor must be aware of these mutations in order that he may interpret each of his subjects' responses correctly. An example:

The open avarice displayed by many of the young men I assess would have been a rarity in my initial years of practice. In those days, British citizens were conditioned to regard greed as evil. The role models they were provided by the state and media reinforced this view. Popular entertainments and government propaganda advocated thrift and a sense of duty. Even advertisements appealed to duty in order to prompt the consumer into purchase. Nowadays, goods are sold on an exclusion basis. An individual is made to feel incomplete, or the victim of unequal treatment, unless he possesses certain branded products. This is a perpetuation of the child's cry 'It's not fair'.

The phrase does not, of course, represent a demand for equitable distribution. It is an expression of the fear that another individual may receive more than the complainant – for if it is impossible to have it all it is better to ensure that no one else is preferred.

I restrict my research to mass-circulation media. This has been created to reflect, as far as possible, universal opinion. It concentrates on expressing sentiment – feeling, if you like. Most individuals are more likely to respond to feeling than to thought. Specialist journals which target a smaller sector of society are close to useless for my professional requirements. It is a ridiculous but common misconception that change results from the agitations of an enlightened few. Dogs bark and the caravan moves on.

You see, true change requires a critical mass. Discontent must spread until it touches each heart with irresistible conviction. Then, and only then, will the crowd speak with a single voice. During my seventy-three years of conscious life, despite the variety and turmoil that have afflicted mankind within the same period I have encountered this collective eloquence but once: last year, upon the dismantlement of the Berlin Wall. When I close my eyes I can see the crowds and hear them chant: 'If not now, then when? If not us, then who?'

Indeed.

Weekends hold little significance for me. My consulting rooms are closed but the two days provide vital time for analysis and research. I rise, as usual, at seven o'clock. It takes me two hours to bathe and dress myself. I have resisted retaining a personal assistant – the illusion of independence is important. From Monday to Friday Miss Younghusband prepares all material necessary for the day's work and it is waiting by my desk in the consulting room when I descend by elevator at nine. Today, as is her custom, she has vanished to the depths of the shires and I sort documents myself. Simon N—'s reconstruction has been completed by the computer overnight. I wheel myself to the printer trays and remove the data. The analytical equipment I possess would be the envy of all but two universities in this country. I have been a master of computer technology since its inception. Its processing powers compensate for my reduced natural faculties.

The anatomy programme I use for reflexiveness tests extracts data from the video images to generate a reconstruction of the muscle groups beneath the skin on a subject's face. As I suspected, Simon's flayed visage demonstrates no unusual development. The Fluvifex cartum are the most prominent muscles, which indicate a gentle smile to be his usual expression. In cases such as this, the model is programmed to provide separate enlargements of each muscle group when in motion, to facilitate analysis.

I am in the middle of executing a complex series of commands to achieve this end, when the telephone rings in my study. On weekdays Miss Younghusband vets all calls. If I have no wish to return them in person, she is instructed to determine the caller's purpose and to relay the appropriate response. On Saturdays I am reduced to answering the instrument myself. It is an unwelcome distraction. I engage the speaker and the soft sweet tones of my goddaughter fill the room.

'Uncle Charles? It's Lydia, Lydia Markham.'

'Good morning, Lydia. What can I do for you?'

My relationship with Lydia results from my acquaintance with her late father. James Markham was a childhood friend, of equal years, who was my closest companion through school and medical college. He was instrumental in assisting my recovery and provided invaluable encouragement throughout my initial research. He married in 1957 and had one child. When he contracted cirrhosis of the liver in 1969 I was appointed Lydia's guardian. I supervised her education after James died and continue to administer her trust fund. Regrettably, she did not inherit the noble bearing and generosity of spirit which characterised her father. Lydia discovered at an early age the power that a short skirt and a good pair of legs can wield over the male sex. As an infant, she colonised the laps of older men. Lydia's guardianship became an increasing burden from her thirteenth birthday – threatened, in truth, to be an intolerable distraction, until fortune threw me a lifeline by placing in her path a man of equally intemperate nature with whom she fell in love and married. His wild character acted to suppress her own, functioning in the same manner, I suppose, as the stimulants dispensed to quieten hyperactive individuals – the combination of two extremes resulting in stability.

Throughout Lydia's youth, the sole reason for instigating communication on her part was to seek money or assistance in extrication from trouble. Our relationship has improved since her marriage, to the extent that, on occasions, I welcome her company.

Her low, musical laugh now fills the room.

'As circumspect as ever, Uncle Charles – trust you to beat around the bush! "What can I do for you?" Why, I might not want a thing!'

At this I cough. I am fond of Lydia, but my affection does not blind me to her true nature.

'As a matter of fact, I do want something, but it's not . . . Oh damn!'

I detect the sound of splashing water.

'Damn! I'm calling from the bath and I've lost the soap. Where d'you think I should look?'

'How's Andrew?' Time to change the subject. Lydia has a tendency towards the provocative, even when it is inappropriate. Besides, there is genuine interest to support my enquiry. I regard Andrew Bruton, Lydia's husband, as a friend.

'He's . . .' She pauses and her tone alters; the cheerful confidence subsides. 'To tell the truth, that's why I called.'

'Is he still working?'

'No.' She sighs. 'It's hard to talk about this, but I suppose you'll find out anyway, unless you already know. Actually, I'd like you to see him. Promise me you will? He respects you, and if you speak to him he'll listen.'

'Of course, Lydia. You know I welcome Andrew's company. The only cause for complaint I may have relating to his visits is their infrequency.'

The rebuke passes unnoticed. It is not in Lydia's nature to acknowledge criticism. She flies from passion to passion, instant heaven to instant hell. But she is always happy when her wishes are met with concurrence.

'You sweetheart! You radiant old saint! I'll send him round at once.'

I can hear splashing as she rises.

'Please don't. I can spare some time tomorrow.'

'This evening?'

'Tomorrow at one o'clock.'

'Oh well, that will do . . . I mean, that's fine! Perfect! Magnificent!'

The bath is unplugged and the noise of turbulent water flies around my study.

'I'm rushing off right now to tell him. Thank you! Have as many kisses as you care! Will a hundred be enough?'

31

And Lydia is gone. The speaker amplifies the interference on the empty line, the whispers of infinity.

The girl is poor at conveying accurate information. She must dismay other telephone correspondents. Her breathless conversation hints at everything, reveals nothing. What is wrong with Andrew? Has he discovered yet another pretext for confrontation with society? I believe he has exhausted the conventional channels of protest, including drink, drugs, door-to-door sales and loose women.

I push the question aside. Speculation is a fruitless occupation. People waste their lives in the dissection of what might have been, what might be. I will find out from Andrew when he calls on me.

My profession is a hard discipline. I cannot afford to be distracted further from my morning's work. I switch the telephone relay to the answering circuit in the consultation suite. Miss Younghusband will sort any calls when she returns on Monday. It is time to return to Simon N—: time to resume the anatomy lesson.

Young Simon appears natural and easy-going, but he is a highly conditioned individual. His extended education, coupled with his successes at organised sport, indicates that he has taken few decisions in his thirty-five years. Most of his life has been dedicated to fulfilling others' expectations. Such responsibility rarely engenders independence of thought – it forces an individual to occupy his faculties with applying someone else's regulations. Head prefect, captain of tennis, secretary of his university debating and golfing societies, ten years as a salaryman . . . Poor Simon!

Please do not consider me a cynic. Cynicism is a luxury I cannot afford. I have examined so much of humanity over the last forty years that surprises are rare. After all, I am not required to provide Simon N— with a simple character reference. I have been employed by a third party to peer into his psyche, to dissect his soul. His material and social achievements are irrelevant. My assessment exists to assist an insurance company to underwrite risk – if Simon N— is pushed, which way will he fall?

Simon's responses in the course of the first interview were complex. His reaction to the picture of the decrepit horse was of particular interest.

Question: Does the subject have religious leanings?

I re-examine his statement and none are evident. He gives his faith as Church of England and his sporadic interest in charitable work suggests humanitarian motivation: he is prompted by concern about physical wellbeing, as opposed to a wish to save his own, or someone else's, soul.

It appears that the data is inconclusive – in other words, incapable of simplification into the binary logic that the assessment programme demands. This happens from time to time and necessitates adjusting future interviews. At the next session I will not play at being Simon's friend.

Perhaps a re-examination of minutes twelve to fifteen of the first interview may remove doubt?

I depress the POWER ON switch to my computer and boot up.

As the mainframe searches for the data, I compose my thoughts and adjust my breathing to assist in clearing my mind. Young people might term this exercise 'meditation' – a ridiculous mystic synonym for self-control. The pattern I prefer is Tantric, although its rhythm is similar to the cyclical pattern of Gregorian chant; whatever, what's in a creed? Religion is the spit that enables us to swallow the grosser morsels of collective living. Meditation methods of all principal religions seek to achieve the same psychosomatic effect, then misapply it in nonsensical searches for abstract deities. I need hardly point out that this is very foolish.

Two bleeps: the search has been completed.

I feed in ACTIVATE instructions and key RETURN. The spirit images materialise on screen: Thursday, 12 February 1990. Time: 16.13.42.

'Tell me more about your year off. That's what you young men call it, isn't it?'

33

'No fits, I'm afraid, Sir Charles.' Simon smiles and waits for me to return the gesture before continuing. 'It was great, really wonderful . . . I sometimes wish I could spend all my time the same way – you know, enjoying the freedom to travel, to explore. Mind you, I've plans to do it again – perhaps in four or five years, when the kids are old enough to come with us.'

'But, in the interim, you must dedicate your time to work?'

'Exactly.' A flash of understanding. 'I hate to talk about responsibilities, but [and here Simon shrugs his shoulders, then leans back and smiles] that's the way it is. I suppose I could always have chosen a less demanding career.' He pauses; his eyes flick up to mine and wait for me to signify I understand. Two point three two seconds pass on the timer clock, then the faint creases in his brow dissolve and he continues: 'Still, you never know. What I saw in just that one year gave me a taste for adventure.'

Damn. Two point three two seconds! My synapses must be disintegrating. It is vital to convince the subject that his opinions are agreed with and understood. He must perceive the Assessor as a benign and sympathetic presence for the course of the first interview. Hesitation, even in the case of serial killers and their tedious 'you-should-have-seen-the-blood/heard-the-screams' insistence on confession to anyone who will listen, can destroy the balance of an assessment.

On screen, Simon continues talking. His youthful face wears an earnest expression. He raises his fine, well-defined eyebrows – an indication he is convinced of my attention.

'But work is important to me. You don't need a crystal ball to see that. Of course, a number of my friends don't have the same point of view. They drift from place to place and talk about "freedom". But it seems to me that freedom is something I have and they don't. I choose to work, but have the freedom – the financial freedom, the real freedom – to leave. You see, Sir Charles, I've been lucky. It seems I've always been in the right place at the right time. I was given equity in Pendle's six months before the Americans

34

bought us out. I arrived and invested in Tokyo literally the week before the market took off. So I suppose I don't need to work for money any more.'

Simon pops his chin on to his hand and pauses to look thoughtful.

'Anyway,' he continued, 'my personal life has been the same. Vivienne is wonderful. The children have inherited the old ancestral health. Nothing in my life gives me cause for complaint.'

'You almost sound as if you'd welcome some.'

'What? No! Of course not! I think when I was single I used to wish I had that sort of challenge. Not any more. You see, it's not just me I have to worry about. I suppose it might be possible to wish some sort of biblical-style trial on my head, but, frankly, it would end up involving my family as well. I'm just going to pray my luck continues, touch wood, and, if it doesn't, hope I have the strength to bear through to better times. I would hate it if I caused something evil to happen to my children. I don't think I could live with myself. The sense of failure would be too great. I know that many people stand up to day-to-day difficulties that I've never encountered. And I admire them.' Simon ends his homily with a discreet nod in the direction of my wheelchair.

How puzzling! Despite the even course Simon has charted through the years, he appears to be prompted by emotional impulse – he honestly loves his family! For many subjects, this would be a real handicap. Emotion troubles mankind – teases otherwise stable individuals into acts of madness. They surrender to the value systems of the primitive brain. In Empire days it was called 'Going native' . . .

Enough. I am beginning to judge the man. Every year, the burden of accumulated knowledge increases. A conviction of futility is enlightenment's twin. I know so much about humanity that every time a person speaks I am tempted to condemn him. There are no revelations in Simon's words. When his sentences are dissected, it is clear that vanity prompted his monologue. He feels no need to confess;

35

rather, he wishes to provoke envy through a eulogy of his privileged state.

I've had enough of Simon N— for this morning. I feed the TERMINATE command to my computer and its screen dies. As my eyes adjust to accommodate the absence of visual stimuli I experience a mild hallucination: a faint negative image of Simon's sly, youthful face hovers on the blank screen. When I blink it vanishes.

Curious.

Two hours spent calculating divergence strings suffice to restore my equilibrium. It is impossible to explain how difficult it is to remain objective. I am, after all, in flesh-and-blood terms, an isolated old man, to whom every other subject could be said to resemble the son I always wanted: idealistic achievers, flushed with good health and material success. When Lydia, my goddaughter, married Andrew, such dim longings were suppressed for a time. But now Andrew seems to seek to surpass her in intemperance, and the animal need for my own son, the survival imperative to have procreated, reappears. It is an unwelcome, mocking vision – the ghost of an instinct – a goat's head floating in the subconscious soup of images.

Fortunately, the extreme dedication my profession demands fully engages even the most sentimental of minds. The conclusion of an assessment must be objective. If I assess Simon N— as bad, this will damage an otherwise flawless career. His insurance premium will be high and the covenants in his bankers' underwriting agreement unduly restrictive. If the conclusion is good, no impediment will result. Simon will remember our interviews with amusement – regale his friends with tales of the strange old man who once gave him epilepsy tests, and perhaps illustrate his account with rolling eyes and jerking frame, or mimic my oddly mechanical gestures.

It may appear unjust that my verdict can so influence an individual's career. After all, it derives from no more than a series of meetings with a stranger, supported by a spurious premise for examination. I content myself with the knowledge that my methods are fastidious, and that the consequences of the assessment are no greater than those of the umpteen other desultory interviews a man must face whose arbitrary conclusions will dictate his destiny.

At noon, as is my custom, I stop work and turn my attention to reading for an hour. Material for perusal in this period is chosen to appeal to me, Sir Charles Barrington, as an individual. It is seldom of professional interest. On Saturdays, I read *The Times*, the *Guardian*, the *Chronicle* and the *Spectator* and compose letters to each. I use five different pseudonyms. Publication affords a source of amusement. I have to change my identities from time to time: the various styles I employ last a maximum of four years. By the end of the period the readership's moods have changed so much that publication in yesterday's prose would be improbable. Occasionally, I am able to recycle. The correspondence of Mr Jenkins, of 12 Albemarle Street, W1, which graced the letter columns of *The Times* in the late 1950s, now finds new life under the *nom de plume* of Roger Bidham, Camden social worker, in the pages of the *Guardian*.

This is a trivial diversion, but pleasing none the less. Hindsight is one of the rare privileges that old age and a deprived existence can confer. It amuses me to observe the reappearance of certain elements of the behavioural cycle. For human behaviour is cyclical. The patterns are inevitably repeated. Each generation strives to commit 'the oldest sins the newest kind of ways'. The cycle, however, is very long. It did not become apparent to me until I had been in practice for thirty-five years – the equivalent of over a generation. A comparison: Hold your face close to a piece of patterned silk and the design will not be visible. Remove it six inches, then a foot, and as distance increases the governing order of the plan is revealed. And in real life, time is a measure of distance. Few individuals live long enough to observe the entire cycle of human behaviour. Those who do are subject to depression. However, once sections become apparent, it is perhaps possible to extrapolate and to predict the pattern of the whole.

It is my habit to give my full attention to every article in the newspapers. The mass of useful information they contain is usually secreted in small columns far from the controlled hysteria of the banner headlines. Indeed, the only item I ignore is the crossword puzzle. This I consider too pedantic to merit adult attention.

I am halfway through my favourite paper – the *Chronicle* – when an article catches my eye: MARDON ON THE WARPATH, says the headline.

Damn! It seems impossible to avoid Simon N— today.

A hostile takeover of a manufacturing company is rumoured, and Mardon Packaging Corporation, his employer, has been named as the predator. I rarely take an interest in my subjects' paymasters. They are, after all, irrelevant to the assessment. At the same time, I do not seek to frustrate innate curiosity by closing my eyes to information the world throws in my path. And the behaviour of Mardon, the corporate individual, is fascinating. I think I will do some research. I have access to the Infotext database through my computer modem. This is a facility I use to manage my own portfolio. It is an efficient service and painless to interrogate, as, having been designed for executive operators, it takes for granted a low boredom threshold. A few key presses suffice to select a general search into the company's affairs over the past three years and, within minutes, material collects in the printer tray.

It appears that Mardon has undergone what my salaryman subjects would describe as a 'change of corporate identity' in the past eighteen months. The company has 'trimmed its cost base' and assumed a 'proactive expansionist stance'.

Indeed.

The poverty of the vocabulary of participants in the financial analysis industry is a perennial source of amusement. Precise use of language appears to be anathema and grown men resort to childish phrases to express complex strategies involving thousands of workers and millions of pounds. Perhaps this is fitting. The fundamental stimuli that drive such machinations – fear and greed – are very simple instincts which do not require eloquence to portray.

It seems from the data that Mardon, an established manufacturer of durable goods, is being used as a vehicle for the accumulation of other companies by one Donald Fletcher, who assumed *de facto* control of Mardon itself just under two years ago. Since then, Mardon's turnover has doubled, its debt–equity ratio tripled, and significant changes in operations and management have been made. The original toolmaking business, on which the company was founded and which carries the famous 'Magnus' brand, has been sold to a management buy-out. Meanwhile, packaging businesses have been purchased on the Continent and in the United States. This expansion has been funded by an issue of preferred shares and significant increases in borrowing.

So! Simon N— works for a predator! This knowledge sheds new light on his move from the cut-and-thrust business of merchant banking to the leisurely environment of a corporate treasury department. Traditionally, this sort of step is considered a 'sell-out' (to borrow a recognised financial term) in favour of an easier way of life with shorter hours, greater job security and lower wages. This cannot be the case at Mardon. It appears that Simon's career move was not prompted by the need to relax and spend more time with his young family; rather, it represents a deliberate increase in risk in order to satisfy his ambitions: he has taken another pace towards the fire.

Simon's resolve is greater than I anticipated. Donald Fletcher is a demanding employer. His selection criteria are rigorous and the qualities he favours in recruits would not be included in any common list of virtues.

Thirty-five years have passed since I last met Mr Fletcher – the occasion, his third interview in my old consulting rooms in Harley Street. The assessment was performed at the request of the Director of Public Prosecutions, but, before I presented its conclusion, the charges that prompted Donald Fletcher's assessment had been dropped and the Crown had no further interest in my analysis.

What has he been up to since? I think I will carry out some research. I adjust the database search criteria and command PROCEED.

Fifty press articles in the last three years.

I scan the headlines and print those that attract my interest. The first to appear in the tray is from the *Daily Telegraph*, dated 22 July 1986.

Packaging Magnate Establishes Arts Foundation

Donald Fletcher, managing director of Mardon Packaging Corporation, officiated yesterday at the inauguration ceremony for the Mardon Foundation at the University of Norwich.

In a speech given at a reception following the ceremony, Mr Fletcher stated that the Mardon Foundation would 'provide new opportunities for aspiring musicians, both locally and nationally'. He also welcomed the chance to contribute to the cultural development of the region, where Mardon is a major employer.

Completed at a cost of £2 million, the Foundation will provide a significant addition to the existing facilities at the University of Norwich music schools. The building, which is of contemporary design, includes rehearsal rooms, recording suites and a concert hall with an audience capacity of 300. The University chamber orchestra celebrated the occasion with a performance of a selection of music by Andrew Lloyd Webber.

[Picture: 120 mm by 80 mm. Caption: Mr Donald Fletcher at yesterday's ceremony.]

The Infotext service cannot transmit the photographs that accompany articles, but, in this case, there is no need. I have a good memory for faces. After all, my assessments extend further than a curt appraisal of an individual's features. With a few seconds' concentration – a search through the memory data bank – Donald Fletcher's image appears:

A physical man in structure, expression, ideas. Sparse red hair, creased forehead, well-freckled skin. Pale-blue eyes, closely spaced, a narrow nose and an asymmetric, thick-lipped mouth. His body broad, with big shoulders above a barrel chest. The usual impression this combination of sharp features, strong build and pale colouring creates is of ugliness and anger. It provokes wariness in observers – instinct places them on guard.

Donald Fletcher was a complex subject. Every action he performed and every word he spoke was edged with a violence only partially controlled. My profession brings me into contact with many dangerous men, yet I have seldom felt so threatened.

I pick through the remaining articles in the printer tray. Most record Mr Fletcher's progress as industrialist and patron of the arts. Adjectives linked to his name include 'respected', 'modest' and 'dynamic'. It is safe to say that not one of these accolades would have been associated with the same man twenty years ago.

You see, individuals do not change. It is prevailing sentiment which changes around them and elevates or ruins them according to the suitability of their temperament to the spirit of the age.

Donald Fletcher is a man whose hour has arrived. This is to be expected; it is part of the cycle. And when the cycle turns away, his fame will not endure.

I am, however, surprised at the speed with which he has advanced. It seems that the human behavioural cycle must be accelerating – each revolution is faster than its predecessor. It is impossible to confirm this postulation. It may, of course, result from a flaw in the observer – as I grow older, each year appears shorter.

Whatever. My curiosity about Donald Fletcher is extinguished. I shred the data, unlock my wheelchair and repair to the library, which benefits from a south-facing aspect. I sleep for two hours each afternoon. It compensates for unsettled nights, when repose is disturbed by cold or dreams, and assists my concentration for the remainder of the day. Sleep usually comes quickly, and as I close my eyes I address myself to my progress with Simon N—. He is a surprising individual. His association with Mardon Packaging Corporation and Donald Fletcher demonstrates a determination which his passive face, low reflexiveness and settled upbringing contradict.

4   Sunday, 15 February. I am rereading a favourite work, which I admire for its certainty and, moreover, respect for its contemporary relevance. On every page I can discover summaries of historical behaviour that might pass for observations on the despotic nature of the modern company executive. I quote: 'But the fierce and illiterate chieftain was seldom qualified to discharge the duties of a judge, which require all the faculties laboriously cultivated by experience and study...' This age is in need of another Edward Gibbon, to measure its greatness and expose its follies.

It is now past one o'clock. My goddaughter's husband is late for our meeting and I am irritable. This is because I enjoy Andrew's company and am impatient for his presence. In my experience, it is rare for men of different generations to form friendships unless the motivation is sexual. I need hardly assure you that this is not the case in the present circumstances. I am pleased to see Andrew because he has an inquisitive mind, similar to my own, combined with an exuberant nature and passionate manner of self-expression. His speech is filled with variety and modulated by emotion. His fortunate marriage to my goddaughter Lydia has given me great pleasure.

Why is he late? In the past, he has arrived drunk, verbose through the influence of a popular narcotic, fresh with the scent of debauch, but invariably punctually.

It is not until two o'clock that the doorbell rings and Andrew's fine, rather delicate features appear on the video screen of my security system. His carriage appears unsteady, and there is an edge to his voice as he announces his name. I will receive him here, in the library.

43

After a few minutes' delay, I hear his footsteps on the staircase, accompanied by the clink of the drinks tray. It is a custom of his visits that he prepares refreshments for us both upon arrival, thus allowing me to be a better host than my physical condition permits.

Andrew has an appealing, mobile face. Emotions chase each other across its features like ripples over water. It seems impossible for him to conceal his feelings beneath the conventional mask of composure. His body, too, is animated. It moves in time to his emotions. When he is sad, it slumps and limps. If he is happy, it is a kinetic expression of exultation. He smiles when he sees me – I believe he draws pleasure from our meetings – but the greeting dissolves into sad lines. Some other matter is of overwhelming concern. He puts down the tray, shakes my hand, then places a crystal whisky tumbler on the occasional table beside my chair. He sits down opposite me and inspects the glass he is holding with both hands.

'I know I'm late and I'm sorry.' He looks up, I nod, and he continues: 'I assume Lydia has explained the problem, so I suppose . . . I wish she wouldn't interfere!'

Andrew springs from his chair, and slips across the room. He turns his back to me and examines the spines of some medical volumes. His quick fingers select a book, spin through the stiff pages, then he slots it back into the shelf. He has outstanding co-ordination. Neurologists would lust for an opportunity to dissect his hippocampus.

He turns and speaks again: 'It's such a shame, a great shame, because this time I thought it would work out. I tried, I really tried. I applied myself, endured those trivial little disciplines, even had drinks with them all after work. And God! Charles, it was dull, simply, monstrously dull, sitting in the middle of a group of charcoal-suited sycophants without a word to say for themselves – not one, I swear! You'd discover quicker-witted company in a graveyard, better conversationalists in the cages at a zoo. I think I'll take up pig-keeping – a year with those Philistine fools must be better

44

preparation for the task than any formal training in animal husbandry.'

Andrew has lost his job again. I am not surprised, but raise my eyebrows and form a light frown to communicate concern. Andrew is too independent to function as part of a collective, and is unable to compensate through establishing a separate identity for the portion of his life spent at work.

He continues speaking: 'You know, Charles, I've searched my actions a thousand times, looked at everything – everything I said and did – been as objective as possible, and I still can't find a fault. It can't have been performance . . .'

'So why did it happen?'

He frowns. 'Why ask the question if you know the answer? I refuse to believe you've been robbed of perception since we last met. It was the people, of course. But, this time, it was a surprise. I wasn't playing at being one of them – I really wanted to be one. I honestly enjoyed my work. It was intellectually pleasing. And, God knows, I'm married just as they are, need the money as much as they do.'

'Perhaps it was bad luck?'

'Bollocks. I'm sorry: nonsense. You know I don't believe in luck or any other arbitrary influence. I take responsibility for everything I do, everything that happens to me. If I blamed other people, or some mad, blind fate, I'd never be independent. I accept the sorrows, and rewards [a smile], without a proprietary hand on my shoulder.'

Andrew sits down at last. 'They sent in some fool from the central finance department who offered me a drink, which he wouldn't share, then gurgled on about cost control and rationalisations before he told me they were going to "let me go". It was ridiculous, Charles: just like school. This hideous halfwit with a child's face was so full of morals he vomited mouthfuls of them across the table. His breath stank of piety. It was surreal. I don't see why he couldn't make do with saying: "Here's your cheque, now fuck off." For some mad reason he wanted to explain. Perhaps he thought I'd fall down and repent – you know, sob out floods of tears of contrition, kiss the vulgar tips of his slip-on shoes and thank him for his heavily accented words of wisdom . . .

'Anyway, enough of this, Lydia was furious. She locked the bedroom door and broke things . . .'

I inadvertently shake my head. Andrew notices and a broad smile illuminates his face. He is aware of the problems that his spouse used to cause for her guardian.

'Come on, Charles, it's not so bad – at least she's taken to venting her frustration on objects instead of people. I'm sorry I've been ranting. How are you? Still sorting out the sheep and goats? I should send you the madman who fired me – stuff him in a box and leave him for that charming secretary of yours to discover on Monday . . . What's her name again?'

'Younghusband.'

'Does she still drench herself with that vile floral scent? I could smell it lingering as I came up the stairs – just like one of those air fresheners used to mask unwholesome odours. Perhaps that's why she wears it. I'm amazed you tolerate her. I wouldn't let her in the house.'

'She performs her duties efficiently, is punctual and is attentive to my routine.'

'Don't bother to defend her, Charles. You know she's nothing more than a raddled old divorcee.'

Andrew's anger – his frustration at rejection – has found a new object. And, quite frankly, I am bored of his frenetic and distasteful observations. He arrives late, drunk, and once he has tired my ears with his own complaints he turns to abusing an individual who is necessary to the efficient management of my affairs.

'Please don't bother to continue. Miss Younghusband is not a fit target for your criticism.'

'And why not?' He glares at me, testing, testing, but it is too late. My own anger has been provoked, and once a passion manifests itself it is best to let it run its course.

'Andrew, your intemperance tires me. Please ensure that your condition is less volatile if you return.'

Shock, consternation and sorrow flow in succession across his face. He mumbles an apology. His hand shakes as he puts down his drink. 'I'm sorry, Charles. You're right. I didn't come here to fight. I think I'm still in culture shock. What I was trying to explain, or trying to analyse, I suppose, was the horrible vacuum in my colleagues' heads. You see, we had the same backgrounds, the same upbringing, but I had a soul and they had none . . .'

Andrew hesitates, tugs his hair, then the words burst forth: 'It was surreal, Charles – almost too much so to explain! They all lived in one dimension. They were dead from the waist down and the neck up . . . frozen loins and empty heads. Only the coarse digestive organs had a say in their behaviour . . . It was un-fucking-real, Charles – absolutely unreal! – a shoddy race of gluttons, all obsessed with the consumer madness, ranting on about vehicles, stereos and DIY. They believed in newspaper headlines. And adverts. Those two things were the sum of their conversation. Can you imagine how dull it was to have to speak to, no, worse than that, pander to them – bend and crawl before, nod and grin and say "Yes!" or "No!" and look and care as if you had any form of interest, apart from a scientist's curiosity, in their morbid and vacuous existence?'

Andrew's speech has accelerated. 'I'll give you an example: one of my old colleagues – Kevin Narg, or whatever the fuck his name was – no matter – it won't trouble historians – once delivered me a five-minute monologue on the seat covers of his car. I wanted to slice him up with a butcher's knife in return, tell him: This is the equivalent of what your pointless, stupid, repetitive statements have attempted on my brain . . .'

Andrew has turned away and is addressing the bookcase. I wish to empathise, but resist this form of mental surrender. He is, of course, quite right in his surmise that most individuals, including those considered to have benefited from an education, are incapable of thought. Darwin has been dead five generations and people still believe in God. It is perhaps fortunate that the citizens of industrialised countries are too occupied with hire-purchase contracts to launch a new crusade.

I am not going to offer Andrew sympathy. He is married to a rich and desirable woman. It is time he ended his quest for the nebulous brotherhood of man and began to discriminate. I will interrupt his chain of thought when a suitable opportunity presents itself.

'You know, Charles, I'm beginning to hate this town. It's as if everyone here dies the instant they get married or take out a mortgage or turn thirty. "That's enough," they tell themselves. "No more adventure. Time to stick the cork back in the bottle . . ."'

'Then why, in your own words, don't you "fuck off"? If the need to work for a living frustrates, you should enjoy your wife's income and hope for productive offspring.'

Excellent.

Andrew spins in his seat to face me. His pupils contract, exaggerating his startling blue eyes. I think he will try to be proud.

'I see.' He swallows, nods, then turns away. He folds his arms protectively across his chest. 'You know, Charles, you know how difficult it is for me. How much I want to give when every day I'm forced to take. I couldn't live with myself if I had to exist on Lydia's money. I don't want to be proud and when I'm earning I have no problem with her wealth. But you see, Charles, I need at least the illusion of independence. I find it amazing that Lydia loves me at all. She's a paragon to both my soul and senses – so much so that at times she seems unreal, too great a gift, so in order to believe in her I have to be independent. And to be independent, I need to earn. You see what I mean, Charles, don't you?'

I don't, but I can feel the strength of his feeling and it provokes emotions of my own. I was in love – once – and the longing in Andrew's voice has discovered a fragment of memory – a seed which flowers into a garden of associations, beginning with lips brushing lips in the endless yet evanescent summer of a sixteen-year-old's heart and launching cascade upon cascade of sensuous recollections from the few adult years of existence I enjoyed as a man.

Enough! I cannot afford to indulge in emotion. For the last six months, any psychologically generated variations in my metabolism have fed my disease. Even memories of physical sensations seem to provoke spasms no drug can control. Soon I will be in pain again. The danger signals are apparent: a tribe of insects has begun to march around my vertebrae. Already the lumbar muscles quiver. How long, how many minutes, will it be before they start to feed? The pain will be shameful. Pain is my familiar. A seven-clawed Satan has his chambers in my spine. When he walks abroad, he is absolute master. He can twist me, wake up muscles I no longer control and bend them with careless violence.

Andrew must leave! No one can know of this new affliction! If they wish, they can write my cause of death on a tombstone – it's not that far away. However, until I surrender, I shall pretend to perfect health in paralysis.

'You know, I'm sorry, Charles,' Andrew says, 'and sorry I always need to apologise. But, what should I do? I need your advice: should I start again or step aside? Should I throw away all the years of trying to conform?'

Why is he persisting? Why ask me? I'm in pain, now, right now – in too much pain. It takes everything to stop crying, screaming.

'You make claims to thought, Andrew. Well, prove them! Sort it out yourself.' The words were hard to produce but I must continue while I can and banish Andrew. 'It is late and I am tired. Please give Lydia my regards. Ask her for a cheque if necessary. Meanwhile, I suggest you be wary of individuals who talk too much about cars without trying to place them in a wider context.'

The insults work. He leaves the room and the sound of his footsteps diminishes as he descends the stairs. Five minutes of madness follow before I find and inject medication. It is a further half-hour before I can think.

One day I will lose control in public, and with that my licence and my *raison d'être*. As my illness progresses, its attacks become impossible to forestall. I should restrict all human contact to the professional and forget my friends. But this is a hard step for any animal to take. Besides, Andrew needed me, and I turned him away. If I had been patient, diverted him, perhaps, his frustration would have spent itself and allowed him to relax. My anger and affliction have robbed me of the only enjoyable company I have had for three weeks. If I suffer an attack again in front of Andrew he won't come back. Friends are hard to make at any age, and most of my contemporaries are senile or dead. A list of my lifelong acquaintances would make a fine guidebook to the cemeteries of England. Individuals with native vigour, such as Andrew, are the rarest form of mankind. His presence is so vivid that, in comparison, the subjects I assess are mere bloodless imitations – pale besuited spirits who haunt the underworld of modern metropolitan existence. Compare him with Simon N—, who has, I must admit, some flickerings of spirit, but moves through the ordered strata of society with ease, gathering laurels, attracting accolades for his half-strength soul. Meanwhile Andrew is treated to series rejection. It seems to me that inspiration has been forgotten as a virtue. Its contemporary substitute is proficiency in repetitive tasks.

Now I am too unsettled to work, and tormented by the knowledge that I could have helped. Every time I see Andrew he deteriorates. He seems to have given up hope. He speaks of yesterday, yesterday, yesterday, with all the passion of a world that might have been. For a man in that condition, even tomorrow is already dead.

I myself have a lonely prospect until Miss Younghusband arrives on Monday morning.

5 Simon N— is my only subject for interview this week. His second examination is scheduled for today, Wednesday, at two o'clock, which has given me plenty of time to prepare. Speculation in the weekend newspapers has proved to be well-founded. His employer has made a takeover bid for Darlington Card, which, in response, has issued a series of statements to its shareholders and the world at large advocating stern resistance to Mardon Packaging Corporation's advances. By coincidence, I am a shareholder in the target, so have instructed my stockbroker to dispose of the holding. I consider any financial involvement in the affair would create an intolerable conflict of interest – my position as Assessor demands I have no personal links, actual or potential, financial or otherwise, to my subjects.

The second interview plays a pivotal role in the success of an assessment. This time, the Assessor is required to be exploitative rather than empathetic. He should already possess an accurate knowledge of his patient's character, and use this second encounter to complete his understanding. This ensures that by the third interview the subject has been reduced to its essence: a human machine, a complex, self-perpetuating chemical reaction, whose functions can be manipulated at will.

The sun has been bright since dawn, the winter air is brisk, and I feel full of energy and purpose. My disagreement with Andrew has rejuvenated me. Exercise of anger is good for the elderly. It floods adrenaline through the system and stimulates its workings. There is, of course, some remorse. But that is the first sentiment I succeeded in subduing. After all, if actions result from innate character, there is no sense in attempting to disclaim their consequences. When the

51

predator is hungry, the predator will kill. Conscience is a luxury of the well-fed.

Two knocks on the door coincide with two o'clock. Miss Younghusband enters, quickly turns her back, and ushers Simon in. He casts his eyes around the room. His glance lingers on the control panels to my left, flicks over my head, then arrives on my face, accompanied with that furtive, juvenile half-smile. He strides up to my desk, shakes my hand, releases it and mutters, 'Sir Charles!' then accepts the invitation of my inclined wrist by sitting on the facing chair.

'Welcome back, Simon. I must say I'm pleased and surprised to see you. I perceive from the newspapers that your time is at a premium.'

'When I make appointments, I make a point of keeping them, Sir Charles. I've taken the liberty, though, of leaving my portable telephone with your most able secretary.'

Indeed.

The hero of the college debating society has been resurrected. Simon evidently has been talking to the press. His delivery has ascended into rhetoric. For the remainder of his takeover campaign, Simon will perform as orator.

'I won't ask if you've been well. You look fit, and I'm not your doctor. As you recall, the affliction for which I am testing can lie dormant for some time, to be resurrected – discovered, let us say – by a sudden, violent impulse.'

Simon nods his head. Good. He is a model of attention.

'Today, the examination will consist of two tests. The first is known as "Colourfield Exposure". Loosely speaking, this means I will show you a series of coloured patterns, with somewhat more striking hues and contrasts than you would encounter in everyday life.'

Simon smiles and settles back in his chair. He is not afraid of colours.

'It is common,' I continue, 'for the intensity of the shades that I will show you to generate a violent physical response. They can trigger primal reactions, so please be aware that some parts of this test may make you feel uncomfortable.

This should not be allowed to be a source of embarrassment. In order for Colourfield Exposure to achieve the desired effect, it is necessary for the individual undergoing the test to be exposed to absolute darkness for an initial period of five minutes. Again, some of my patients find this unsettling.'

I search Simon's face. A certain tension is discernibie. I coincided the termination of my last sentence with the elevation of both eyebrows and a sideways tilt of the head, to indicate I anticipate a response.

Silence.

Good. I think he has been pushed off balance. No more fireside chats, Simon. Today you will have to work for release.

'Have you any questions?'

He shakes his head.

'In which case, we shall proceed.'

I unlock my chair and wheel it smoothly to a panelled door to the left of my desk.

'Follow me. If it makes you feel more comfortable, please feel free to remove your jacket.'

Simon's feet shuffle and I hear the sound of his arms sliding out of his sleeves. Then he is beside me, to assist with the door. The Colourfield Exposure room is little larger than a cubicle – about eight feet by six. It is furnished with a single, central armchair. The walls, ceiling and floor are painted black. The chair faces a large, curved screen, intended to fill the subject's entire field of vision.

'You will be subjected to a total of six exposures. There is a thirty-second period of darkness in between each. Every exposure, including the first, will be preceded by a single tone – a bell, a gong, that sort of thing. You can see that both arms of the chair are fitted with a button. These form part of the test. They enable you to signify your response to each exposure. If an exposure creates a pleasing sensation, you are to press the button by your right hand. If, however, the feeling it prompts is disagreeable, use the one on the left.'

'And if I press both at once?' Simon enquires, smiling hopefully. I think he wishes to introduce levity into the proceedings.

'I shall assume the impression is disagreeable. You may practise, if you feel the need. The circuits are not activated before, or in between, exposures.'

Simon steps forward and takes his seat. His posture is rigid, formal – a schoolboy on parade. He is determined to perform his duty.

'Please remove your watch. I shall keep it for you on my desk outside. Do you wear contact lenses?'

'No.'

'Good. These, too, would have to be removed. Simon, it is necessary to monitor a patient's impulses during the course of these exposures, so I am going to fit a measuring device to your temples.'

His mouth opens – an indication of apprehension.

'Please sit back – lean back in the chair. That's right. Once you are comfortable, I shall proceed.'

Simon shifts a little to his left – not, I suspect, in search of an improved posture, but to demonstrate that I have his attention and he is taking pains to co-operate.

The monitoring device consists of an expanding steel template with three sliding sensors which are placed against the temples and the forehead. It is fitted to the back of the chair by an adjustable bracket to allow for subjects of different heights. It measures EEG activity in the cortex during the course of the tests.

Simon is nervous. His neck is rigid and a sheen of perspiration has appeared below his hairline. The variety of responses this essential preparation provokes is a perennial source of amusement. Executives are always apprehensive, in particular when I coat their temples with graphite paste to improve the contacts. They fear that I will interfere with their most vital resource – their brain. Occasionally they ask me to check the fuses, unable, in their state of terror, to differentiate between a device that generates current and an instrument which measures it. The criminals, however, take a very different view of proceedings. They are flattered by the attention paid to an organ whose workings they generally ignore. Every rapist feels he has something strange going on inside his head which will explain his antisocial behaviour and somehow assist in absolving him from blame. This misdirected spirit of co-operation lends a practical advantage to preparations.

Simon is sweating quite freely by now. I suspect he will try to reduce fear through speech – make a 'joke', perhaps – but I forestall him by asking for his hat size, which, of course, he doesn't know.

'The contact should be firm but comfortable. There: how does that feel?'

'Fine, thanks.'

Answered in a low tone – the uncomfortable affirmative.

Simon's head is surprisingly small for his undoubted intellect. I wonder if I should tell him. No. The knowledge will irritate him, make him rebellious instead of afraid. He would resent the implication that small is inferior. It is, after all, a common misconception. Mankind persists in equating size with success, where no such correlation exists in nature. Phrenologists thrived on this superstition a century or so ago in Paris. I think it is enough to add that the same individuals favoured lobsters as pets.

'I'm finished. Now, have you any questions?'

Simon shakes his head. A faint, sour odour emanates from his armpits.

'Good. If, for any reason, you need to leave the room during the course of the test, please press the lever beneath the right arm of the chair. This illuminates the room and releases the door. Undo this chin strap to remove the monitor. The entire procedure takes just under ten minutes. You may find the initial period of darkness soporific.'

For an instant we are seated side by side, chairs parallel, in a black room, staring at a blank screen. Then Simon turns

55

his head and says with a thin smile, 'I'll do my best to stay awake.'

'Excellent. Let us commence.'

I wheel myself out backwards, drawing shut the door as I leave the room. The control console for the exposure test sits on a pedestal by my desk. The room itself is illuminated through the screen. Light is programmed to fade slowly until extinguished, allowing the subject time to adapt naturally to darkness. If he should appear unsettled, there is a facility to provide background noise for comfort – I favour a recording of breaking waves.

The usual exposure period of each Colourfield is set at five seconds. This can be reduced for sensitive individuals. During the course of an exposure, the subject's face is photographed from the sides and from beneath. The cameras are concealed until the room is in darkness, when a control mechanism automatically releases the lens covers.

The Colourfield Exposure test is an elemental experience. It would not appeal to casual pleasure-seekers – the stimuli are too extreme. The initial period of absolute darkness and silence (the room is soundproofed) disorientates every subject. Approximately 20 per cent find this highly disturbing. The complete absence of physical sensations unsettles the brain, usually leading to the release of adrenaline, which increases the discomfort of a restricted, stationary position.

An LED meter on the control panel displays a moving average of the EEG activity in Simon's cerebral cortex. It is also recorded on paper by an oscillograph bank in my study upstairs. The EEG activity meter is graded from 1 to 100 and at present reads 69, indicating that Simon is nervous, but unafraid. I anticipate that after three minutes of darkness it will have risen to approximately 86, then subside towards its present level in the fifth and final minute.

The first exposure causes severe trauma in over 90 per cent of subjects. It consists of an 82-decibel scream combined with a violent orange fireball which appears to explode out of the screen and engulf the viewer. As these constitute the first sensations an individual encounters after five minutes of total deprivation, very few consider the experience agreeable. In truth, I can recall only one – Jason S—, a particularly unbalanced serial killer, who claimed to enjoy a spontaneous ejaculation. This, however, was such an unusual response that I declined to have it substantiated.

Subsequent exposures are less alarming, though equally extraordinary. There is a wonderful luminous phosphor green, accompanied by the sonorous beat of a gong, which many patients claim provokes sensations of reverence, even of awe. There is a radiant yellow, which bursts forth like the warmest sun on a summer's day. It generates excitement and happiness. The photographs taken while a subject is undergoing Colourfield Exposure constitute perhaps the strangest images of mankind in existence. Every facial expression appears in its most extreme manifestation – joy, fear, sorrow, fundamental grief. I have no doubt that the majority of individuals would find such pictures alarming. In any event, all negatives are destroyed at the conclusion of each assessment, as are most prints, although I retain some that demonstrate emotions with particular clarity. The only other representations of the human form that approximate these photographs are contained in the work of a contemporary painter – Francis Bacon. I possess a number of his canvases – indeed, one hangs in the reception above Miss Younghusband's head. I suspect few of my clients realise I own them for their verisimilitude.

One minute remains. As anticipated, Simon's activity level has subsided. Good. There is a certain element of risk involved in Colourfield Exposure tests. They cannot be performed on subjects with weak hearts. In addition, if an individual is genuinely prone to epilepsy, the stimuli are almost certain to provoke a seizure.

Thirty seconds. Simon's EEG rate has ticked back up, as if in anticipation. Perhaps he has been counting? I have had a number of criminal subjects with experience in the boxing ring who were able to count off the adjustment period with a high degree of accuracy. Most people have trouble determining whether a single minute has elapsed, let alone—

There it is! A green light on the console coincides with a violent blur in the LED – 80, 95, then 70, 90, and the rate settles close to 83. Meanwhile, the response indicator lights up – Simon found the first Colourfield unpleasant. Nearly every subject does. It is a simulation of birth, a recreation of the moment when the foetus is ejected from the slumbering comfort of the placenta into a strange world of violent impressions – the instant when each human receives, and is forced to process, its first sensations. His recovery, however, is quick. Very quick. Most subjects undergo an aftershock, which occurs ten to fifteen seconds after the first exposure, when the brain has recovered from the initial sensory overload and begins to try to quantify the experience. But Simon has none.

It is as if he had been forewarned of the nature of the tests.

This is most irregular.

Responses to subsequent Colourfields are less predictable. It is usual that at least one will provoke a response as violent as the first. This is revealed either through EEG activity rates or by relative reaction speed to the appearance of the new field. But here, once again, Simon's behaviour is strange. Each response is registered approximately two seconds into the exposure. As the test proceeds, his EEG pattern becomes increasingly stable. Colourfield Exposure tests were developed to ensure that a subject's reactions are spontaneous. The human animal learns very quickly: the shock of the new does not last. It becomes accustomed to its environment, however strange, and reason soon regains dominion over instinct. Hence this test is short and extreme, mixing pleasurable exposures with the unsettling. But Simon has reacted as if he knew what to expect. This alarming hypothesis merits further investigation, which will have to wait. The test is over and light is being restored to the room, accompanied by soothing music. In less than a minute, it will be time to release Simon N—. In the interim, I shall compose myself and prepare for the remainder of the interview.

I am master of my profession. I do not expect surprises, in particular from commercial patients. It is true that responses vary greatly between individual subjects, but they occur, in essence, within fairly limited parameters. If I am to succeed in manipulating Simon at our next interview, I must establish control today. Perhaps the Exposure photographs will help resolve this unexpected problem. Meanwhile, I shall have to be patient.

I wheel myself to the test room. When I open the door, Simon is standing, waiting to receive me.

'Daylight!' he announces, and smiles that irritating smile. 'At one stage I wondered if I'd see it again.'

He walks out past me. His face is a satisfactory shade of pale, and there are large damp patches under his arms.

'It's warm in there,' he tells me, then pulls on his jacket and sits down at my desk. Evidently executives do not like to be seen to sweat. I roll back into position and pick up his watch. It is a Rolex – an expensive present, I would guess, from Simon to himself.

'How did you enjoy your test?'

'Well . . .' He smiles and rolls his eyes. He utters a nervous laugh. 'What can I say, Sir Charles? Strange, I suppose, though some of the pictures were . . .'

'Appealing?'

'Not exactly. I can't say they made me comfortable. How are they made?'

'With considerable ease. In comparison with 1980s technology, the mechanism is rather crude. They depend, to a large extent, upon the initial darkness for their effect. People rarely experience sensory deprivation. If someone had lit a cigarette in there beside you, the surprise would have been as great.'

'I don't know' – a frown – 'but if that happened, I would've pressed the left-hand button very quickly.'

'Don't smoke?'

'Never have.' Said with conviction.

'Why not?' I am seeking to provoke Simon. I need to test his equilibrium.

'I'm surprised to hear a doctor ask that question.' His reply is quite rapid, and he blinks a couple of times. I think he is unused to having his judgment questioned. Remember, Simon has never failed an exam, and he has been placed in positions of responsibility through school, university and career. By now he must be touched with creeping righteousness: he has not done wrong, therefore he cannot do wrong.

Time to change the subject. Simon still believes I am a doctor. I would hate to disabuse him of this notion.

'The Colourfield Exposure test makes many of my patients nervous. Even the light smokers among them then feel a strong urge to light up a cigarette.'

'Slaves to their addiction,' replies Simon with a smile, without humour.

'Perhaps I can tempt you with a little caffeine?'

'No coffee, thank you, Sir Charles, but tea would be great.'

'How taken?'

'With milk and two sugars – conference standard.'

I manufacture an appreciative smile for his industrial humour and instruct Miss Younghusband over the intercom. She informs me she has received a number of messages for Simon. My eyes meet his across the desk and he waves his hand and says, 'Later.'

'Mr N— will take his messages at the end of the interview.'

I switch off the intercom and lean back in my chair. 'I'm grateful for your full attention,' I tell him.

'My pleasure, Sir Charles.' He gives me a gracious nod. 'After all, it's in my best interests and, besides, I think it's tacky to interrupt important meetings with other business.'

Ideally, at this instant, I should blush with pleasure. A financial director, mid-takeover, a merchant prince of his generation, has condescended to dedicate precious moments to an unusual search for an improbable ailment . . .

Indeed.

The true balance of power rests in my hands. Insurance is an essential condition of his company's funding contracts. Interest rates are high and banks are nervous. They have fought for the favours of the corporate whores, and now that the results of their profligacy manifest themselves they have become suspicious. A surfeit of healthy-looking corpses puts even scavengers on their guard. Simon needs my approval.

I wonder what he might do, could be made to do, to win it. A bribe? Is Simon N— a stranger to bribery? He appears to be moral, perhaps believes in moral conduct, but it is quite possible he would carry out actions in his employer's name that he would consider reprehensible in personal life.

Enough. I am speculating. This must be a consequence of the unusual responses to the Colourfield test.

'In twenty minutes, Simon, you'll be your own man once again. We have one further set of tests in order to complete today's examination. You may find them disappointing – no more animals, no more colours.'

Simon makes a little *moue* – purses his lips – intended as a counterfeit of distress. I think he would be surprised to discover that the gesture originated in man's animal past as an expression of sullen aggression. It still can be observed in this role on the faces of certain primates.

'I can't claim I'm too upset, Sir Charles. It's already been quite a day. What did you say these next ones were called – Logic something?'

'Logic Simulation.'

Simon appears puzzled. 'Sounds like a contradiction in terms.'

'Perhaps. Let me explain. Logic can be defined as reasoned thought applied to the solving of a problem. It is the systematic analysis of a given set of circumstances. However, any logical inference is made on the basis of a number of fundamental suppositions which are, in truth, beyond proof.'

Simon is the picture of earnest attention. His eyes shine from his pleasant, youthful face.

'So what you're saying is that logic is flawed?'

'Precisely.'

'We were told something along those lines in the mathematics section of my degree.'

'Good. That will help you to complete the examination. Consider Logic Simulation to be a sort of intelligence test – although somewhat different from those you may have encountered at school.'

Simon nods his head thoughtfully. He is still aware that brighter individuals than himself exist. I do not think he finds this knowledge pleasant. Time may save him. If his present successes continue, the synapse paths will alter and the discomfort vanish. He will no longer acknowledge his innate limitation.

'The Logic Simulation test presents a series of problems which appear capable of solution through conventional rational methods.'

Simon unfolds his arms and leans forward over my desk. He rocks his head gently from side to side while I speak. He is wearing his 'thinking cap'.

'But in fact they're not?'

'In fact they are.' My tone is sharp. 'Each problem, however, has a second solution.'

'And that is the right one?'

'No – a better one. These tests may seem irrelevant to epilepsy, and in most cases they are.' I smile reassurance with a conspiratorial glance, as if to confide to Simon he is not at risk. 'You see, there have been rare instances of fits being prompted through mental confusion. The sufferer's brain is unable to accept a simple proposition and it panics as a result – responds with a series of violent motor actions.'

Simon sits back, folds his arms and smiles. He knows this cannot, will not, happen to him. He is wrong, of course. As I anticipated, he has not applied any thought to my words. It would be very easy to confront him with a simple proposition that provokes violence: if I called his mother a prostitute, perhaps? Still, the brief 'explanation' of the intention of the test has succeeded in its true purpose: to tell Simon nothing about Logic Simulation, but simultaneously to cause him to relax and feel confident. Logic Simulation measures a ratio known as Kappa. In essence, this quantifies the ability of the adult brain to construct and maintain new neural networks, which in turn determines how far each subject resorts to dogma when solving a problem, as opposed to employing rational thought. Does he approach each difficulty as if it is new, or does he apply a programmed response that prior experience has taught him is successful? Kappa ratios decline with age, when the brain cells become set, and, in effect, it is physically impossible to develop new mental reflexes. The test makes an important contribution to the master assessment model. *Per curiam*, a definite correlation exists between a high Kappa ratio and a positive assessment conclusion. In plain speech, this relationship can be expressed as 'good people tend to be open-minded'. This, however, is a mere statistic, to which there are a very great number of exceptions. It amuses me that if it could be proven it would demonstrate that all religious individuals are intrinsically bad.

A knock at the door. Miss Younghusband has arrived with the tea; also, I note with irritation, Simon's portable telephone.

'It's your chairman, Mr N—. He insisted that you speak to him.'

Simon looks mortified. The corners of his mouth drift downwards in embarrassment. An instant ago, he was in command: master of himself, master of his time – a benevolent monarch, dispensing favours. Now he has been overruled. His eyes meet mine as he accepts the telephone from Miss Younghusband's rather masculine hand.

'Yes, Donald.' His body tenses. 'I see. Of course.' He examines his watch. 'In fifteen minutes.' He turns away. 'So soon? I see. Very well.'

He switches off the telephone and drops it in his jacket pocket. He looks at me, opens his mouth, closes it, clears his throat, glances down at his lap, then speaks. 'I hate to say this, Sir Charles' – he looks up and I detect anger: his features display a fierce resentment – 'but I have to leave. As you know, my company is involved in an acquisition, and something has come up which requires my signature. At any other time, I could have postponed, but now . . .' And Simon opens his hands in appeal. His face is twisted with frustration.

If you require a car, Miss Younghusband will see to it.'

'One is already waiting, Sir Charles.'

Simon rises quickly, leans across the desk and shakes my hand. He searches for eye contact, and speaks. 'Thank you for your understanding. I promise you I will make up for this. Perhaps we could meet on a weekend? That way I can guarantee my freedom.'

I nod my head. 'That may be in our best interests, Simon. Much as I welcome your company, I am aware our meetings impose demands upon a precious resource and therefore it would satisfy us both to conclude the examination in the shortest possible time. I believe I am free a week on Saturday. Should this be agreeable, please make the necessary arrangements with Miss Younghusband.'

Simon makes a little bow – the traditional gesture of submission – and follows Miss Younghusband out of the room.

Bloody man! Simon has created a genuine impediment to the progress of the assessment. He has left me no margin for error at our next interview. In such circumstances, there is only one sure way to establish control. I shall have to gain command through artificial means. From time to time an assessor is forced to resort to administering narcotics to a subject. Deliberate doping of an individual without his knowledge or consent is, of course, immoral and considered serious malpractice in most branches of the medical profession. For an assessor, it is an occasional, if regrettable, necessity. Fortunately, a loophole exists within the ambit of our governing statute which could be interpreted to place such an action within our powers. As it is legal, it therefore can be said to be ethical, but I must stress we drug patients infrequently, and only in circumstances where unforeseen or insurmountable hindrances impede the orderly course of an assessment.

Hence Simon's offer of a weekend interview is welcome. The agent I employ is a mild hallucinogenic which can continue to act upon the subject for some hours after the conclusion of his interview. It is not advisable to return such an individual to his place of work while his conscious mind is in an altered state. It is not that the drug interferes with his ability to perform his duties; rather that he may question the need to perform them at all and resign on impulse in order to dedicate himself to a higher purpose.

This really is most irritating. I shall have to salvage what I can of the interview from the video tape and the Colourfield photographs. There were a number of false notes that will require meticulous investigation. What was wrong with his EEG rate? It should have rocketed out of control on at least three occasions. I have never known such a difficult subject.

No. If there is a difficulty, it lies with the Assessor. Simon is a simple case: an ambitious little salaryman. I am inventing problems. Perhaps it has become impossible for me to remain objective? And now, on reflection, I am conscious that all my recent assessments have seemed unusual. Either humanity is mutating (which is improbable) or I am losing my analytical powers. I should retire. I am holding on for all the wrong reasons. My profession is my sole indulgence. I have no hobbies, no other interests. In a sense, I am the prisoner of my own achievement. I have dedicated my life to objectivity, identifying and eradicating personal sentiments one by one, in order that I may perfect my ability to assess. Without that expertise, I am nothing. I have proved, biologically, that the soul is nonexistent; that mankind is an animal species, no better or worse than any other. As a result, I have destroyed any chance of personal happiness in an idle state: the man has gone; only the brain – the calculating machine – remains, and now it seems that that is faltering.

6 The telephone is restless today. Miss Younghusband called in to claim she was suffering from influenza and hence unable to perform her duties. I am not convinced of the veracity of this excuse. She is a robust, somewhat coarse woman with great natural resistance to such inconsequential maladies.

This is an unexpected hindrance. On the penultimate Tuesday of every month I take lunch at my club. This is often the sole occasion that I venture out-of-doors and I hate to leave the house unattended. Equally, I am loath to destroy my routine, even though the fixture is seldom an exercise from which I derive pleasure. Most of my old companions are dead and new members treat the club premises as an extension of their offices. The games room and library resemble a business park. They have been appropriated by grey men in grey suits, who tap away at their lap-top computers and mutter the occasional expletive when their fingers hit the wrong key.

It is small changes like these that make the old sad. We are tormented by the persistence of memory. When places were once filled with the palpable current of genius, we cannot accept them as being occupied in any other way. The tedious repetitive duties that challenge modern working minds suffer in contrast to the adventures undertaken by their predecessors. It is as if these rooms have been given over to caretakers – menials – to drag out their hours with petty tasks, oblivious to the wonder of communication or the stimulative power of creative thought.

I close my eyes to picture the games room and it materialises, *circa* 1952. Fedor Orlovsky, refugee victim of revolutionary fools, leans back from the chessboard. He shakes his head and his lank Slavic hair whips across his forehead.

'Aha!'

Then the hand darts out and the knight slots into its destined place. Checkmate – the signal for a further glass of vodka . . .

Orlovsky would play any of the members, regardless of their standard. If his opponent was weak he would provoke him to compensate with wit. If his opponent's skills approached his own, he turned his concentration on the game, expressing his intellectual grace through the placing of his pieces, the deft movements of his slim fingers.

He died five years ago – too soon to see his native country freed, disillusioned with the soulless complacency that had become commonplace in his adopted home. *Sic transit gloria mundi* . . .

A car collects me at twelve o'clock and delivers me to St James's in time for the first sitting of lunch at half past. The preparation required for this expedition is exhausting and I am invariably in a bad mood when I leave the house. This morning, it appears my acquaintances are involved in a conspiracy to vex me. First Andrew telephoned to offer belated apologies for his behaviour last weekend. He seemed to be sincere, though his manner is remarkably casual. I am not surprised he is unemployable.

'I'm sorry I lost it, Charles,' he told me. 'I won't try to foist the blame on to hard times or phases of the moon or other such madness. I was feeling low and vile. I'd been indoors all week, summoning up courage to look for work again – hating myself, hating everything in fact, even London. I'm just sorry I offended you. I'd like to make up if I can. What about lunch out? I'll make all the arrangements . . .'

I declined the invitation. Though pleased that Andrew felt sufficient attachment to attempt an apology, I am disappointed he chose self-pity as a justification for absence of self-control.

The next intrusion came from Regal Insurance, who likewise selected the telephone as their instrument of harassment. They are sponsoring Simon N—'s assessment, and requested 'an expedition of the examination process, due to certain unforeseen matters which have arisen since our last communication'.

Fools! Practitioners in that industry seem incapable of expressing themselves in plain English. 'Hurry up' would have sufficed.

Finally, at eleven o'clock, Lydia Markham appeared on my doorstep, uninvited, and as careless with my time as if, like her, I had no other purpose to my hours but the casual pursuit of pleasure. Lydia has a somewhat slack appearance. She favours expensive clothing, but contrives to seem dishevelled. It is as if she wished to taint her natural purity of feature with unnecessary artifice. Perhaps she is frightened of her beauty.

She was applying lipstick when I examined her through the camera of the video system. I registered surprise at her visit, but invited her to ascend. I was *en route* to the library to receive her, when, as I traversed the landing, she intercepted me by springing up the staircase, taking two steps in each stride, having rolled her dress up her thighs, no doubt to assist her in the execution of this endeavour.

Then there she was before me: fragrant, breathless, a childish grin of delight distorting her even features.

'Uncle Charles! You must be delighted to see me! Poor thing – rolling round the house on your own all day – you must be screaming with tedium. Anyway, I have some news. Look!' And she stood before me, hands on hips, legs apart, staring, it appeared, at her belt. 'Well?'

'What is it, Lydia?'

'Can't you see? Here – light my cigarette and I'll show you.'

She then pressed matches and packet into my lap, stood back, unfastened her skirt, and revealed her abdomen. There is no doubt that this portion of Lydia's anatomy would have a powerful effect on most men. Her stomach is flat, the skin smooth and golden. The lines are firm, yet delicate – feminine.

'You must see it, Uncle Charles? No? Well, feel it, then! Give me your hand!' Whereupon she took my fingers and placed them forcibly against her belly, slightly below the navel. 'I'm pregnant! I think it happened in December, during our anniversary jaunt in Paris. We've narrowed it down to any one of seven tries that weekend. I remember telling Andrew seven was my lucky number. If it's a boy, we'll call him Charles. Isn't that wonderful? You must be pleased!'

I was silent, which Lydia interpreted as assent.

'I've spent the morning buying maternity clothes. I'm going to swell out like a peach. But now I'm tired and need a drink. What will you offer me? Will it be champagne? Call Miss Younghusband! No – of course, she's out. I saw her this morning in Bond Street. Poor thing – you really should employ an errand boy.'

I was forced to endure a further twenty minutes of Lydia's ungovernable good humour before she could be persuaded to leave. She insisted on extracting a promise that I would dine with her and Andrew. I have no intention of keeping this. An evening expedition in my condition is unthinkable.

It came as something of a surprise to hear of Lydia's encounter with Miss Younghusband. I had assumed my assistant was immobile somewhere. It is possible, of course, that she visits a general practitioner in the vicinity of Bond Street.

It is now twelve o'clock and another obstacle has emerged to impede the smooth passage of my routine. The car that takes me to my club is waiting outside, yet the photographs from Simon N—'s Colourfield Exposure test, due to arrive by hand this morning, have yet to appear. Wilmots, the developing laboratory, is usually prompt, but I am not prepared to hold the car and wait. Their nature is too sensitive to allow delivery to an empty house. I am forced to make a telephone call with instructions that a courier deliver the pictures to St James's Street.

Needless to say, the weather has added its weight to this conspiracy of vexations. As I open the front door, it begins to rain. There is nothing quite like the rain to enforce the misery of handicap. The elements highlight the futility of a second-class existence. My fingers dig into the padded arms of my chair in displeasure as large, cold drops fall on my uncovered head. It makes a mockery of the sustained effort required to rise, bathe and dress, only to discover oneself stupid, immobile and useless; unable to protect oneself against something as simple and commonplace as rain.

The deluge ceases an instant before I am handed into the car and the damp earth releases a sour smell. The air fails to circulate in winter London. It is suppressed by the chill, absorbs the traffic filth, then collects into a sump – a poison pool which suffocates the city. The plane trees are bare as we drive up Ladbroke Grove. Absence of vegetation emphasises the width of the road, leaches brilliance from the white terraces and so reduces the vista to uniform grey. When we turn down Holland Park this impression of chill isolation is reinforced. The painted mansions appear abandoned – boarding houses in a seaside town whose season has passed. I listen for the gulls, whipping past with the breeze, to cry lament into the empty streets.

The sun appears when we reach Hyde Park, harsh, white, low on the horizon. It penetrates without warming, casts long, flat shadows, gives sharp definition to the office blocks across the park, the spiked railings close to hand, but nowhere illuminates. It is a monochrome world, as if the unforgiving vision of my interview tapes has been extended to encompass London.

I am really pleased to reach St James's Street, to ascend the ramp by the club steps, and roll slowly into the hall. So many members, like me, are infirm, that the pace of the institution too is slow. A longcase clock draws out the seconds, chimes the passage of each quarter-hour, strikes the hours with sonorous pomp, as if to accord the same importance to these little periods as the record of some great event – a virgin birth, a tyrant's death, the advent of a new millennium.

My wheels are soundless on the marble floor. The hall attendant stands behind the counter, a uniformed statue amidst the polished brass postal trays, the letter-crowded order of the pigeonholes. He is at once attentive and immobile, respectful of my need to propel myself, ready, when I reach the lift, to float across the floor and withdraw the iron grille so I may enter and ascend. The lift rises at the same stately pace at which all activity, human or mechanical, proceeds in the club. From the instant I enter, it appears as though I have been dropped on to the conveyor belt of some vast and antiquated machine, which rolls with slow precision through the steps of its programme, its actual productive purpose long forgotten.

The dining room is on the first floor. Jenkins is waiting by the lift and accompanies me to my table in silence. He has been with the club for thirty years and his familiar, quiet presence is a comfort. We must be close in age – his footsteps are slow and deliberate, his back is hunched beneath his livery jacket. I think Jenkins gains pleasure from my visits. Perhaps he registers them as a natural phenomenon. Man is a creature of instinct, whose nature imposes itself on the artificial calendar – ordains that on the relevant Tuesday of each month Sir Charles Barrington will return from his wanderings to take luncheon at his club.

My table is positioned in the centre of the dining room, backlit by two great windows. I sit facing the door, flanked by these twin, curved pillars of light. From time to time I have company. Usually, I eat alone. My club, above all, is a place of repose – a sanctuary from the frenetic, *fin de siècle* existence outside. It is the last refuge of empirical thought – a calm seat from which the serene individual can contemplate, with pleasure, a Creation founded on immutable order. The club embodies security. Here I am treated, and enabled to behave, as Sir Charles Barrington, eminent senior member, without the need to endure the stares of strangers who derive amusement from my appearance and immobility. The food is plain and makes no demands upon my digestion, which, frankly, is a relief: an upset stomach in a wheelchair is a humiliating condition. After lunch, I invariably retire to the library, occasionally to converse or play at chess, usually to sleep. I perform this exercise with a book opened on my lap, to dissuade opportunists from attempting discourse. At three-thirty I am collected for the return journey to Elgin Crescent.

Today the dining room is full. The average age of occupant is, I would estimate, approaching sixty. For these men, a visit to the club is a necessary tonic during winter. I nod my head in greeting to a few familiar faces – judges, surgeons – professionals whose careers are linked closely to my own. My eyesight is acute, and though the dining room is large I am able to recognise individuals upon entry. Strangers stand out immediately. Some are overseas members, with half-closed eyes and saurian skin, who squint as if still fighting off an unforgiving tropical sun. Some are businessmen, and move with awkward poise, determined not to be in awe, desperate to belong. They cannot apply their customary domineering manners in a club: there is no *maître d'* to bully; staff cannot be tipped to ensure preference. At table, they resemble meek schoolboys. They fiddle with the cutlery and speak with artificial composure, hoping to impress through reserve.

Now then, who is that? A group of three has entered. The short man in the middle is a stranger, but he is confident, very confident. He has an arrogant, no, more than that, *aggressive*, bearing. I know him, but there is a false note: the face is wrong. The features have been changed, and they contradict his posture. How curious!

The trio proceeds to a central table and the stranger stands for a moment with his back towards me, but, as he takes his chair, he turns in my direction and smiles. It's in the mouth, and the nose – the nose in particular – but the work is very good, so good, in fact, that if I could not visualise the original the alterations would be impossible to detect. The change to the lips, however, cannot be concealed. That smile betrayed the false symmetry of corrective surgery. Skin, after all, is no more than a mask. Expressions are created by the muscles underneath, whose motions will contradict a synthetic surface. I am astonished the man was admitted to the club, even as a guest, in the company of two such eminent sponsors – Lord Tendor and James White, respective pillars of the banking and broking communities.

Donald Fletcher is indeed a man whose moment has arrived. He recognised me, I know: communicated it through that arrogant smile. Enough. So he is here, and here in good company. He will not be the first man to change his fortunes through an altered appearance. It is too much to expect his companions to be aware of the true nature of their guest. Perception is a rare gift. All three are relaxed and in good humour. Any business between them evidently has been concluded. This lunch is a celebration. I return my attention to my rib of beef and the glass of claret before me. This is a strange and unwelcome occurrence: I do not expect to encounter the subjects of my profession in the course of my leisure hours. The club membership ballot takes place in March. I shall examine the list of proposed entrants with great care.

Thankfully, the library is quiet. Two ageing peers are perusing bound copies of *The Field* from 1937, no doubt intending to settle a wager on the result of a forgotten sporting event. Otherwise, the panelled room is empty. The tick of the mantel clock and a gurgle from the boxed-in radiator are the only sounds. The club cat peers round the corner of the oak door, then withdraws its head when its intrusion is met by three hostile stares. It is not permitted to enter the library. The tip of its tail flicks against the door frame as it leaves.

Three o'clock. Three little silver bells chime and, in the

distance, a base echo from the longcase clock repeats the hour.

I have been asleep. The peers have gone, but I am not alone. In a leather chair, opposite my own, Reginald Boyce-Duncan is waiting. He holds a magazine; his eyes rest on my face. He seems impatient. I think he wants to speak to me: there is a certain restlessness, a quiver, in the slack folds of flesh below his jaw. Very well. I am indifferent to his company. The present Director of Public Prosecutions is not renowned for either wit or perspicacity.

He clears his throat and commences conversation with the weather. We agree it to be changeable, but tolerable. Mutual enquiries are made as to health. Thanks are returned for each solicitation, conditions are allowed to be passable.

Reginald is an ectomorph, perhaps the purest example I have seen of this basic physical type. He is short, narrow-shouldered and fat-rumped, with small, soft hands, which protrude like cotton wool from the tight confines of his dark suit. His voice is weak and contains an impatient quiver. His eyes are very pale, and whether blue, grey or green, it is hard to say.

Luncheon is discussed and compliments are delivered as to the food's wholesome qualities. The presence of mutual acquaintances in the dining room is mentioned, and then it arrives: Reginald's offhand manner cannot mask the eagerness in his voice.

'Jacob seems to be hungry for company – his third new guest this year.'

'Indeed?'

'Red-haired fellow – d'you know him?'

'Yes.'

Reginald waits, frowns, then leans forward, elbows on knees, chins cupped in palms. 'Listen, Charles, I'm sorry to trouble you, but the Crown has an interest here.'

'In Donald Fletcher?'

'Yes.' He straightens up, then begins to speak quickly. His tone is confidential. 'We know you examined the man in

74

1955. Certain circumstances have arisen which may make your conclusions relevant. It seems, however, that your report has been mislaid – quite possibly when we moved offices a few years ago. You've always been an efficient sort, Charles, and a copy, if you have one, would be of great assistance.'

'No copy exists.'

A frown. He looks at me steadily, employing the lawyer's courtroom gaze in an attempt to determine if I tell the truth. As a matter of fact, I do.

He tries again. 'I don't know what you remember about the man, but he's been causing us some trouble in the past few months. We've been forced to keep a sharp eye on him. There appear to be irregularities in his business methods, but sadly' – he shrugs his shoulders, expressing frustration – 'we haven't been able to resolve them.'

How typical. A government servant appeals to an outsider for assistance in unravelling his department's own incompetence.

'He seems to keep good company.'

'Yes. That's a problem. His companions today, for instance. I know them both and regard them as prudent men, who could not allow themselves to be associated with a person of uncertain reputation. But times have changed, Charles. Confidence has been shaken and relationships between my office and senior members of the financial community have deteriorated. There are too many new faces, and the opportunities for gain are far too great. It's a poor show really. They seem to treat us like the Revenue these days.'

'An unfortunate comparison.'

'Precisely.' A sour smile. 'It's becoming a game of us and them. Frankly, I'm looking forward to retirement.'

He shifts in his chair, looks at the door, which is closed, then taps lightly on the table in front of him with his forefinger. He wants my opinion. He is frustrated that he has to ask, and irritated that I appear to be evasive.

'Look, Charles, we think it's likely that Donald Fletcher will cause us some embarrassment, and not just us. I know that, in some quarters, we have a reputation for being rather flat-footed, but in this case we're not the only ones who stand to lose. Some very senior people, including members of this club, may end up looking foolish. Investors will be disappointed, and in the current economic climate that is not something this government would welcome.'

How melodramatic! If I refuse assistance, I will betray not only Reginald but the club, the man in the street, the Government (and thereby the nation) . . .

Reginald is a worried man. I am not surprised. The Government was foolish to decline my assessment when it was submitted. In accordance with the 1967 statute, it has long since been destroyed. I remember the conclusion. I will not divulge it. It has no value as evidence. In fact, I am amazed that Reginald has humbled himself to beg for such scraps. But flattered too. It indicates a certain confidence in the predictive nature of my work.

I open my hands, palms outwards – a gesture of concili- ation. I explain, with regret, that I am unable to provide assistance. This is received with scrupulously controlled anger, but as my car is due shortly we exchange polite fare- wells and I roll away towards the lift. Reginald's behaviour is amusing, yet perplexing: he entreats me, in confidence, to break another confidence. I have no great respect for ethics, but the need for absolute confidentiality in my profession is a matter of practical necessity. The conclusion of an assess- ment is dangerous knowledge. The potential for misinter- preting it is immense. After all, to be certified medically as bad carries perhaps more stigma than to be judged insane. The latter implies an incapacity, the former an active nega- tive intent.

My car is waiting and I am handed in. The manufacturer and model seem to change with every visit. I have used a contract company since my last driver retired, and although they are punctual I detest the inconsistency.

It seems to me that modern automobiles are designed to minimise the pleasures of driving. As is the case with many other contemporary innovations, comfort is the only test of excellence. It saddens me that manufacturers do not seek to appeal to the spirit of endeavour. Everything is made to be 'fail-safe' and 'foolproof' and, if possible, fashioned to dissuade humans from independent motor action. It is over forty years since I have driven an automobile – James Markham's Jaguar SS 200, which he kept in a barn near the airfield at Hinton. It possessed a large engine, no roof, and was painted in the same matt black colour as the reconnaissance planes we flew by night. On those rare evenings of leave in the summer of 1943 we would roll back the great wooden door of the barn and fire out into the lanes, gathering speed and purpose as we approached London. The pleasures of travelling in this manner often exceeded those waiting at our destination in the ruined capital. While it is fitting that now, a cripple, I am carted round in a conveyance resembling an air-conditioned coffin, I am filled with scorn by the pusillanimous fools who circle London nose-to-tail with their electric windows and power steering. Surely they realise that there is more – that a car which makes demands on them could increase their pleasure in motoring? But no, they insist on choking the streets with their gaudy little toys and I am forced to endure an hour in this distasteful 'limousine' as a consequence.

There exists a further source of irritation: such was my eagerness to flee the company of Reginald that I omitted to collect the Colourfield Exposure photographs of Simon N—. My afternoon will be wasted. It is imperative that I examine them. I cannot entrust their delivery to a courier company – they are too sensitive. Miss Younghusband is feigning illness, hence cannot be directed to collect. Besides, she is a woman, and would not be admitted to the club premises. There is no one else whom I can trust. I shall have to turn back and endure another eternity in this wretched car. The rain, of course, is pouring down. It's only three-thirty, but already dark. The oncoming cars wear blazing headlights.

Perhaps Andrew? Must I ask him a favour? He has a motorcycle. It is infuriating that I have to rely on others! I only have to make a few mistakes, behave like an amnesiac for an instant, and my whole world falls apart.

Very well, I have to do it. The car is provided with a telephone, which makes this choice the line of least resistance. I speak first to Lydia, whom I think is drunk. It is very difficult to tell when she is in high spirits. Then Andrew, who agrees instantly to my proposal, listens calmly to my directions and leaves at once. A telephone call to the hall porter at my club alerts them of Andrew's arrival and purpose. Now I feel I can relax. The car at least is comfortable, which serves to reduce the frustration caused by congested traffic. Once home, I will take my medication, then concentrate on Simon N—. I am resolved to avoid creating complications. The case is simple: a young, successful married man who has spent much of his life on the side of the angels. He is as greedy and vain as would be expected of a pleasant, healthy individual of above-average intelligence. His imagination appears to be dormant, but I would not be surprised if he indulges in many fantasies of material success. This is the favourite pastime of aspirant capitalists. They thrive on dreams: copulation with film stars, a round of golf with the Governor of the Bank of England, that sort of thing. There is nothing uncommon in Simon's behaviour. He is prompted principally by conditioning; hence, he is systematic in his approach to life: he acts through applying patterns he has learnt. Last week I was overreacting. When I sit down to examine the tape of his second interview and the Colourfield photographs I am confident that any anomalies will be resolved.

The rain halts for a short while. The driver keeps his windscreen wipers working, in an attempt to disperse the greasy slick that covers the screen. The brief absence of precipitation allows other sounds to penetrate the car from

78

the streets: the hiss of tyres over Tarmac, the rumble of a bus engine as its driver selects wholly inappropriate gears to pull away downhill. My driver ignores the red traffic light and his passenger's comfort as he deliberately rolls the limousine off Ladbroke Grove and into Elgin Crescent. I cannot admire such manoeuvres. If the man had spirit and desired to drive with style, he would emigrate to Italy tomorrow.

Why are those policemen outside my house? Have they nothing better to do than stand around residential areas in the rain? Do they not realise what an eyesore they create, like so many crows, hunched over roadside carrion . . .

No. They are expecting me. Waving and pointing. One steps into the road as the car draws up. What has happened? Is it a break-in? I must get to my house immediately. The security is very good. The alarms connect to the station in Ladbroke Grove, but nevertheless I am nervous. What is going on?

A tap at the window. I rub away the condensation and am rewarded with an emotionless face under a peaked cap. Its skin is the colour of veal. I depress the button and the window opens, admitting cold air. What is that fool of a driver up to? It is imperative that he releases me!

'Sir Charles Barrington?'

I nod my head.

The policeman calls over his shoulder to his colleague: 'This is him, sir.'

The other officer approaches and removes his cap. He intends to speak to me. What is going on? Can't they see I'm trapped in a state of discomfort?

'Inspector Evans, Sir Charles. There has been an attempted burglary in your house, sir. They tried to start a fire.'

'Who?'

This question stops him in his tracks. Of course he doesn't know. Policemen amaze me. They are exomorphs to a man: heavy, with overmuscled frames, a prominent ridge of bone

79

on the forehead, zero reflexiveness, and the ponderous thought processes of a dog. I am not convinced they possess secondary consciousness. This Evans opens his mouth again, no doubt to assure me his colleagues are in hot pursuit, but I intercept him.

'We will achieve more if you conduct your explanation inside my house. It is imperative that I examine the damage.' I hold up my hands. They are shaking with anger. Do I have to explain I need assistance, spell it out word by word, or are they waiting for a miracle? 'For God's sake, help me out of the car!' I phrase it as an order – something he can understand. At last! The door is opened, strong hands reach within, and I am carried to the porch.

The front door is unmarked. Perhaps the lock has been picked. The security camera is smashed. There is the crunch of broken glass under boots as I am manhandled over the threshold.

Meanwhile, Inspector Evans is pouring information into my ear: 'We think we surprised them. It looks as though they wanted the paintings. They had a good go at that door . . .' On my right, the door to the reception has been knocked off its hinges. The Bacon portrait is missing . . . No, there it is, lying on the floor. A strong smell of smoke. '. . . And, as you can see, there's been some damage to—'

'Fucking hell!' I say this out loud and the policemen put me down, in the centre of the consulting-room floor, and stand around me in surprise. The room stinks and damp ashes are scattered everywhere.

'The sprinklers caught them off balance. This is as far as they got,' concludes Evans, cap still in hand, and his meat face peers at mine.

Violation! I am furious, utterly furious, shivering in my chair, a red pulse of anger thumping in my temples. I am on the edge of rage, which is a dangerous condition. I must regain self-control. A warning tickle has appeared in my spine. Its resident demon feeds on emotion. I have to lull him back to sleep. *Exhale slowly, Charles, slowly! Now. Do it now! There.*

'When did it happen?'

'At some time between one and two o'clock, sir.'

'What about the alarms?'

'None given, sir. I'm afraid—'

'What do you mean?'

And they explain to me that the systems were disabled one by one. I am then subjected to a series of questions: names of visitors, frequency of their visits. Do I lend my paintings to exhibitions? If so, are they displayed as my property? Wretched things! I shall call Christie's tomorrow. Put them in the next auction and forget about them. Time has made them so valuable, they now endanger my work. What if my records, my equipment, had been destroyed? Unthinkable!

Mid-question, Evans peers over my shoulder and lowers his notebook. His face assumes a belligerent expression. I turn my head and see Andrew in the doorway, dishevelled, dripping water, a package wrapped in plastic under one arm.

'What's going on, Charles?'

Evans frowns. He does not enjoy being pre-empted. 'Who are you?' he says.

I intervene, explain, and invite Andrew into the room. He puts down his crash helmet, takes a seat on the edge of the desk behind my right shoulder and listens in silence as the police continue their questions. Evans informs me he suspects this is the work of an international gang of art thieves. I am not interested in his speculations. He has been reading too many novels. My immediate need is to repair the damage and restore the alarms. It is a full hour before I am rid of them.

'Why don't you stay with us this evening?' Andrew speaks for the first time since entering. He reads the rejection on my face and changes his suggestion quickly. 'Or I could stay here and help make a start on clearing up.'

'Don't bother. I'll arrange that with the agency. I have to

make some telephone calls.' My voice sounds very sharp –
too much like a rebuke. But I am glad of Andrew's presence.
I have no wish to drive him away.

He steps forward and offers me the package. 'Here.'

'Thank you. What about a drink?'

'I'll find out if the cabinet's intact.' He strides off, a tall,
slim figure, surprisingly light-footed in his heavy boots. I
hear glass crackle as he enters the sitting room. A pause,
then, 'Untouched!' he calls.

'Bring the bottle.'

I make my way up in the lift. Andrew is waiting for me
outside my study, malt whisky in one hand, two glasses in
the other.

I dig into the waistcoat pocket below my ribs for the keys.
'Here.' I attempt a throw. Damn fingers are shaking and the
keys fly low. In an elegant instant he tucks the bottle under
one arm, drops his hand and closes his fingers. He straightens up, unlocks the door, and holds it open. I flick the light
switch as I roll in. It's set low in the wall – waist height for
the average man.

A quick scan to ensure no material from my current assessment is on display, then I call out the invitation: 'Come in.'

Andrew enters slowly. His mouth is open and his glance
sweeps the study. Other practitioners and contract cleaners
aside, he is the first individual to have seen this room in
twenty years. It appears to make a powerful impression. I
try to see it with his eyes, and admit it is unusual: a hybrid,
with leading-edge, twentieth-century technology mixed in
among the inkwell-and-paper-scroll disorder of the creative
retreat of a Victorian man of letters. Group photographs of
sporting teams hang above high-resolution VGA screens. A
glass-walled cubicle with an elevated steel floor occupies one
corner – a surrealist aquarium where vivid plastic cables
wind around white boxes like fantastic-coloured serpents . . .
Elsewhere, blotting pad, silver letter-opener, crystal water
flask, laser printer, teletext printer, oscillographs, leather-
bound anatomy volumes, microfiles, floppy discs, video tapes

in three formats, occasional religious paraphernalia: a shrunken head, a voodoo totem, a crucifix. A single, comfortable armchair, where Andrew comes to rest, after spinning on his heels in fascination.

I lock my wheelchair into position by my desk and commence a series of telephone calls: the insurance company, the operator of the security system, the cleaning agency. Appointments are made for each tomorrow morning. I use the speaker-phone system, which leaves my hands free to take notes and accept the drink that Andrew has poured.

The insurance company show particular interest in the attempt at arson. 'Most unusual,' repeats the idiot on the other end of the line. He asks as many questions as Inspector Evans, so I refer him to this slow-witted guardian of the peace in the hope that they will exhaust each other with interrogatives.

'Bloody man,' I remark to Andrew. 'I fail to see how it can be considered unusual that thieves would wish to steal property valued at several million pounds. What does he expect them to do? Dedicate their hours to petty theft?'

Andrew looks thoughtful, but makes no reply. He draws his knuckles across his forehead and returns his attention to his drink.

My final call is reserved for Miss Younghusband, to inform her of events and determine her state of health. I mention this to Andrew, then tap in her number. Before the line is connected, he walks over, flicks the cut-off button and says, 'Wait.'

What has prompted this desire to interfere? I must indeed now wait – for two matters: an explanation, and communication with my assistant. I watch Andrew's face closely. He is hesitant, wondering, I think, where to begin what he has to say. He stares at the tumbler, which he swings to and fro in his fingers, spinning the cinnamon liquid around the crystal.

'Charles, is it possible that ... I mean, have you considered the possibility that she may be involved? The police and the insurance are looking for the same thing – a frequent visitor who has your confidence, or has at least had time to gain some knowledge of the alarms – and, Younghusband aside, who else could there be?'

'You.'

This silences him. He swallows, then stares at me. His posture indicates that his muscles are tense.

He licks his lips and speaks again: 'That's true, and in my case you'd have little trouble establishing a motive. No need for a gypsy with a crystal ball – plain poverty would suffice.'

'Be quiet. Enough public servants are being paid to speculate about this crime. There is no call to add amateur voices to their babble.'

'Listen, Charles, don't shout me down. Other people will say the same.'

'And I shall answer them in the same manner. Younghusband is a wealthy woman. I pay her well. Besides, she gained her divorce in the 1970s and benefited greatly in the settlement. She is too proud, and too stupid—'

'To attempt to rob a vain old man?'

'I beg your pardon?'

We are both silent. Andrew is breathing heavily. His pupils are contracted with anger.

'I'm sorry, Charles – I need you to listen. It may not be money. Lydia told me she saw her with a man.'

'Enough. This is ridiculous. I am grateful for your help, but if its price is insult, then I will do without it.'

'Very well. I understand. I see you wave your hand – "Be off" – I know what you want. But this is important, Charles. You must realise that other people can be compelled by passion, a motive to which you seem quite blind. Even a creature as hideous and unpleasant as your halfwit secretary can fall in love . . .'

'Andrew, I must warn—'

'No, Charles, you must listen. I admire you more than any other man, but you're being blind. You're being manipulated. She knows you so well she can work you just like a machine.'

'Enough, Andrew! You have said enough!'

I am successful in silencing him, but not, I suspect, in derailing his speculative train of thought. My next step must be to get rid of him. An attack is imminent. It is too late to take pre-emptive medication. The tension of these last hours has awoken pain. If I am to avoid another night of spiritual disintegration, I must be calm and dismiss Andrew at once. In prior years, I could have achieved this objective with ease, but now, for perhaps the first time, I feel unequal to confrontation. I have lived through handicap, but disease is new and frightening in its power. It advances to a monstrous yet natural – predictable – rhythm. My cells have altered their pattern of build/decay/replace into a sinister endgame. Most of happy, foolish humanity profess no alarm at death's approach. They seem to believe that at the terminal instant, the soul will float free from its dead-flesh temple towards a pure existence. I have no such consolations: kill the body and the head will die.

I must hide all this from Andrew: no fist-clenching, nail-biting or other distressing gestures can be admitted to the public view. Time for control. *Right hand, pick up the tumbler. Deliver same to mouth. Mouth open wide, to diminish risk of spillage. Drain, pause, then replace on desk.* There! Another algorithm accomplished.

Andrew appears to be shaking slightly, but his eyes are very bright. He picks up the whisky bottle, looks at me, then my glass. 'Another?' The voice is eager. This, evidently, is a topic Andrew has rehearsed and he feels he must seize his moment. 'Because, you see, Charles – you must see! I'm sorry I'm going on, but what I say deserves at least consideration. I can see you've been thinking about it. But no, now you frown. You were trying to forget me. You're the most perceptive man I know, but I'm disappointed you won't admit to flaws.'

'Had you chanced on one, Andrew, I'd congratulate—'

As I am speaking, a spasm strikes. The entire room shifts, then settles back into place as a tremor of pain shakes its way through my senses. Even my hearing twists: voices are distorted, words in transit are caught and squeezed by the disease. I can no longer be sure of their source. The syllables spray round the room, then regroup in fantastic combinations.

'I know (know, know) you hold her in low regard (low regard) . . . But contempt, Charles (Charles, Charles), is no barrier to deception. She manipulates you; she feeds on you . . .'

And I have a vision of the parasite. It is strangely clinical. I know too many of its secrets to feel fear when I observe it at work.

Astonishingly, as if a hypnotist had clicked his fingers and restored me to my senses, control returns, and there is Andrew, stamping up and down, still talking.

'Contempt is no barrier to deception, Charles. Feel free to hate her, by all means. But for God's sake, keep up your guard! She manipulates you – no, worse than that: she feeds off you, she is a parasite . . .'

'At last you speak from experience!'

Good! That shut him up. A hot flush spreads across his pale face. I might yet make him violent. Question: would such anger spring from conditioning or instinct?

Shame is the reference point. I'm too close to my own edge to play with other people. No one may hear me scream. Can't Andrew see what's happening? It's absurd: I've no motor control, but still he stands in front of me and frowns. Perhaps this is what all people look like when they're dying – so normal as to be unworthy of comment.

The hallucinations recommence. Now time itself is falling apart. The numbers, then the hands, melt and drip from the wall clock as Andrew continues to prance to and fro in an idiot dance.

His arms twitch at the elbows, his mouth babbles: 'Exploitation! That's the word I was looking for. But there's more, isn't there?' He pauses, strikes his forehead. 'Now I understand why you insist on supporting the creature! Why you speak of her with evident affection – or more, more than affection: love!'

'Don't tell me about affection, love or exploitation. Only one of the three means anything to you.'

'What did you just say?'

Andrew's voice is suddenly quiet, his face surprisingly blank. These are extremely dangerous signals. I grab my chair with my left hand, while the fingers of the right scrabble at the package of photographs in my lap. Could I use it to repel Andrew? I shall have a last try with words. I curl my neck towards him. I have to move like an infant, like a hatchling, to make an awkward reply.

'One of three: exploitation. E-X-P . . . Ask Lydia . . . ask her for a cheque . . .'

The effort required for expression is too much. Suddenly, my entire circulatory system is pumping agony into every limb. Instead of liquid, my arteries, capillaries and veins distribute countless splinters of broken glass. The Colour-field photographs seem to float in the air around me. My eyes select one and follow the image of Simon N— as it descends, in seesaw motion, to the floor. Where is Andrew?

Pain strikes again! I am at the centre of a soundless explosion. In an instant the walls around me are dust and accelerate away into space. The furniture spirals off on separate orbits, diminishes from chairs to icons to distant points of light. The carpet flows into an emerald, wave-furrowed sea, moulds to an enamelled globe, which itself drops away beneath my feet. Now there is a rushing sensation – as if I, too, am travelling.

The telephone is ringing. Its disembodied tones float through my dreams and drag me into consciousness. I struggle to open my eyes. The lids are crusted, swollen. I have to blink repeatedly to separate them. What appears is meaningless: shapes too close for resolution, and a soft white glow. Moonlight fluoresces the carpet. My cheek is numb, but the woven filaments tickle my nose, cause my face to twitch up. The inclined woollen plane fills my field of vision. Now both ears are clear and the telephone echoes at the base of my skull. I raise my head further. Why so dark? I think the lights were on when I fell. I am lying on my right arm and that, too, is numb – cramped and useless.

Free it. I push down on my left hand . . . harder . . . then the effort overcomes and I subside. Still the telephone rings – *da da . . . da da . . .*

Pain has vanished. An astonishing calm prevails.

What happened? I have no idea, no concept. The sensations were so violent that the brain cannot, has not the capacity to, remember.

This must be a value system – hopeless optimism, implanted before birth. Man can only remember the pleasurable; otherwise, suffering would overwhelm. A child would cry once – forever . . .

Da da . . . da . . . The telephone ceases abruptly, though my ears manufacture an echo for the brain. My pulse speeds, but now my body is cold – useless, immobilised flesh. The silence grows, seems to roar round the room, then I isolate the ticking clock, focus on each eternal second. What is left? Can I move my head?

Yes! I can see the tip of my right foot. Is it mine? I can't feel it. How can it be mine? It's as if some mindless fool has stitched an alien lump of meat to my torso to vex me!

The irritation subsides and a single emotion rests across my thoughts: sadness. It is gentle, yet complete, and is accompanied by resignation. This time, the damage is beyond repair. Not enough of this organism remains to remake a man.

Now I understand the melancholy. It derives from a knowledge of futility. I have no will left to preserve myself in favour of further pain. It is time to let go, to let the cells perish, one by one, until the luminous sheen is extinguished.

I wonder, can I stop my heart? Can the brain issue that

command? If only consciousness were absolute master, if only it were more than an innate capacity for wonder, wonder at the marvels of proportion the world contains, the embedded values which write hope over all our actions . . .

Indeed.

I will be brave. I have controlled my life, and now I choose to die.

Farewell, Sir Charles.

The ageing physician presents his compliments to his heart – exemplary organ! – thanks it for its years of faithful service, and bids it goodnight.

2 Dissection

7   'Today, we practised slowing down our heartbeats.'
    'Why?' I ask.

Selina hesitates before she answers. 'I don't know. Perhaps I'll live longer. Anyway, listen to this: when I become an adept, I'll be able to release my bowels and wash them by hand!'

'Charming.'

'Agreed. That's the trouble with yoga – it's so serious and practical. I found out that I have to wait two years until we start Tantric sex . . . and, Lydia, this is the worst part: before I'm even allowed close to that course I have to learn to control my breathing!'

'Impossible.'

Selina confirms my last word with an explosion of giggles.

'Tell me more about your class. Are there many men?'

'Only one – the teacher. He's a strange Indian whose body is full of surprises. He has no muscles to speak of. His bones seem to have been rolled in loose rubber, which hangs or stretches according to which contortion he selects. He can do that trick you used to perform.'

'Which one?'

'With your legs. Behind your ears. Can you still do it?'

'Hang on and I'll try.' I wrap my forearm around my calf, tuck my fingers into the arch of my foot, then raise my leg until I'm staring at my stockinged toes. 'Selina? I'll have to put down the phone.' It's simpler with two hands. The foot pops into place on my shoulder. 'I've done one leg.'

'Was it easy?'

'Quite. I'll try the other.' I balance the receiver between the sole of my foot and my ear and reach for the other ankle.

'Lydia?'

'Hang on.'

'Have you done it?'

'Yes!'

'How does it feel?'

'Painful. If you hear screams, call an ambulance.'

'I promise. Where were we?'

'Before yoga? Men. Your new man. Tell me all about him. Is he gentle?'

'Not at all. It's like being charged by a bull!'

'Selina!'

She giggles.

'Tart!'

'I love it!'

'Good for you!'

'And good for my skin too. Everyone says that.' In the background, a doorbell sounds. 'Lydia? Listen: I think it's him! I have to go. So long, darling. It's been wonderful talking to you. And, Lydia . . .'

'Yes?'

'Congratulations!'

She hangs up, leaving me in a tangle of numb limbs, which I slowly unthread.

Selina's my only remaining unmarried friend – the last single, the last wicked girl in all of London. The others are so tedious: great big lumps of brain-dead flesh who trail around after their husbands. They've been ringing all day long to tell me about the joys of pregnancy. First Julia, next Celia, then Anna – in fact, any girl whose name ends in 'a'. I suppose I should be proud – I'm the new sister initiate. Well, I am! It's excellent! Even so, I think they're trying to scare me: they make it such a mystery. It's so far away – nearly seven months – but if they're speaking the truth, my hormones have already gone berserk.

I think, another drink to celebrate. These bottles don't hold very much. Perhaps it's all the bubbles – less room for liquid. Then again, I suppose I might be drunk? Never mind! Too late! I'll have to give up next month. My doctor was adamant. He handed me a printed list of Do's and Don'ts, mainly Don'ts, and explained carefully how he would monitor my progress. We are going to meet monthly, then weekly. I will be weighed, measured and scanned. It was a strange encounter. I left the clinic feeling more and less human at the same time. My poor body – nothing but painful withdrawal for half a year! I'm not sure I trust that calculating doctor and his formulae for perfect health.

Keys! At last! Andrew is here! Sweet one! I'll run and catch him. On second thoughts . . . Damn table! Far too low-lying. One day I'll chop it up for fire wood. I hop into the hall and arrive as Andrew closes the door behind him. He bends at the waist to place his helmet on the floor. His beautiful eyes meet mine sideways and his mouth tries a smile.

He's unhappy. What is it? He looks handsome when he's sad, but I mustn't say that. Poor thing. Perhaps they had another argument.

'Wonderful one!' I sweep back my hair and catch him with my arms and he kisses me gently behind the ear. His lips are so soft. I love his presence – his simple, physical presence: I could stay like this for days. But he's upset. He needs to speak. Better prompt him. 'How was Uncle Charles? Did he try to bite you this time? Can I search for wounds?'

He smiles quickly, distracted for an instant. 'The same result as at the last fixture: told me to sod off and bombarded me with the contents of his study.'

'Senile fool! How did you provoke him?'

'In the usual manner – by attempting to tell him the truth. But this time there was more. He was burgled today. Someone broke in and tried to take his paintings. They trashed the ground floor, even started a fire. He was surrounded by policemen when I arrived, and giving them considerable grief. A lecture on their duties, complete with extracts from the statutes.' And here Andrew holds out both arms in front of him, his hands clasping an imaginary wheelchair, in imitation of Uncle Charles: 'Am I given to under-

95

stand, officer, that your rigorous methods of examination lead you to the confident prognosis that this is the work of a gang of "international art thieves", possibly operating from a warehouse on the outskirts of Vienna, and no doubt possessing many aliases? Indeed.'

I laugh aloud, then check myself. Poor old man. I must call him. He's too fragile to be picking fights with everyone – like one of those cross-tempered little terriers . . .

I have a surprise for Andrew! Shall I tell him now? No. His face is still unsettled. Let him talk some more. Mustn't interrupt.

'I tried to help – first asked him here, then offered to stay over there. He wasn't interested. I think he's still tripped-out on that wartime sang-froid: soldier on and disregard the odds against. He's well organised, though. I'm sure that by this time tomorrow there'll be no sign of damage. All the same, I feel I should go and see him . . .' He looks at me enquiringly as rainwater drips from his motorcycle leathers.

I have to kiss him. 'Come here, sweetheart,' I say.

His body is warm and strong. When I squeeze him, the leather squeaks. Excites, too. I'm definitely horny. Bath time, I think. I whisper the proposal in his ear and he nods gently, slips a finger in my blouse and tickles my stomach. Wonderful! Andrew disentangles, rises to undress. He shakes his head a couple of times, still distracted.

'Why don't *you* call him? Give him a ring – just to see.'

I nod my head and hold out both my hands. He throws me the phone. What time is it? Nine o'clock. That's not too late. I dial the number. No reply. I wait for the answer relay. Its message lasts just long enough for me to forget to say what I mean to say and the tone catches me unprepared. What shall I say?

'Uncle Charles? It's Lydia! I just want to say . . . I'm sorry to hear what happened. I'd come round right now, but . . .' I can't. Where's Andrew? Good: out of range. I'll whisper anyway. 'We're going away tomorrow for a week. We're bor-

96

rowing Selina's cottage in Suffolk. But, God bless! Keep yourself out of trouble. Ten thousand kisses!'

Grouchy old man! I'll speak to him when we come back. He was sweet this morning – pretending to be irritable, but secretly so pleased to see me.

Bath time! Clothes are worse than chains when you're in a hurry to escape. Buttons, in particular, were invented by a sadist. Worse still are spiteful zips, which trap shaking fingers and refuse to give way. Next door, Andrew has opened the taps. His uncontrolled Lydia must catch him before he steps into the bath. I abandon my skirt and dash through, just in time to intercept.

Andrew is naked. I love his body – his pale skin and smooth limbs. He's strong and slim, with the square shoulders of a boxer. He looks as if he had been cut out from a magazine. His black hair flops forward and I have to peel it back to see his eyes. Shall I tease him? No. My own need is too great. Tomorrow there will be time to play. He'll be so happy! I've got the keys to Selina's cottage for a week.

8　Andrew usually wakes at dawn. It's as if he's still got to rise and march off through the rain to some squalid office. So do I, but sometimes I pretend I'm still asleep. I lie still and try not to tremble when he gives me gentle kisses on my neck. This morning I can't control myself: I roll over, with eyes wide open, pin him down like a tiger and climb astride his back.

'You've nowhere to run,' I whisper in his ear. He smiles, still half asleep, and mutters something. My hair is quite long at the moment. I can shake my head from side to side and flick tresses across his face. A sleepy hand reaches up and catches some. Wake up, wake up!

His irresistible body tries to turn beneath me but I clasp my legs and hold him, which feels joyous.

'Perfect one.'

He opens his eyes and turns his face.

'Sweetness! Today is special day! Today is holiday.'

An eyebrow rises.

'I have the car. I have the keys.'

'Keys?' He tries to push up on one elbow but I hold him down.

'So get up! Wash! Dress! Anoint yourself! But first . . .'

'Make love.'

'Exactly.'

He rolls over beneath me, erect and ready. Perfect!

I feel a little shaky when I dress – warm and tender, but hollow. Andrew is ecstatic – really, really pleased.

Selina has a new man who gives her many toys. So she has lent me the keys to her cottage in Suffolk while she looks after her lover in London. We have strict instructions to drink all the wine and soil the sheets. The cottage even comes with shooting rights. When I told Andrew that, he was so excited he immediately ran off to find his gun. He can spend the mornings trying to kill the birds of the air and the beasts of the field, while I do sentry duty in bed. It's a shame we can't borrow a dog. Someone must have one to spare? A Labrador would be perfect – something sleepy and obese. Then we'd probably be accused of corrupting it.

A week in the country! I've even had time for homework. I listened to the Archers yesterday and bought a new head-scarf. I'll wear it every day – with sunglasses. We can pretend to be married, but I'll hide my wedding ring. Mr and Mrs, ahem, Smith. Of course! Selina tells me that all the Suffolks – all the folks in that neck of the woods – are mad with curiosity. And that their eyes fall out of their heads – literally, litter the roads, no, cart tracks – if you wear a short skirt. It's a shame it's so cold. Answerphone on? Windows locked?

'Away! Away!' I shout to Andrew and we race each other downstairs.

Nine o'clock. The rush hour is dying. It's wonderful to roll through London when everyone else is charging around trying to get to work. Look at them all! I'm amazed they don't trample one another to death. Perhaps they do, but it's hushed up. I drive while Andrew fiddles with the map.

'Light me a cigarette.' I lean across and kiss him. 'Then sing me a song.'

'What about?'

'Love! Adventure!'

He hands me the cigarette and clears his throat. ' "She was poor, but she was honest/Victim of the squire's whim . . ." '

Complete with mock cockney accent. Excellent! I swerve deliberately towards an oncoming car, which shuts him up.

'You tell me such sweet things.'

Selina's cottage proves a nightmare to find. It's hidden in some woods, at the end of a very muddy track. It's miles from the village. No electricity, no telephone. The gas comes in bottles. There's something called a Ray-Burn to heat the water. You can use what you like for fuel – apparently it burns anything. Perhaps that's why there's so little furniture. I can't fault the bed, though – that much is true to the owner's character: it's large and firm like an exercise mat. I think Selina bought the place when she was going through her Action Man phase – she had a parade ground's worth of wild country types. They all hunted or played polo or jumped off cliffs for fun.

Time to get organised. I release Andrew into the fields with his gun. I'm going to drive back to the village for food. Can't wait to examine the Suffolks. Do they really, truly interbreed? I shall keep my eyes open for extra thumbs. I wonder if they bother to conceal them.

What if . . . ? No, I'm sure ours won't be. The perfect lover must make an ideal child. I hope it looks just like Andrew. Can't wait for the patter of tiny feet. If only. In my case it'll be the screams of a despairing mother as she's turned inside out. I'm going to take lots of drugs – before, during and after.

The car starts first time and I manoeuvre it to the end of the track. Which way? Left, I think. Left gets the vote. Oh, look! There's a local! Towing a little cart behind his tractor. That looks like fun, but rather slow. Perhaps they race them in the summer.

I return with a hundred stories for my beloved. Everyone stared at me. They were very friendly, though. I wish they'd been more threatening – no, mysterious, or something – with high-pitched, singsong voices and the odd hunchback.

The food I bought in the village covers every surface in the kitchen. What shall I do with it all? I wish I was a better cook. Those ridiculous nuns used to warn us we'd never marry if we couldn't cook. They had very many strange ideas. It looks quite cold outside. It's cold in here. Fire time. Where's Andrew? Perhaps he's in a ditch somewhere. More likely he's found a pub. Pub first, then ditch.

Four o'clock. Time for a drink. Where does she keep it? She talked as if there'd be an avalanche of bottles when you opened the front door. Kitchen? No luck. Drawing room?

That cupboard looks promising – could hold at least a small hoard.

Well! Selina! What a lot of leather! I wonder if any will fit me. I'll try that skirt. If I make a mistake with the boots I'll need surgery to escape. Must be toys for her new man. She mentioned he liked games. I hope it's been washed. Do you wash leather? I could always ask in the village: 'Excuse me, Mrs Hayseed, but I've got a troublesome stain.' I bet all the locals share the same name. Mirror's in the bathroom. This skirt fits quite well. A bit cold, though. Never mind. Andrew will be pleased.

A knock? No: the door closing. He's back! A high-speed tiptoe to the kitchen and I catch him round the waist.

'Creature!'

'Sweetheart!' I receive a long, whisky-flavoured kiss.

'Hip flask,' he explains, then holds it upside down to show it's empty.

'Party-sized.'

'For the cruelty-free sportsman. I missed everything. Even the gatepost.'

'But it was fun?'

'Outstanding.'

I release him and wave my hips.

'Good one! Is it new?'

'Not mine. It's Selina's. Bought to excite her new lover. He's a high-stress businessman.'

'Nightmare.'

'Agreed. He sounds horrible. He's called Donald and has red hair.'

Andrew feigns a shudder. Then, 'Drink?' he says, with irresistible sweetness in his beautiful voice.

'Can't find it. You look, I'll cook.' I really have to pay the kitchen some attention. That familiar burning smell is already sneaking out from one of the pans. Crashes sound in the background as Andrew searches out the alcohol. That means he's drunk already, or he's thinking – whatever – one of the two always sets him on collision course.

'Aha! Prepare for re-entry! Seek and ye shall find! Look at these! A matching pair from the House of Bollinger, magnum calibre, dated 1982. Note the delicate scrolling on the labels and fine gold foil. The ambient temperature of a February shed has ensured they are in prime condition for immediate use. Prepare the glasses!'

The perfect husband!

We make love twice before dinner. It must be the country air. No wonder all the Suffolks smile. Andrew is on wonderful form. He seems to have forgotten London and those vile people who made our last month so wretched. He's so sweet and conscientious – determined to work. He needn't really. I have enough money. For the present, at least, it seems the career madness is off his mind. Good thing. Careers are for old people who have nothing better to do with their time than lock themselves away in offices and push round bits of paper and fuck their secretaries or whatever else goes on in those ant-hill buildings.

We should move to the country, I tell my loved one. Sell out in Kensington and take to the road. 'I could be an Earth mother and wear dungarees and give birth to twins behind the barn. They'd come out sideways – I wouldn't even flinch. Andrew, you could get a job like Uncle Charles . . .'

He stops laughing. 'Do you know what your godfather does?'

'He's an assessor. Why?'

'But do you know what that means?'

'Well . . .' Shall I bullshit? Yes. Why not. 'Of course. It's a type of pioneer. That's how Daddy used to describe him. "Charles Barrington", he would say, "is one of modern medicine's greatest pioneers." Then he'd look very stern. He was trying to stop me teasing him. So there it is: Uncle Charles is a pioneer. In a wheelchair.'

Andrew smiles at my answer, then suddenly frowns. 'Listen, creature, I'm going to tell you something. It happened yesterday when I went round. But first I'd better explain what Charles really does. It's quite unusual. I think there are only seven others like him. In some ways, he's a very powerful man.'

I lean back in my chair and cross my legs. Scratch any itches, then settle down to listen. Fix Andrew with a look of adoration. He wears his stern storyteller's face. How wonderful! I am going to be attentive. All men like explaining serious things to girls, whether they care to listen or not. I'm not a very good listener. Nothing is so important that it can absorb me for very long. But I love to listen to Andrew's voice – watch his face as he searches for words, for he tries to entertain as well as to impart. I hate it when other people don't. They may as well send each other letters – read that and reply in due course.

'Charles is a scientist, a pure scientist, who measures other people's characters. Your father was right to call him a pioneer. In effect, he invented his own branch of medicine. He acts as a sort of judge. If the Government or a company want an analysis of a man's character – say, if they're anxious to know how someone is likely to behave in the future – they call in Charles and he carries out an assessment.'

I nod my head. How true! Uncle Charles is forever staring at people and making cryptic comments. I used to find him very fierce. He was good at making me feel wicked.

'I don't know how he carries out his tests, but he's very high tech. I saw his study yesterday. It's a wild place. Full of strange machines and voodoo symbols.'

I nod my head again. I've seen it too, but don't want to spoil Andrew's story. It was back in 1970, when I was still at school and Daddy had just died and Uncle Charles could still walk. He didn't know what to do with me – no one did. But he was kind in a forbidding sort of way.

'He was in a vicious mood after the break-in and we started arguing again. He threw that package I'd collected at me.'

'Sweetness! Did it hit you? Did it hurt?'

'It hit. He has a surprisingly good arm for a seventy-three-year-old.'

'He's very naughty. I think we should retire him to the coast. He might take up biting people. Some people are like that by nature. Arabella was telling me her son – Amos, or whatever he's called – has just started. Apparently you can cure it by biting them back. What a horrible family! Imagine them at dinner!'

'It's possible that he's already started. That parcel contained photographs – it broke open when it hit me. The man in the pictures looked in plenty of pain. It was quite surreal – unreal, really – because it was the same man who "let me go" – you know, that nightmare I told you about, who fired me when we were taken over?'

'The head prefect?'

'That one. No doubt still longing for dormitory Bible readings and a spot of buggery after lights out. I don't know what Charles was doing to him – he was off-camera – but it seemed to hurt. His face was a wild green colour and he looked pretty savage.'

'Perhaps he was biting him down there!'

'Lydia!'

'I'm sorry, sweet one – too much wine. Besides, I think it's very brave of Uncle Charles to take revenge.'

Andrew raises his glass in agreement. 'Anyway, what I was going to tell you . . .'

A car, no, two cars arrive on the drive. Their headlights shake as they ride over the uneven track. Where are they going? A farm? No – there's nowhere else but here. Perhaps Selina forgot and double-booked? How disappointing. Andrew looks at me and shrugs his shoulders. Footsteps, crunch, crunch, on the gravel, and a knock. He rises and walks out of sight into the little hall. It's probably the Suffolks to invite us to the village orgy – every Wednesday night in Mrs Hayseed's barn.

The latch clicks and cold air rushes into the room. What is it?

Voices:

'Mr Andrew Bruton?'

'Yes.'

He sounds tense. What is it?

'You're under arrest, for burglary and serious assault.'

'For what? I . . .'

Sounds of a scuffle follow and the door slams shut. Before I can move, there's a policeman in the kitchen, dragged by a violent dog on a chain. When it sees me, it goes berserk – it's not even nearly under control – hackles and saliva and teeth, head snapping back and forth, jerking out its handler's arms. It barks and barks and the cutlery rattles. Each time it barks it jumps forward, knocks something else over. What the fuck is happening? I can feel that dog's breath across the table. It carries a sour, meaty smell, which makes me want to retch. The policeman keeps saying 'Down, Scouser!' as if he's in control. The whole room is moving, seems blurred with motion, but this is real, an affair of the senses. Now a policewoman walks in with Andrew's gun. She's wearing surgical gloves. She puts the gun down and nods in my direction. Now a third comes in, older, with a peaked cap under one arm.

'Lydia Bruton?'

Who the fuck does he think I am? Some nameless little tart? That evil-eyed bitch is staring at me and smiling. I follow her eyes down and remember what I'm wearing. Damn! That can't help.

'You have some questions to answer. You're coming with us.' He looks at the dog-handler and jerks a thumb over his shoulder. It has to be dragged out of the room. The remaining pair sidle round until they're standing either side of me. I can't help staring at that bitch's hands. They look like dead flesh – white sausage-meat fingers wrapped in Clingfilm.

'Where's my husband?'

'Outside. In the van.'

'I want to see him.'

'You'll have to wait.'

The woman grabs my elbow, digging in her corpse fingers.

'Let go! Let me go!'

I shake her off. Hot tears sting my eyes. She looks across and spreads her fingers, ready to snatch, but the old one shakes his head. He puts on his hat, sidles up and stands before me, too close for focus, pushing me back with his presence until I'm pressed against the range. I'm shivering and fold my arms across my chest. I look from the policeman to his vicious accomplice, then at the lines between the flagstones on the kitchen floor.

'Your husband stands accused of a particularly nasty crime, Mrs Bruton. This is not a game. We are the Metropolitan Police and we would like some answers from you.'

I nod my head. Better to go with them. But this is madness! Real madness. What can they think he's done?

'This is a bad mistake,' I say, but my voice sounds so hollow, so false. They both smile, as if that was exactly what they were expecting from me, and we walk together in silence to their car. At the end of the track an indicator flickers, then headlights sweep off into the darkness. Where are they taking him?

I'm burning with heat, though the February wind stings my bare legs. They squeeze me in between the woman and another policeman in the back seat.

'What are you accusing him of? I want to know. He's been with me and—'

'Be quiet,' says the bitch. 'Wait until we reach the station.'

This turns out to be in London, but meanwhile I am just so furious that they can be so violent and rude and wrong, so absolutely wrong, that I'm shaking with anger for the whole hour or however long it takes to get there, firing down the fast lane with blue lights strobing the white lines and Tarmac, constricted by two stinking, sweating lumps of meat.

I can't believe the room they take me to – a windowless cell with a boxwood desk and flickering fluorescent lights that make my head hum.

'Sit down,' says the old one, but I'm tired of this charade. I stand up very straight and fold my arms across my chest and begin to shout at them. *Why am I here? Where is my husband?*

'Your husband is under arrest for a serious crime, Mrs Bruton.'

'This is madness! I can't believe this. Just can't believe it.'

'*Sit down!*'

Now he is shouting and his face is red with anger. Then the policewoman grabs at my arm and forces me to sit.

'Your bloody husband has nearly killed a man.'

God! The vitality drains out of me and my arms flap, useless, by my sides. *He can't have hit him back. That's impossible.*

'So, you know what we're talking about?'

He is suddenly alert. Did I say the last part out loud?

'No! I mean, please explain. What is it? Is he hurt?'

'Is who hurt?'

Fuck it. I've lost it. Everything I say will sound incriminating. Think. No – it's impossible: Andrew would never hit anybody. When I throw things at him he laughs or just looks grim and waits for me to calm down. But what about Uncle Charles? Is it him? What has happened to him? It just goes from bad to worse. I'm crying now and they watch and wait in silence.

'I'm going to ask you some questions. You'd better think very carefully before you answer. Do you understand?'

Nod the head.

'Good. First I want you to tell me all your movements on the seventeenth of February of this year. Where you went. What you did. Everything.'

'When?'

'*The seventeenth of February! Yesterday!*'

How sordid. Lydia under the microscope.

'I went out at nine to go shopping. I'm pregnant. I found out yesterday. The doctor sent me a letter. Then I went to tell Uncle Charles.'

'Who?'

'Uncle Charles – Sir Charles Barrington. He's not a real uncle – he was my father's best friend and he's my trustee.'

'Your what?' asks the dunce to my left, but the inspector – constable, or whatever he is – motions silence.

'Go on.'

'I was there for, oh, half an hour? Then I went to 190 for lunch.'

'Where?'

'190 – 190 Queens Gate. It's a restaurant.'

'What time?'

'Twelve-thirty, I think. I—'

'Who with?'

'Selina Johnson-Scott. She's a friend. It was her cottage, in fact . . .'

'We know all about Selina Johnson-Scott. How long did lunch last? How did you get there?'

The questions go on and on. I can feel the woman next to me sneer at every answer – as if I'm inventing everything that I tell them. If I try to ask about Andrew, they won't answer. He must be in a cell close by. I hope he's alone. They might have put criminals in with him. My heart swells when I think of his perfect form confined by windowless walls and a locked door.

'And after drinking coffee in a Knightsbridge flat, you took a taxi home?'

'Yes.'

They repeat everything I say, as if it's the most incredible of lies.

'And is this an average day, Mrs Bruton?'

'No . . . I mean, yes.' No two are the same. What can I say? And Uncle Charles – what has happened to him? I have to know.

'How is he?' I ask. I'm feeling lost. My eyeballs are burning up from the bright lights. The room is too hot. The walls are bulging inwards – too close. If I stretch out each arm I'm sure I could touch them both.

'If you mean Sir Charles Barrington, the answer is very

108

bad. You'd better hope he comes to, or you'll find yourself married to a man on a murder charge.'

So vicious. I slump my head to hide the tears; then, unbelievably, that bitch grabs me by the shoulders and rams a hand under my chin.

Violation! Anger gives me strength. In an instant I feel clear-headed. I push her hand away and stand up suddenly. 'I'm not under arrest?'

'You're helping us with our enquiries.'

'So I'm free to go?'

'No.'

'If I'm not arrested, then how can you keep me?'

This seems to surprise them. The old one clasps his fingers and stares at them, then looks very hard at me. 'If you want to help your husband, it would be better that you stay.'

Shit. He's got me. I'm Andrew's best hope. But now I know they won't arrest me. They can't: no evidence. Stop it! Of course there's none. It's not as if we've committed some crime.

More questions: When did Andrew return in the evening? When did we leave for Suffolk? Why? Isn't it a coincidence that the place we chose happened to be so isolated? Perfect for lying low. Each new question insinuates, twists. By two o'clock I'm exhausted. Just want to be at home in bed with my husband and sleep for days to forget this madness.

At last, the old one stands up and tells me I can go. 'But not too far, Mrs Bruton. I've a pretty good idea what's going on here, and we'll be watching you very closely. I can recognise a dirty pair of hands when I see them.'

The policewoman jostles against me as I walk out of the door.

I run from the station. The night is clear, the stars are out. Each one has a halo from my tears. The frost is crisp underfoot.

Taxi. No. It gets worse: everything is in Suffolk. They made me rush and I left my bag behind. I've no money, no keys. Just a ridiculous leather skirt and cold, cold, legs. I'm not going back in. I'll walk it, wake the neighbours, and sleep outside the door. It's not so far. Probably only two miles. That's not too far to walk, even in London. The streets are quiet.

Headlights tip over the crest of the hill. A car approaches, creeping down Ladbroke Grove: a dark Mercedes, on a slow cruise close to the kerb. Nightmare. Worse than that. I'll have to go back to that nightmare station. I can't take this.

A hiss as the nearside window descends in an even electric glide.

I start to run.

'Lydia!'

A middle-aged face projects from the window, forehead creased. The voice is sharp and anxious.

Mr Travers!

I say his name aloud and it sounds like salvation. He's my family lawyer. Andrew must have called him. Perhaps he's even seen him?

The door swings open and I walk to the car. At every step, the remaining distance grows. I'm nearly on my knees when I reach the door and climb in. Mr Travers leans across and pulls it to. I cry quietly as we drive.

'Lydia, I'm taking you to my flat. You can have a wash and something to eat. Then, I'm afraid, we have to do some talking. Andrew appears to be in serious trouble, and if Charles . . .' He hesitates, looks at me, then his eyes return to the road and he continues: 'Things could get worse. I'm going to apply for bail as soon as possible. They'll probably charge him tomorrow morning.'

His voice begins to drift away. I am utterly exhausted, a zombie. Can't unlock my eyelids. Can't hold up my head. The car rolls smoothly, engine whispering like distant seashore waves. It halts, and Mr Travers helps me from my seat. My legs won't work – keep crossing, tangling.

'There,' he says.

A blanket falls across my body as it reclines. Sleep.

9   It's hard to play at the game of love, but everyone must: the body commands it; only reason resists. I was always affectionate – wanting affection, and ready to give in order to find: in the hope of return, you make yourself the bait. I started hunting at about thirteen. My mother found this hard. She herself had dried out when my father died. She forgot about love, forgot about passion. And without its aura she seemed less human: a worried spirit drifting through a world of flesh and blood. She warned me not to give myself away or sell myself too cheap, as if I had some single golden treasure only one man could possess and that the wrong commitment would result in irretrievable loss.

When she died, Uncle Charles stepped in and guidance was removed further – from spirit to machine. I think he thought me quite delinquent, and his observations became provocation – if you can't stop doing what you're told is bad, then you accept the title and continue with the deed.

I think Andrew was my twelfth lover – rather, twelfth partner and first lover. All the others wanted simply to possess; one or two, perhaps, were in love, but in love with someone else – some other Lydia. Their affection was conditional. They wanted to remake me and littered their conversation with phrases such as 'Can't you . . . ?' and 'Won't you . . . ?' as if whatever flaws they saw were accidental impurities which persistence could remove – as if I were a box of chocolates and they were free to consume what they liked and discard the rest.

Because I started young, my mother tried a thousand ways to calm me down. Her favourite method was exposure to art. Paintings made her feel serene – those dry spirit images of carnal scenes. One in particular became an obsession. It

111

appeared in an exhibition just before she died. She took me to see it at least ten times. It was called '*Fleur Mystique*' – a pale virgin on a lily stem, fed by the ruby blood of saints and martyrs. It became her idol: the pure woman sustained aloft by sacrifice, by loss. I hated it. That empty baby-doll face, that wasted, misdirected passion – the madness of forcing men to their knees to prevent women falling on their backs.

Andrew was a revelation – so gentle, so forgiving – a talking idol, or, better still, the physical ideal that idols are created to represent. He didn't try to change me; he simply accepted me. Now I love, and live for, his presence. It makes me calm. He is the only thing of value I possess. All those stupid toys like wealth and class which mother, teachers, even Uncle Charles, would parade before my eyes, usually to provoke guilt ('Lydia, you can't behave like that. Remember who you are, who we are'), are worthless in comparison.

Mr Travers is a member of that disapproving chorus – the frivolous Lydia brigade. He's the family lawyer, my father's executor, and, like Uncle Charles, one of my trustees. I find him hard to talk to. His own wife is virtually silent and I think it amazes him to find a woman capable of speech. You can tell him the most reasonable things, could shout them at him from a pulpit, and he'll behave as if you'd never spoken. Nowadays, when we have to meet, I bring Andrew with me. Because he is a man, he gains an audience.

I think Travers finds the present situation impossible. His interpreter is in prison and his stupid, pompous face wobbles with uncertainty when he looks at me. *Will she understand?*

He woke me up this morning at seven with some tea. Every movement he made, every word he spoke, was engineered. He'd rehearsed the encounter all night. *Will she answer (a), (b) or (c)?* In between exchanges, I could hear his mind click as it moved on to the next sequence. He began his inquisition before my tea had cooled enough to drink. He pulled an armchair across the carpet until it touched my sofa, then started to speak. In retrospect, I can see it was important to him that he caught me unawares.

'Lydia, I have some very important questions to ask you, which you must do your best to answer truthfully. Do you understand?'

I nodded yes. More questions. I had so many myself but knew I'd have to wait my turn.

'Good. Very good. You're doing well. Now, firstly, do you have any knowledge of, or involvement in, the crimes which Andrew is alleged to have committed?'

'No.'

I caught sight of my own face in a wall mirror behind Travers's shoulders. I smiled self-encouragement with my eyes as he continued.

'Secondly, do you think it likely, or even possible, that Andrew could carry out such an attack?'

'No, Mr Travers.'

We remained in silence for some time, minutes, perhaps, while Travers kept his gaze on my face. It was as though he was sure that if he were to stare long enough he would see more. I concentrated on that fortunate mirror and waited, knowing if I passed this petty ordeal I would be one step closer to reunion with my lover.

'Very well, Lydia. I'm going to believe you, and every one of my actions hereafter will be founded on the presumption of your husband's innocence. I must say, though, that the evidence against him appears strong, if circumstantial. In order to help me to help him you must tell me everything you know. I want you to think first about Tuesday as carefully as you can.'

I had to interrupt. The prospect of repetition filled me with despair. Another old man treating me like some simple recording machine – locate and press the play button, then the pretty girl will sing.

'For the last twelve hours, Mr Travers, I've faced questions, imprisonment and humiliation. My husband has been locked in a cell, my father's oldest friend is injured, and I have yet to discover how or why or where any of this happened. I need someone to tell me. I have more questions than answers.'

He watched me in amazement, shaking his head, opening and closing his mouth, as if I were firing off a string of mad profanities, and then, when I paused, he jumped straight in, with: 'You mean you don't know?' or some other such absurd question. But at least this meant I was at last getting through. I bit my tongue and told him quietly No, of course I didn't know. Asked why Andrew was under arrest, what had happened to Uncle Charles, and this seemed to work some gentle magic on the man – locked him into courtroom mode. A stern expression appeared on his face, he inflated himself, cleared his throat and finally, at long, long last, I received an explanation.

'Yesterday, at midnight, I received a telephone call from Andrew. He told me that he was under arrest and being held for questioning at the police station in Ladbroke Grove. I drove there immediately and the duty officer informed me that Andrew had been charged with three offences: burglary committed at your godfather's house, and two charges of assault against your godfather, one of them with intent to cause grievous bodily harm. This is a serious crime. It carries a life sentence. The background to the charges is as follows. On Tuesday afternoon, Sir Charles returned to find that someone had attempted to break into his home. As you know, he has a valuable collection of paintings, and these were assumed to be the object of the intruders. The police were already present and after interviewing Sir Charles they left him at about seven o'clock in the company of Andrew. On Wednesday morning – yesterday – your godfather's assistant, Miss . . .'

'Younghusband.'

'. . . Younghusband arrived for work to find the premises in a state of disorder. She proceeded to the first floor, where she found Charles unconscious in his study. An ambulance was called – in the event, two were needed, as the discovery

114

caused severe shock to Miss Younghusband. The police examined the room and found evidence of a struggle. They knew that Andrew had been present the previous evening, knew the initial break-in had been carried out by someone close to Charles, and when they discovered that you had both left in a hurry for the country they followed up. Andrew has been fingerprinted and his prints match those found in Charles's study. Incidentally, they were the only prints that did not belong to Charles, who regrettably remains unconscious. It appears that the attack was sudden and violent. He was struck with great force by a heavy object. Among other injuries, his spine has been damaged. He's being treated at St Thomas's Hospital, where he was taken into intensive care. All this is new to you?'

I was too sad to speak. Poor old man.

'I see. Very well, I must warn you, Lydia, that at the present time the police declare themselves satisfied with Andrew's arrest. In plain English, they're not looking for anyone else. I must add that they consider your involvement likely. Miss Younghusband has made a statement which comments on the difficult relationship that existed between you and Sir Charles. There is more: the police know Andrew visited your godfather last Sunday. They know, too, that Andrew was recently made redundant and believe he may have been seeking money. Younghusband stated that Charles appeared unsettled after Andrew's last visit. It is fortunate that you don't have any children, otherwise the police would consider the case against you, at least, in terms of motive, complete . . .' Here Travers paused and stared at me hard. 'You were aware, of course, that on condition that you married and bore offspring, you were to be the principal beneficiary of your godfather's will?'

'He never told me.'

'I see. This, at least, should be of some assistance to our case.'

I shook my head. 'I'm two months pregnant.'

'Did Charles know?'

'I visited him that morning, just after I found out. I was so pleased.'

'Do the police know this?'

'Yes.'

Travers looked shaken, very grave. 'Now, Lydia, you must . . . No. You have told me you are not involved and I accept that. I'm afraid that you have a very hard time ahead. You must prepare yourself for an ordeal. There may even be interest in the press. I will apply for reporting restrictions, but there is little hope of these being granted. Now, if you will excuse me, I am going to examine some papers. The judicial process has begun, and we must prepare a defence.'

That was half an hour ago. Travers left the room, leaving me to try to sort my way through the madness – reason out 'the judicial process', which at present seems to have no reason, seems no more than a machine out of control, created by men to consume other men, eating into our lives with measured bites. I keep thinking of Uncle Charles. He always looked so very old – that strange, set face and flat voice. But this was just a disguise, as if he'd resigned all hope of contact, realised that once he had been crippled he would face isolation so chose to leave in advance, set off on his own, in his own little boat, until he reached a safe distance from the rest of humanity. It's appalling to think of him in some hospital ward, surrounded by strangers who probably can't wait to pull the plug and free up the bed for someone else, someone with relatives and friends and smiles and thanks and flowers.

Sir Charles Barrington, a powerful man – as Andrew, as everyone, told me – but rolling around in solitude, forever on the edge of despair, a full heart in an empty house. I think we were similar: I'd lost my parents; the security that the rest of my friends took for granted wasn't there. And Uncle Charles had sympathy, had compassion. He didn't try to push me into things, tell me that I'd be a beautiful bride, as my mother did, or a scientist, as my teachers once pretended – things I knew would not come true.

116

I wish I hadn't found out about the will. Money ruins affection. You have to show a horrible, crawling gratitude, until, of course, repeated charity turns thanks into disdain. It's a shame, a bitter shame, for if he lives I won't be able to behave as I would like in front of him, because, somewhere in my brain, the money thing will be there, the craven expectation; no more chance for teasing, no more tantrums.

A smile. I'm amazed I still can. I have to pull myself together. I'm chasing all these wild thoughts around in circles but doing nothing to solve them. It's like staring too long in a mirror: you get obsessed with details and forget why it was you looked. Time to act. Today I will set Andrew free.

How?

Jailbreak. No. Andrew is innocent. Travers will be my key. I'll sit him down and make sure he explains. If he tries to gloss things over, I'll hire another lawyer – a woman, perhaps.

By the time he returns I feel better, calmer. I know what I want to do and Travers represents a weapon to achieve my aims.

I pre-empt him before he can open his mouth. 'I need to get into my flat, but the keys are still in Suffolk. Do you, or does your firm, have someone who could be sent to fetch them?'

'Yes, Lydia, that's possible. However, the police took away a number of items as evidence, and the keys may be among them.'

'Do you have a list?'

'Not yet, but—'

'Please get me one. Meanwhile, I would like everything that's left up there to be brought down – I'm sure that there's a limit to what they can consider evidence. Have you a pen and paper I can use?'

He's going to ask why, so I frown hard and the question dies on his lips and he pulls from his case a small pad with his partnership's logo stamped on every page.

117

'There's the address. In the interim, there's no point in waiting. I'll call the locksmith to let me in. Can you drive me over?'

'Of course, Lydia, but, first, some questions remain.'

'No more questions. What time is it?'

'Eight.'

'They'll be there already, won't they?'

'Who?'

'The police, in our flat. There's no need for keys. Will they leave a guard, or retreat once they've done their work?'

It appears that Travers hadn't thought of this. Flustered, he removes and polishes his glasses to give himself time to think. He looks up. 'In the event, I concede it is highly likely a search warrant will have been applied for and granted. I shall telephone them immediately to confirm.'

'Don't bother. We'll surprise them.'

I stand up, brush down the skirt – a gesture really, as the creases seem to stick – collect the pad and walk out of the front door. I can hear Travers rummaging in the background. I know he'll follow.

The bright light in the dawn street is a shock. After the eternity of the last twenty-four hours, time once again has started to run. It's one of those clean, still, winter mornings – so refreshing, like a crystal glass of clear spring water. Mr Travers lives in a neat white Chelsea square off the King's Road – not far from home, fifteen minutes' walk at most, but the dawn air is cold and it's better to drive than arrive on foot alone. Travers has not yet emerged and I walk over to the square. Sugar-white frost holds the grass blades stiff on the lawn. A blackbird hops on to a wooden bench and shakes out its feathers at the rising sun.

The hazard lights flash on the Mercedes and its door locks click. I turn to see Travers with briefcase under one arm, the other held aloft, matador fashion, brandishing the car key. He looks a mess. He has that lanky, middle-aged hair, mousy going grey, flapping across his forehead, and wide-framed I-see-the-world lawyer's spectacles. A drop of perspiration rolls out over his collar. How can he be so warm?

We climb in and the engine starts to hum. The windscreen is frozen over. It seems that Travers is going to wait until his superfluous heat clears the frost, so I dig around for a cloth, then leap out and do the job myself.

It's quiet in the car, which rolls slowly over the smooth roads, its padded floors and heavy doors insulating us from the rumble of the rush-hour traffic. We live in Ifield Road – just across the street from Nikita's Russian Restaurant. Andrew once suggested a tunnelling expedition to its vodka cellar; but we decided against it. Our flat is on the first floor so we'd have to start through the downstairs neighbour's chimney.

When we draw up outside No. 122 the front door is wide open, so I tell Travers to park and I start to climb out, but he restrains me with a soft, damp hand on the elbow.

'Lydia, in these circumstances, and as your lawyer, it is best that I accompany you.' He nods across the street at a police van on the corner.

He's right. I'm pleased with him. At last he's acting as paid adviser – it's lawyer/client now, not parent/child.

Nerves return when I walk into the hallway. The shock of violation is repeated. It seems we're just in time. Perhaps 8.30 is visiting hour. I lag to let Travers catch up and we climb the stairs together. We find a policeman in a black viscose jumper stretching plastic blue-and-white tape across the splintered door frame. The white section is stencilled POLICE POLICE POLICE in the same blue – to make them feel comfortable, I suppose.

'Who are you?'

'John Travers, of Perkins, Bulwhite. I represent Mr Andrew Bruton.'

The policeman turns. His moustache quivers. 'Sergeant!' he yells. 'There's a bloke here who claims he's his solicitor.'

Really! What a horrible, suspicious world they must inhabit.

'Ask for some identity,' comes a voice, and shuffling, sniffing noises. God! Another dog! They must employ them to do their thinking. Travers gives the man his card. He frowns and turns it over. Looking for clues? Perhaps it just reads better upside down.

'And who's that?'

'Mrs Lydia Bruton – the owner of these premises. I assume I will find her name on your search warrant.'

Travers breaks the tape, takes me by the hand and shoulders his way in. Good man. As soon as I'm inside, the uncertainty vanishes. This is my flat. I virtually run into the sitting room, but Travers beats me to it. One policeman is occupied with a pile of plastic bags on the table. Each contains one of our belongings. He's sealing them with nylon ties and little labels. Another is standing by the mantelpiece, my wedding photograph in his hands.

'Put that down!' Travers and I shout together. Travers really looks quite fierce. His face is flushed and his forehead is creased into a terrific frown.

'Who are you?'

'Where's your warrant?'

A fourth policeman emerges from our bedroom. His upper lip is hidden under a walnut-coloured moustache, whose bristles protrude horizontally. He looks at Travers and says, 'Sergeant Tomlinson.' He produces a folded piece of paper from his jacket and waves it to and fro. 'I am empowered by this warrant, issued at . . .' His speech sounds as if a legal document had been programmed into him. Words flow out in an unpunctuated monotone, full of 'said premises' and so on.

Travers steps across, grabs the piece of paper and spreads it out on the desk. The sergeant looks offended, but he breathes heavily and says nothing. I'm sick of this. Every part of my life – husband, house, self – has been peered into, pawed over, violated by uniformed strangers. My skin is grimy, my hair stinks: contaminated by the hours in the interrogation room.

'I'm going to change and have a shower,' I tell Travers. 'If that's all right with you,' I add, for the benefit of the policeman. He opens his mouth . . . unbelievable! I think he's about to protest! 'If you're worried I'm hiding evidence, then come and watch.'

'I don't think—'

'Be quiet, Tomlinson. It appears to me that this warrant is flawed, and that you, and your colleagues here, have committed a serious breach of procedure. Without prejudice to my client's rights, I demand that you remove yourselves immediately, before you carry out any further trespass.'

Excellent! Somehow, Travers has got them. I'm not interested in the logistics of why they're at fault. He can show them the door. The need to be clean and kempt and composed is overwhelming. It hits me again when I walk into the bedroom. They've emptied all the drawers, all the cupboards, on the floor. Even turned over the bed. No order remains other than that represented by a neat pile of plastic evidence bags by the door. Bloody people! As I strip I can hear Travers bawling them out of the house. Good man. Evict the vermin! They can take their tapes and radios and bags and moustaches back to their dogs and lights and their who-the-fuck-are-you questions in that midden of a station.

10 February is the best month for murders. People work hard and spend their evenings indoors. The sunless days and cold, damp nights are claustrophobic, and as the tension builds they learn to hate.

February's my busiest month. There's so much violent crime, we can pick and choose what to publish. For most cases, we stick to formulae. We give them half a paragraph in Home News, beginning with a factual header in bold: **Mother Faces Death Inquiry** and so on. We refer to the circumstances of death – list multiple wounds, note evidence of a struggle, reveal condition of corpse in understatement: 'badly burned', 'severely lacerated', 'identified from dental records'. It's only when the case reaches trial that we begin to burn up column inches. Even then, the whole affair is pretty hit-and-miss. It's hard to tell which case will catch the public's fancy – unless there's a good-looking woman involved. Everyone's interested in a beautiful face. This is nothing new. A century ago, when newspapers couldn't write about sex, people were curious to an unbelievable degree about crimes involving women. We used to print special editions which described every gesture when a young female appeared in court. If she was the victim, my predecessors would fill the pages with maiden blushes and well-timed swoons. If she was in the dock, she was credited with the most wicked character they dared invent. She was the witch who seduced men from reason and made otherwise faultless citizens cast aside civilised restraint.

This fascination persists, even with tits on every other page. I welcome it; after all, it keeps me in a job. I've been on the crime desk of a national newspaper – the *Chronicle* – for nearly twenty years. I started after grammar school as a runner, did my time, worked my way up, and now I'm in charge. This means fewer hours on the streets, less time spent begging for interviews and sitting around in police stations. If a big one happens, people call me. I'll turn up for the trial with a ticket for the front row. I know all the coppers, all the silks, the judiciary, and most of the regular criminals too. Some cases are like reunions: we nod to each other every morning; there's respect on all sides. The only misfits are the social workers, whom everybody hates, but nowadays they're usually in the dock and get sent on their way with a 'hope you get buggered in prison'.

Usually, I start work at eleven o'clock. If I'm wanted earlier, they call me at home. Used to send up a runner when we published out of Fleet Street. I live in Soho, always have. It's quite upmarket nowadays, but still a crossroads – where East End meets West End. I run a staff of five, including one trainee. He's an Oxford boy – a failed philosophy student, as it happens but he has a good instinct for the work. He does the dawn patrol: calls all the major stations – Vine Street, Blackheath, Ladbroke Grove, the Yard – to see what's come in. He breaks the crimes down into a score sheet – Rapes 2, GBH 0, and so on. Public interest switches between crimes from month to month. Depending what's in fashion, we follow up. For instance, if it's taxi rapes, we'll check out all the charges to see if cabbies are involved. Connections make for extra column inches. Otherwise we set up the usual one-inch fillers, which the editor can print or spike. At the moment, it's a strange mix: racial violence and arson – a hard appetite to feed, unless, of course, they're rioting again in Brixton.

We publish out of Docklands. It's a regular piss hole. I travel over by bike – Norton Commando. One day the piles will win and I'll trade it for something with suspension. Meanwhile, it's quicker than a car and I don't work in a suit.

This morning I had a clear run in. Nice day for the time of year; ice on some corners, which made the ride that little bit more interesting. The roads around Docklands resemble camel tracks. The surface has been wrecked by the construction traffic, so I have to dodge potholes in between miles and miles of empty high-rise offices. It's the city that never was. Our building's got a bloody great foyer like some Arab palace, which makes a change from the old days when we used the backstairs.

As I walk on to the news floor, Pritchard, my trainee, is buggering around with his computer terminal. He looks flustered, so I surmise the machine is winning. He hands me his morning score sheet and a couple of other pages. Nasty handwriting – he can't have learnt that at Oxford.

'What's this? An essay?'

He cringes, but only for effect. What's the little bugger up to?

'It's a feature I'd like to do ... No, Roy, wait – it's a perfect case. It came in this morning from Ladbroke Grove. Remember the DeStempels?'

I do. As a matter of fact, all too well. It was buried by my editor in Other News – two bold inches – nothing more, then the quality Sunday papers picked up the story and gave it full-page colour spreads. Instead of being leader, we had to follow with the tabloid pack. I'd screwed Pritchard's essay into a ball, in preparation for its final resting place, the oval file – the waste bin – but decide to hold on for an instant.

He sees the hesitation and speaks: 'This is the same style, Roy – GBH on a crippled veteran. Murder attempt for inheritance.'

'Go on.'

Pritchard can be a pain in the arse. Tries to speak the language, but he's too long-winded. Slang sounds ridiculous in an Oxford accent.

'There's love interest, too, Roy. The wife of the accused is a real sex kitten.' The way he says this, it sounds like 'sax carton'. 'He was charged yesterday morning – Sections 18 and 20. Committal proceedings are set for this afternoon. I'd like to go.'

He keeps talking, but I drop the crumpled sheets, turn

my back and walk away. 'Hate Fire in Ethnic Ghetto' is what I need. There's no immediate market for blue-blood crime. Lord Lucan was sighted again in December and that killed off all demand. Besides, it can't be 'love interest' if the woman is a wife. Still, I'd like to find out Pritchard's taste. It's the first time he's ever mentioned a female person of the opposite sex.

'What time is he in court?'

'Two o'clock, at Horseferry Road. Can I go?'

'If she's so pretty, I might go myself. What's her name?'

'I don't know.'

'All right, what's *his* name?'

'Bruton, Andrew, aged thirty-two and unemployed.'

'And what about his wife? How old is she?'

'Don't know.'

'Then how do you know what she looks like?'

'Charlesworth told me. He's the duty constable at Ladbroke Grove.'

'And you took his word for it?'

Pritchard can't answer this, so I take a walk around the finance desk to clear my mind. You should see their trainees. They try to imitate their counterparts at the merchant banks by dressing up in Continental suits and speaking into two telephones at once. They look like some Mafia hit squad on speed. Bernie Hayes, the economics editor, is a close friend. His area, like mine, is inviolate. Both are ninety per cent news, ten per cent speculation. That's what fills a paper day to day. And he pulls in revenue – bread-and-butter adverts – corporate results, a weekly appointments page, so that together we account for a third of each edition. Lately we've been working closely. City fraud is big news. By contrast, common theft is now so common it no longer even makes the inside pages. Who cares if Sid Nobber knocks off his local post office when Lord Fauntleroy is caught with his hands in the till of UK PLC? Our co-operation started with the Lloyds scandals. The PCW affair put the Kray twins and their kinder in the shade. We have to split these cases. My desk does the counterwork and Bernie's deals with the socio-politico-economic consequences for his nervous City punters who've just been shafted. The legal fees his team faces are tremendous. It's hard to call someone who drives a Jaguar and carries an attaché case a thief. Silly, really: if a national newspaper named Ronnie Biggs a master criminal, he'd raise his glass to them in Rio. If it's some balding director, the defamation writs come flying. Even as I speak, there's one such story that Bernie's been sitting on for over a month. But he's got two injunctions pointing at his head and six writs tied around his balls and can't publish a single word.

Bernie looks up from his screen when I saunter over and gives me a wink. He rolls back from his desk and we sidle over together to his glass-walled edit office on the edge of the production floor. Bernie Hayes reminds me of Fleet Street. He's short, badly shaped and perpetually dirty. He chain-smokes roll-ups and disgusts, I think, his present generation of hacks. All they seem to aspire to is lunch at Goldman Sachs and a new Versace suit. None of them can write, of course. In comparison Pritchard is the Shakespeare of the folded page – the column-inch bard, his polished prose sold in daily folios. In the best tradition, Bernie keeps whisky in his desk. Think about it – why else do they make a bottle-sized bottom drawer? A slug in the tea refreshes the morning tonsils: Lysterine for the soul, as my friend is fond of saying. He pours out a couple of measures and plonks them down among his files.

'Anything up?'

'Quiet days, Bernie. We're looking for arsonists.'

'Can't help there, my friend. Jewish bonfires are a thing of the past.'

'And you?'

'Still sitting on Mardon Packaging Corporation. It's like a bad dream, Roy. That bastard Fletcher is out and about, walking up and down, as the Bible sayeth . . .'

'Amen.'

'Up to no good, new woman in tow, new company in his sights, redundancies planned, and accounting tactics that would make a Brick Lane whore blush for shame.'

'Too bad.'

'Agreed. Especially because, as far as I know, we're the only ones with the evidence. More tea?'

I nod yes. I like Bernie, like his sense of humour. Besides, a shandy in the morning sharpens the mind. You can throw out all those studies we publish – the twenty-one units of alcohol a week. Stick to that, and the *Beano*, let alone a quality national daily, would never reach the press.

'And who's the woman?' I ask.

'Selina someone.'

'What's her story?'

'Standard Donald Fletcher trophy. Thirty-something. Likes leather. Runs a love nest.'

'Which you're watching?'

'Telephotos at dawn. Perkins is on to it. He's moving up to Suffolk tomorrow. He's staking out her cottage in a place called Peasenhall. Know it?'

'I've heard of it. There was a celebrated murder trial there last century . . .' Bernie waits for me to elaborate, but I can't. 'Peasenhall equals murder. That's all I know. It was probably a vicar and a choirboy.'

'Or choirgirl?'

'Unlikely. The Victorians saved them for different crimes.'

'What did they do to the girls, then?'

'Taught them how to sing. I'll show you the law reports one day. The public was so innocent they could be convinced to do anything in God's name. Listen to this: there were two vicars, in distant parts of this country, both of whom had one very pretty girl in his choir. Each vicar took each girl to one side and told them that if they had a simple operation, which the vicar would perform, they would have perfect-pitch singing voices for ever.'

'What sort of operation?'

'To make a passage for the air.' I demonstrate the rest of these true stories with gestures and Bernie laughs.

'I'll remember that one for Tiffany. Where were we?'

'Donald Fletcher and his unproven crimes. Have you found anything new?'

'No gold as yet. I'm hoping for something this afternoon. Why don't we meet at lunch?'

'I can't. I'm at Horseferry Road.'

'What for?'

'A committal.'

'Why?'

'Love interest. If she turns out pretty, I'll arrange some photos.'

'Send us a copy.'

'You old bastard.'

Bernie smiles and pours round three. 'We are all in the gutter . . .' he intones.

'But some of us are looking up passing skirts.'

It's four hours later and my mood has improved beyond recognition. Pritchard's case may have some mileage in after all. I went to the committal at the justices' court – the Queen *v.* Andrew Bruton. It was a good old-fashioned one too: defence pleading no case to answer, barristers practising their reading voices, policemen making clockwork statements. I got a good look at the accused, and by the by some words of wisdom from my old friend Detective Inspector Evans. The wife was in court – Pritchard's 'sax carton'. She wore a black skirt and looked her respectable best. The reports were right: she is beautiful. Just like Lauren Bacall in *The Big Sleep*, but of a lighter build and with a bit more speed in the legs. Best of all were her eyes – green eyes – and her wide starlet lips. Perfect colour-supplement material. She was smoking a fag in the corridor when I arrived, having the pants bored off her by some fat little ambulance chaser with a pompous voice and an armload of books. She saw me straight away – gave me the once-over, the old floor-to-ceiling measurement, blowing smoke at her lawyer as he read her chapter and verse from the statute book. She was curious – intrigued, call it what you will. I think she thought it would be a family-and-close-friends affair. Anyway, I took a seat in the stalls at the back. Horseferry Road has an unusual atmosphere. The air inside is very dry, the grain stands out on its plank seats and a single wooden panel on the wall behind the magistrates looks suspiciously like a blackboard. During the silent moments in between depositions and witnesses the court feels like a classroom and every person present is overcome by remembered oppression. From my vantage point in the back row I had the best view in the court, which gave me the opportunity to observe all entrances and exits and, most importantly, to get a good look at the face of the accused.

You see, it's a universal truth that all the punters in the underworld (or underclass, as my brethren in the Society and Home columns prefer) have criminal faces. You have to learn to identify the look, but, when you've seen it once, you can always recognise it. It's a flat kind of face. I don't mean literally flat, as if they'd been too long pressed against a window – Tiny Tims staring at things they can't afford – but flat as in expressionless. You see, every last one of them has been in trouble since the cradle, and they've learnt how to cope with authority: say nothing, know nothing, deny, deny, deny, and hope for a soft jury or a witness who fluffs his lines. When Mr Andrew Bruton, accused of causing grievous bodily harm (with intent), was hauled out to make his statement I could tell in an instant that Evans had pinched the wrong man. Just like the criminal, the honest man has a recognisable look about him, unless he's born with a squint – but modern juries can sort that out. After all, it's years since we burnt women whose noses were too long. This Bruton looked everyone in the eye, including yours truly, spoke clearly, answered truthfully – he'd have won the Bible prize in any Sunday school you care to mention. When he wasn't being asked to confess, he watched his wife. They worked in synchronisation. Wherever he looked – say, at a policeman reading out a statement – she looked too. When he introduced his alibi, she faced forward and watched the bench.

The evidence against him was mainly circumstantial, but just enough for the justices to do what they do best – namely pass the buck and vote for case to answer. The coppers produced a few durables for the touch-and-tell show: a Moto Guzzi bike boot with glass fragments in the heel. Two hundred quids' worth of prime accessory – or, rather, one hundred, as they had only the one. Wouldn't mind a pair myself. Followed by various household ornaments with Mr B's fingerprints. Finally, for the icing on the cake, a grand conspiracy theory they lifted from the television involving premeditation, planned pregnancies and missing millions. All too fanciful to repeat, but the justices were impressed.

Next came the bail application. The prosecution ran objections in alphabetical order, commencing with abscond. Once again, they stole the script from the pictures: Sir Charles Barrington, renowned physician, lies close to death in a hospital bed. To the accused, this represents unfinished work. And if the chance to have another go fails to tempt him, why, an armada of yachts, a private heliport and a one-way, first-class, anywhere-in-the-world airline ticket are at his disposal so he can whisk himself away to a new identity and life of crime elsewhere. And if any of these very real threats to the public at large and basic human decency some-how fail to materialise, then sureties for an unemployed natural sciences graduate should be set at no less than a hundred grand. It was a masterly performance. I'd give that prosecutor a place on my copy desk any day. They eventually settled for £5,000, a curfew and a restraining order prohibit-ing Andrew Bruton of 122 Ifield Road from approaching Sir Charles Barrington or otherwise doing or causing such acts to be done as may be likely to hinder or otherwise obstruct the true course of justice.

When bail was granted, the girl slid from her seat and

slipped across the court so quickly, so soundlessly, that no one realised she had moved until she was there, at the dock, leaning over the parapet, careless of the spikes, holding her husband's face in her hands and kissing him fiercely. The policeman on guard didn't dare touch. Perhaps he got out an 'Excuse me, miss', but it seemed she preferred not to be interrupted, and when she finished she spun around, turned her bright green eyes on all the punters, then beckoned to her lawyer, who trotted after her out of the court room.

All this drama gives a man an appetite. My belly was crying out for nourishment. I held it tight to muffle the symphony and set off to find a café. I'd spent last night in reverent contemplation of a whisky bottle, which, combined with Bernie's 'tea', left me in real need of some swill to soak up the poison. I ordered full English with a side plate of chips. I love chips and I'm buggered if I'm going to give them up, whatever my doctor might suggest. You need warm meals in winter, and savoury food rejuvenates our little grey friends. I was tucking into a fresh egg, slightly runny, fried in butter, accompanied by crunchy white toast, when I was joined by my old mate Inspector Evans. He's a traditional copper with all the good and bad characteristics which that label implies: forthright, diligent, fearless and thick, thick, thick. He patted my shoulder in a clumsy sort of way and pulled up a stool opposite so we faced each other across the Formica. He lit up a fag and blew smoke all over the place. Policemen seem lost to know what to do with their arms when they're not feeling someone's collar – this, at least, is my theory why most of them smoke. I've known Patrick Evans about fifteen years – since he was a copper on the beat. No one would mistake him for a poet, but he's learnt not to blunder into everything when he opens his mouth, and if he wants to speak to you he usually tries to kick off with a joke. I don't need to tell you that policemen have a very limited range of gags, though from time to time they produce some gruesome gem. Today it seemed he wished to cut out the middlemen and got straight down to business.

'Ten-bob seats for the matinee, Roy? I thought you was a gala man these days.'

I told him in between mouthfuls that I had my box reserved for the trial, if there was one, and waited for him to get to the point.

'And what did you think of our little friend?'

'Not guilty as hell and I admire his taste in women.'

'Ah.' Evans tried to look thoughtful – a grievous mistake for a man blessed with a face the same colour and texture as the sausage then impaled on my fork. 'You may have a point there, Roy, a very good point indeed.'

'So you know he's not the one you're after?'

'I never said that, Roy, never said that at all. I was merely commenting on your perception. Women like that sometimes fall for a man with a fuller figure. Who am I to judge what brings your good self to a magistrates' court on a Friday afternoon?'

'Innocence, of course.'

'I'm surprised to hear you use that word, Roy. Forgetting Mrs Bruton for an instant, why do you think her husband is clean?'

'He looks it.'

'Is that enough?'

'You don't sound so sure yourself, Patrick. He hasn't been in trouble before, has he?'

Evans shook his head.

'And he answered all your questions, didn't he? He doesn't look to me like a man with something to hide. Is he intelligent?'

Evans started fiddling with a vinegar bottle, so I presumed he'd been outwitted by his captive. I waited for him to change the subject.

'Now, tell me this, Roy, how many have you got on the case?'

'Only three.'

'For a Section Eighteen?'

'We have to cover all the angles.'

Evans shook his head and lost his smile. 'Too many, old son – too many to watch a guilty man hang.'

'But enough to help someone clear his name.'

'It depends on what you know, doesn't it?'

I wasn't in the mood to argue. 'Or how good you are at finding out the truth.'

That seemed to please Evans. 'Very good, Roy. Make sure your boys stay on their toes.' He followed up with a wink that would have stampeded a herd of elephants, gave me another push on the shoulder, slid back his stool and left.

Was he trying to tell me something, or was he just surprised to see me in a magistrates' court? I think he wants publicity, but why?

It seemed logical to puzzle this one out so I decamped to the Victoria, sank a pint, ordered one more, then summoned up my mentor, Bernie, on the mobile phone. He's the past master of motive, and since I'd decided to cover this case I needed his help. He wasn't at his desk, so I tried him on his mobile and caught him, coincidentally, at another pub. I could hear him wipe froth from his lips, and his sentences were punctuated by the occasional click as he opened or shut his tobacco tin.

'It's a trap, Roy, but no doubt they'll make a fuck-up of it.'

'So you think the public schoolboy's a decoy?'

'Just that.'

'What's Evans up to, then?'

'He's playing for time.'

'I'll do the same. I'll dress the report up with mystery.'

'Why not glamour?'

'How?'

'Well, is the woman beautiful?'

'Certainly is.'

'It's easy, then: get some pictures, my friend. Where does she live?'

'Off the Fulham Road.'

'Call it Knightsbridge. Turn her unemployed husband into a playboy. No one will know or care about the difference.'

After we hung up, I had three more pints to celebrate. In the taxi back to Docklands, I contemplated motives and came up with many. You see, it's a ridiculous truth that the reading public has very little interest in facts. People don't want to know *how*; they want to know *why*. My first editor drummed this into me over a few beers in Carey Street. He pointed out that the Nazis killed six million Jews, but, since no one understood this fact, very few could believe it. 'So if you want to sell newspapers, make sure your criminals have reasons.'

I wish the same man was alive today to help me deal with Pritchard. Since my arrival in the office, he's been hopping up and down like a frog on heat, eyes bulging behind his scholar's glasses. 'You'll never believe this, Roy,' he begins, 'but I know, I mean I've met, the victim in this Bruton case. What do you think about that?'

Dear God! It's the confessions half-hour. People Pritchard knows.

'Does he use the same local?'

'I beg your pardon?'

I give up. Humour is wasted on academics. 'All right, where?'

'At Oxford. While I was doing my degree. He came up to lecture us. He's an assessor.'

'Weights and measures?'

'No, at least . . . well, it's more complicated than that.' He pauses, removes and polishes his glasses, replaces them, then sort of peers down at me. He's one of those tall, shapeless bastards, about half a head taller than yours truly, all too visible when he'd be best advised to keep low. So condescending – 'it's more complicated' indeed! What does he think I am? Some underprivileged halfwit who's spent all his life kicking cans round a housing estate?

'Wait a minute, Roy! I've got something here which could do a far better job in explaining.' He fishes around his desk and retrieves two pages of grubby type from the wad in front of him. 'Here – I went to get my lecture notes at lunch time.'

I snatch them from his hand. Typical bloody student. I bet he keeps them under his pillow. They're a right bloody mess – two photocopied pages, underlined in several colours and highlighted with a fluorescent marker pen. I note that Pritchard has scratched his mark on the top right corner: J. M. P. Pritchard, Jesus Coll. Jesus Christ is what I say. The pages come from the middle of a book: Chapter 13 'Applications'. The font is Franklin Gothic 12 – a popular script among our brother typesetters throughout the 1970s. Your modern journo wouldn't know that, of course. Too busy playing computer games to worry about the nuts and bolts of the printer's trade. Needless to say, the printed wisdom is about as fucking boring as a book can be.

'Did you have to read this?'

'Yes.'

'All of it? I mean, the rest of the book too?'

'Yes.'

No wonder Pritchard's not all there. Poor sod. Anyway, it tells me something, or rather two things: that Sir Charles was famous, at least to other boffins, and that I should have noticed him at some time in the courts. He was an important man in an obscure trade. I hand the pages back to Pritchard and belch politely.

'A quarter-page obituary,' I tell him, meaning that scientists only interest the public when they're dead. 'Unless, of course, he has a sex life.'

'H-h-hardly,' stammers Pritchard. 'He's paralysed from the waist down.'

'I thought he was in a coma?'

'Yes.'

'Then he's paralysed from the head down.'

God deliver me from fools. I think I'll have a post-prandial kip. It's hard to stay in training in this pub-free environment. Besides, all the computers tend to make a man sleepy.

'Roy?' What the fuck does he want now? 'When, er, when should I start the assignment?'

'Right now. Fuck off immediately. Go and sit on Mrs Bruton's doorstep. Get an interview. Bribe the neighbours.'

'Does that mean . . .'

'You get expenses? Yes. Now fuck off. And bring me some aspirin when you come back.'

Pritchard pisses me off. How's a man supposed to work when that sort of cretin is dancing around his ears? We've not got any great stories on the go. Quite a lot of muggings – at least, a lot for February. These are usually sunshine crimes, when the Blackies are warm enough to leave their ghettos and venture forth. Can't print that, of course. We'd be drowned in complaints. We have to phrase it coyly: 'Police are looking for two men, both described as being in their early twenties and [surprise, surprise] black.' It's not that niggers do anything for circulation – not one of the buggers can read. But it would blow a bloody great hole in advertising revenues. All the companies monitor our columns for prejudice. You know the sort of thing: 'Another Sambo cartoon and we'll take our business to the *Telegraph*.' Go on, then: fuck off. Sanctimonious bastards. I suppose, though, in a funny sort of way I see their point of view: all their employees – for that matter, the whole fucking population – need their reading censored. They're already such a godless lot – forever bleating about welfare and morals, then abandoning or buggering their children or stabbing each other sixty-seven times with the bread knife when they can't change the channel to watch the omnibus *EastEnders*. Honestly, that's the truth. There was one just like that last month. Still, where would I be without them? Out of a job, no less. 'Neighbours swear eternal friendship' or 'Scientists predict global harmony for next May' would never sell. Strife, or at least its illusion, is essential to circulation. Our punters pay to feel uneasy. They know they're bad and pay six bob each day to have it confirmed in black-and-white. Television is, of course, far worse than us. Look at all the violence. More people are killed on the screens each week than in the streets in a year – good copy, in fact, when we've no real murders. I do a nice little line in earnest leaders on declining standards: the 'why oh why do we endure a ceaseless barrage of mindless violence?' Answer: because it's what you all want. And don't believe those old tosspots when they dredge up dreams of a better age – the days when little Johnny played street cricket with his little chums in tow. It's bollocks. The pensioners forget the violence and the world wars which made it all such fun. And now that they're old and senile, instead of just hating their contemporaries they hate everyone. Even the grannies with their knitting needles and pet cats and electric fires with one bar on low to save money have heads stuffed with animal hatred. It's part of them, that's all; part of everyone, really. That's why everyone has a hobbyhorse – a pet cause, which they can use as an excuse to vent their hate. The cause itself is nothing more than a safety valve.

'Long live the RSPCA!' I say aloud and raise an imaginary glass.

11 The kitchen doors swing open and a huge roast is wheeled out on a trolley. It's rib of beef, with all the trimmings. The smell of it has been driving me mad. I'm too hungry even to think straight. And it's just what I always wanted – all for me. I'm the only diner. I hesitate before picking up the silver. Did I order too much? Impossible! Besides, you've got to look after yourself.

I'm not so sure about that waiter. He bears a strange resemblance to Evans.

'Roy.'

It is! I recognise that voice. What's the bugger up to?

'Roy!' A pause. '*Roy!*'

It's Bernie! Grinning at me across the desk. Fuck it! I'd fallen asleep, hadn't I.

He's rustling a bit of paper under my nose, but snatches it back before I can grab. The side whiskers on his little rodent face are quivering. What's he up to?

'The fat is in the fire, my friend!'

'All right, all right, don't get personal. What's that, then?'

'Evidence.'

'Of what? Queen Anne's death?'

'No, Roy. Better than that. News from the Continent.'

I close my eyes and squeeze the bridge of my nose. Time to get things back in working order. There's no harm in an afternoon kip after a few pints, providing that when you wake up you're on the ball.

Bernie's still there, smiling from ear to ear. This makes the obligatory roll-up droop until it's in danger of setting fire to his chin. I can see it all now: 'Economics Editor in Office Fireball'. He keeps moving his bit of paper back and

138

forth under my nose so I can't see what's written. Looks like a fax, which I tell him.

'Very good, my friend. It's a communiqué from our Luxembourg correspondent. Went to visit his Uncle Gustave in Liechtenstein, didn't he.'

Aha! Looks like Bernie's got some news. He sees the interest in my eyes, takes a step back and beckons: follow me.

When we're inside his office he closes the door and the newsroom chatter cuts out. Despite the filth of occupant and his effects, Bernie's office is a regular clean room – soundproofed, direct lines, swept once a month for bugs.

'Take a look.'

It's not my day. First Pritchard, now Bernie, hand me strange bits of paper and ask me to make sense of nonsense. Besides, it's in French, isn't it. May as well be Chinese – it's all Dutch to me.

'What's this about, then?'

'Look at the signature.'

'And?'

'What does it tell you?'

'What's it supposed to tell me? All right, all right. Number one: an accountant signed it.'

Bernie twitches. I think he's surprised.

'They all write the same, don't they? Exercise-book signatures.'

'Anything else? No?' Bernie can be a vexatious bastard when he wants to be. What's he got? 'It's a Certifikay Dassymont, my friend.'

'Come again?'

Bernie shakes his head. 'I'll explain over a cup of tea.' He reaches for the bottom drawer, pours out a couple of man-sized measures, lights another roll-up from the butt of the last, then speaks. 'It's a Liechtenstein legal document. You need to fill one in to set up a trust . . . Wait! Not there!' He snatches back the fax before my cup comes to rest on its surface. 'That's no tea-coaster. It cost us four grand.'

139

'And who wants a Liechtenstein trust?'

'Someone who wants to keep a secret.'

'Then how did you get hold of it? Some bloody secret!'

Bernie looks pleased with himself and raises his drink. 'No one need ever know. You won't be the only one to ask that question. It's going to piss off plenty of people for many years to come.'

'Like who?'

'Donald Fletcher.'

'Fletcher!'

'The one and only.'

'That's not his signature.'

'No, but it's the missing link.'

'For fuck's sake, Bernie, get to the point!'

The fag twitches. His mouth opens – about to tell – then it snaps shut. He shakes his head. 'I'm sorry, Roy, I can't. But all will be revealed, my friend.'

'When?'

'On Monday. Mardon announced a press conference this evening after the stock market shut. It's scheduled for nine in the morning. I'll be there. I've got some questions for our old chum. Meanwhile, I'd like you to do me a favour. I need a feature in Saturday's edition – half a page or so.'

'Concerning?'

'Insider trading.'

'Easy enough. Guinness is still in the news and we've got the space.'

'Can you put it on page twelve?'

'Why?'

'I've arranged a decoration for the Arts section on page thirteen. Here.' Bernie flips a photograph across his desk.

'You old bastard!'

'I thought you'd like it.'

'I do. A toast . . .'

'The hanging man!'

We touch cups and knock it back.

'Fancy coming along?'

140

'On Monday?'

'Why not? Sadly, Fletcher won't be there in person. He's got a puppet to make his speeches.'

'Is he involved too?'

'I think so, and he's young enough to take fright when I start asking surprise questions.'

'I'll come. Where is this conference?'

'The Brewery, in Chiswell Street.'

'I'll be there. Don't drink too much this weekend.'

Bernie grins as he shows me out of his office.

A big bike's the best way to get round London. I'm not one for ducking-and-dancing through the traffic, though – I'm too old to be a boy racer. But it's not a bad way to travel. You feel you're part of the city, part of London. I watch the girls in the summer. It's amazing what comes out from beneath the overcoats when the weather warms up. English girls have the best legs in the world. Speaking of which, what about Mrs Bruton, then? Her husband's out on bail so I suppose she's getting hers. Lucky bugger! I wonder what she gets up to between the sheets. She looks the wild type. You can always tell – there's no way of hiding it. The way she looked me up and down with those big green eyes of hers. I've left Pritchard orders to give me a shout when he dishes up some dirt. I'm sure there's plenty, and Pritchard – I have to hand it to him – is the man for the job. Nosy bastard, but he looks so stupid, bug-eyed and inoffensive that no one suspects. They tell him everything, and slowly too, just in case he doesn't understand.

The bike finds its own way home. Spin round the *Mirror* building – nasty-looking place with its red-for-the-voice-of-the-workers colour scheme – then down High Holborn. Hold-up at the lights. The paper stall's still open with some old boy barking out: '*Standard! Standard!*' We used to have three evening papers in London. All the sellers would shout their wares – so you could locate them through the smog. One of the old cries of London.

Short cut round St Giles to Cambridge Circus, Shaftesbury Avenue, right up Old Compton Street, and home in time for nine o'clock.

It suits me, living on a corner. It's noisy, true, but you do see the world go by. Soho's picked up in the last few years. There was a time, a little while back, when that wasn't the case. The piss artists and the Latins had moved out, the whores and fairies were moving in. But since they did up Covent Garden the tone's changed. It appeals to a different sort of punter, one with more style, but less depth. We have wine bars now instead of pubs, poseurs instead of characters. But it's a cosy place, especially in winter. The streets are narrow, so they don't seem so cold, and there's usually the odd brazier going here and there.

I park the bike in Sam's lock-up, then it's only two flights of stairs and I'm home. That tosspot doctor of mine tells me to take these easy, so I always have a breather on the landing to admire the landlady's taste in floral arrangements. She keeps a bowl of flowers on a table. Changes them every day. Has to: they never see any light.

I'd better be getting on to dinner. I always eat out on Fridays. Tonight, I've got a table at Simpson's. I fancy a roast. I might walk over – it's only fifteen minutes. I like a walk in this part of town. There are so many cooking smells from so many different restaurants, you can go round the world in a couple of streets. Then again, it's a bit cold to be out on foot. It looks like snow. I like snow. It's a shame it never settles. But it's nice to see it whirling under the street lamps. It soaks up the noise, doesn't it – the tyres on the roads, the voices in the air. It makes London peaceful: rolls back the years to the days of fog and footpads – and iron horseshoes and carriage wheels on cobblestones and screaming kids and shouting beggars and rattling trams. It can't have been any quieter then. It's funny how we mystify the past, isn't it?

12 I remember the moment when Donald Fletcher gave the go-ahead. It was close to four on a December morning. The board meeting had been going for ten hours. It was a claustrophobic event – six middle-aged directors and me, confined in a conference room. By midnight, fatigue was showing up their age; creeping into their sentences and ambushing their eyelids. By 2 a.m., the air had become stale and the monotone hum of the air-conditioning system was an irritating reminder that it had failed its purpose. Then Donald tapped his water glass twice, turned off the overhead lights and sat up straight and alert in his chair. For some reason, this simple action had a mesmerising effect. The room fell quiet at once while our eyes adjusted to the diminished illumination supplied by a few lamps on side tables. This semidarkness hypnotised us and created illusions. Strain vanished from faces; the blotches and wrinkles, which had been highlighted by the fluorescent tubes, melted away. It seemed in the lamplight that we were seated round a campaign fire, sharing the dreams of a visionary.

Donald explained how long he'd been waiting for this opportunity. How he'd built Mardon from a regional industry to a multinational, taking over other companies one by one, until he was ready for this bid. It all made sense. It seemed then to be the inevitable climax to a master plan – as if he'd worked to a single-minded timetable for his whole life, and its final triumph was approaching.

Fatigue gave way to attention, conviction and, finally, exhilaration.

'We are the new merchant princes,' he told us. 'Running a large company is the last great adventure. Think about

143

it. There's nowhere wild left in the world, except in the imaginations of fools and madmen. There's no *terra incognita*, nowhere for people to lose themselves, to rediscover nature, to search for lost civilisations or hidden treasure. No true opportunities remain for man to prove himself outside society... And as for society, what's left of that? The common people worship pop stars and chat-show hosts. Even old-fashioned social ambitions have become devalued: who'd want to marry a princess in the 1980s? Politics, too, is a waste of time. Governments are five-year frauds. They have no real power – only its illusion and the ability to enact petty legislation. Whether you want adventure, honour, prestige or influence, industry is the only place to be. We control the wealth. We employ the workforce. Their happiness, their ability to buy the things they want, is in our hands. Whatever your ambitions may be, they can be satisfied here. This is the real thing. This is an opportunity to live a life commensurate with your own high expectations...'

At that point he seemed to single me out. His eyes were telling me: 'This is your chance, Simon. Seize it.'

I did. We all did. The motion to proceed with a takeover bid for Darlington Card was carried unanimously.

For days afterwards, I remained haunted by Donald's words. Those long hours inside the conference room were condensed by my memory to a single tableau. Within that scene, the directors had become abstracted. No longer tired executives in shirtsleeves, they were apostles, and I was among their number. I felt other people could sense this too. They made way for me in the street. They could see my power. They could recognise my station. Which is why, six weeks later, I'm still at my desk after an entire weekend of intense bargaining, ready to announce a new direction to our campaign. We've decided to raise the stakes: offer more money, and price the opposition out of the game. The press conference is this morning and now I need to forget the bargaining with our banks and think business.

First things first: where's the market?

The Reuters screen on my desk will tell me. I depress the ON switch and it begins to irradiate green light. The phosphorescent glow composes itself into symbols and figures: CBOT 99 3 – 7 . . . FTSE 2378 . . .

Brent is $18.1/barrel spot. Cable is $1.8263/73. 6 Month LIBOR is 14 1/8 – 1/4. The June Long Bond is 7.42% S.A. Greeks yield 11.78 annual.

The human brain is wonderfully versatile. When I first stared at one of these screens I couldn't make sense of it. After nearly ten years' practice it's become an ingrained habit – no, more than that: an instinct. How else could I make sense of it in this state? I'm so tired that my eyes feel as if they've been boiled dry in their sockets, yet still the screen carries meaning.

In combination, all those figures – oil prices, currency prices, interest rates, share prices – amount to a portrait of the human sentiment that lurks behind. This is the hardest part of City life to explain to outsiders: how a good trader can picture the intangible. When someone asks you 'Where's the market?' he's not looking for the price of a commodity. He's trying to sniff out sentiment – that amorphous feeling which pervades each dealing day. What he's really asking is: What's everyone out there thinking? Do they feel good? Are they strong, are they the bull? Or are they treacherous and uncertain, like the bear?

This Monday morning it looks like a nothing day. There's been no volume or direction in the Far East overnight. It's a good day for a press announcement. The players are bored, so they'll listen.

Directing a takeover bid is more demanding than a marathon. When one company wants to buy another it's no high-street shopping trip, it's war! And far closer to the real thing than I'd imagined. Every element of conflict is present, particularly propaganda. The press releases we issue are fantastic. They trumpet capitalist benevolence and just cause: 'We will manage better!' 'Our only concern is the' shareholders!' But the fighting itself is a messy business. After all, who'd start a war they couldn't win?

The number of people with an interest in this takeover is amazing: 20,000 employees, 48,000 shareholders – and add to that number the vultures: the banks, the merchant banks, the pension funds, the speculators. Then multiply their total by ten thousand for the individuals they represent. It adds up to enough to elect a government – with a comfortable majority.

However, resources aren't enough. You need commitment as well – a readiness in the executive to put in long hours, to take a risk, to test and harass the opposition.

Time for a visit to the men's room to freshen up. It's no good appearing in front of the national press looking as if you've just finished a shift in the coal mines. The men's room at Mardon is functional and no more: four basins, two urinal bowls and three lavatories in a row with low blue doors. This is deliberate: egalitarian. It encourages *esprit de corps*. The room holds one extravagance – a floor-to-ceiling mirror for executive staff to confirm their appearance before meetings. I'm pleased with my new suit; I just hope it doesn't look too new. It's Prince-of-Wales check from Chester Barrie; neat without being ostentatious. I sent out for it on Saturday when the old one began to smell. What's going on in the mirror? Fortunately, things don't look too bad. I feared I might resemble a vampire. That would give the conference something to think about! The papers would pick up on it straight away: 'Mardon Packaging managed by the Undead.' Darlington would load their HQ with wreaths of garlic . . .

Over my reflection's shoulder, I can see that one of the cubicles is in use – at least, the door is locked: the Engaged sign shows. But it's very quiet. Perhaps someone is sleeping in there? I'll take a stroll round the desks when I get out and see if anyone's missing. We don't pay people to sleep on the job.

Wendy, the executive assistant, brings breakfast to my

146

office. A hot, golden croissant, a little dish of Normandy butter and a honey pot. This is the sort of attention most of the world would envy, though one which, in my present state of exhaustion, I can barely acknowledge. But it's gone eight o'clock, our press conference is in less than an hour, so I pick up my attaché case, take the lift to the foyer and call to the taxi driver, who's leaning across our reception desk.

As soon as the cab starts to move I feel even more sleepy. That's the nightmare about transnational deals. Someone's always waking up and demanding to know what's going on at the same time as you feel like going to bed. It's thirty-six hours since I last went home. My children will start to treat me like a stranger: 'Mummy, who's that man?' Thank heavens that Viv understands, but even she's started to tease me: makes enquiries about the 'Mayfair Model', six feet, skinny, and just turned twenty-one, who keeps me from my marriage bed. Time is too short, however, to allow my thoughts to drift. I need these minutes between our offices and the conference to get my brain into gear and reorder the hours of cramming last night. First, our new deal:

Ladies and gentlemen, I am pleased to announce that Mardon Packaging Corporation has raised its bid for the ordinary shares of Darlington Card Limited. The new offer comprises one Mardon share and one debenture for each two shares of Darlington, thus valuing Darlington at £312 million. The offer is supported by a new revolving credit facility, signed last night with the company's lenders . . .

That, more or less, is the gist of it. Our most important task is to improve sentiment. People should feel comfortable – no, more than comfortable: pleased – with this new deal.

I stretch out when I leave the cab and can feel some strength returning to my legs. Good! I need to be really switched-on for this one. Our new offer has to be seen as the knock-out blow – if nothing else, to keep the world's eyes away from the dirty punches aimed below the belt.

The press conference has been set up at a standard City greeting zone: the old Brewery on Chiswell Street. We

147

resisted hiring the principal banqueting suite and opted for a side room. We're expecting sixty; it seats forty. It's easier to communicate excitement to a crowd. The admen (God bless their silk suits!) have set up a small podium, draped in the company blue. There are five chairs – we like to face the press as a management team, then they immediately see consensus – like an even row of masks on a wall: these men mean business!

The hall's half full already. We've arranged for coffee and fruit juice to be served. The atmosphere feels surprisingly good, but not propitious enough to smother my nerves. It's rather like those last few minutes before a school golf match: butterflies start dancing around your stomach even when you're sure you're going to win. To be honest, I'm grateful for the tension. It's waking me up and forcing me to relax. It's a luxury to be able to sit back while other people run around and make things ready. It wasn't always this way, of course. A mere three years ago it was me out there, handing out the press release, checking the microphone wires, calling away late executives from their Mayfair Models' arms . . .

Dreyfuss, our PR man, is patrolling the aisles. At five to he'll close the doors, hit the lights and stroll up to the podium. At the same time the Stock Exchange notice will be released to catch the opening bell. This part is exhilarating. It's like the start of a race – when the clock strikes, the gun fires and news shoots out across the globe.

Ten minutes before kick-off, the executive team assemble and go into a huddle. At five to we walk out abreast, shoulder to shoulder, and take our seats together. Whenever I participate in an event, whether it's a sporting occasion or any other when I'm called upon to perform, I always feel a tremendous sensation of relief once it's started. Then there's no going back – the game is under way – and only then can I relax and get on.

Three minutes to go . . . I settle into my chair and observe the auditorium. It's nearly full. City folk are pretty silent on their feet. Orderly lines file in through the doors, filling up the gaps in rows until all the seats are taken, then flow round the aisles at the sides. It reminds me of a game of chess – played at speed in rewind. The people are the pieces and they wander back across the board through their maze of moves to regroup in silence and good order.

Thirty seconds . . . Dreyfuss has taken up position by the doors at the back. One is closed already, so when the clock strikes all he has to do is pull the other to. A couple of latecomers squeeze past him – a middle-aged Japanese in one of those funny, flapping suits they favour, followed by a pretty young girl wearing a Hermès scarf round her neck. Dreyfuss clicks the handle shut behind them and strides towards the podium. All the faces turn his way as he passes along the central aisle. Just before he reaches the microphone, he looks up at me and winks.

Action! 'Ladies and gentlemen, thank you for sparing some time to be with us this morning. The directors of Mardon Packaging Corporation have called this conference to announce revised terms for their offer for Darlington Card Limited. Mardon is represented here today by Arnie Eaglebaum, director, North American Operations, Serge Cartouche, director, Europe, Mr Simon Norton, finance director, and his treasury team. Mr Norton will run through the revised offer; his associate, Mr Jason Fairacre, will provide some logistics. If any time remains, the directors will take questions from the floor. So, without more ado, I'm going to pass you over to Simon.'

Polite applause.

'Ladies and gentlemen, I'm pleased to announce that Mardon Packaging Corporation has revised its offer for the issued and outstanding share capital of Darlington Card Limited. The new terms are as follows: one Mardon share and one debenture for . . .'

Thank heavens it's automatic. The words run off my tongue.

'. . . Thus the total value of the new offer has been calculated by Mardon's advisers at three hundred and twelve

149

million pounds, based on last Friday's respective closing prices for Mardon and Darlington on the International Stock Exchange of England and Wales . . .'

I could do this asleep. Still, I mustn't rush: got to keep things steady, upbeat and even.

'In the opinion of the directors of Mardon Packaging Corporation this improved offer constitutes an attractive opportunity for the shareholders of Darlington Card. We believe we can extract better value from Darlington's existing business and invite you to share our success.'

Perfect! Over to Jason. As I turn round to take my seat I can hear the pencils scribbling.

Time for a squint at the audience. Up to now I've been wearing my Harvard face – a standard US postgrad-school expression which aims to convey boundless optimism. It's amazing the rubbish they come out with in the States; they all know how to pose, even if most of them can't read or write. Still, one has to admire their attention to detail.

Now, who have we here? Who has come to the feast? Let's see: some asset salesmen from the syndicate banks. The self-elected wild men of corporate finance. As if. In truth, they've got no guts at all. They'll spend all afternoon jamming the phone lines trying to sell down Mardon. 'We want fifty million to hold,' they tell us, and the next second we find they've novated the lot to some dodgy little Continental banks with an eighth skim on top for good measure.

Who else? Analysts. I spy analysts. Easy to spot: they're all in such poor shape. Too low-ranked to qualify for corporate health-club memberships.

Last of all are the journalists – a motley crew! Only the *FT* and the *Wall Street* make theirs wear suits. The rest slouch around in corduroy jackets with coffee stains and cigarette burns on the lapels.

Jason is well into his speech. He sounds a little earnest, a little flustered, but he shows he's in command of the figures, which is the hallmark of a true professional. He's winding down now. Another instant and it'll be question time.

Who will have the first one? An analyst, I'll bet. They like to show off knowledge – think we'll be impressed by their diligence and reward them with a preview of our interims.

Aha! Here's a question – a hand is raised way at the back on the left. Dreyfuss points to its owner, who then stands up. This has a funny effect. Until he moved, the audience looked like those cardboard cut-out figures you get with toy theatres – flat rows of people, frozen in the act of observation. Now they've gained depth: motion has added an extra dimension and brought them all to life.

Let me see: quite tall and bulky, red face, charcoal suit, untidy hair – an analyst! I guess before he opens his mouth and the Oxbridge vowels that emerge confirm my judgment. His question is about good-will write-downs. The English always ask about that. Needless to say, we're well prepared and I let Jason answer. He's brighter than a rocket scientist and nails him with statistics – blows the analyst right out of the water, and the fellow retires, muttering in confusion.

Anyone else? I'm still on edge, even though these conferences should be no more than formalities – clockwork feeding times. Digestion follows later. I shuffle my papers as if I'm about to leave – another Harvard trick designed to distract the foe. Silence reigns. The audience are cardboard cut-outs once again.

Dreyfuss spots another hand – right at the back, by the refreshments table. He points a regal finger and his assistant forges over with a microphone.

Who is it?

I don't like the look of this one. Could be some old tramp they dragged in out of the rain, so therefore it must be a journalist, or, rather, two journalists. He exchanges a smirk with an equally ill-dressed fat man by his side, then they both stare at me. The smaller and shabbier of the pair takes the microphone.

'Bernie Hayes, the *Chronicle*.'

I was right. He is a newsman. What can he want?

'Could the management of Mardon Packaging please

explain the role in this offer of Millwork Limited and Massfund Investments?'

What shall I do? Pretend not to hear? I'll pretend I didn't hear.

'Could the gentleman repeat his question?'

'Millwork and Massfund. I'll spell them if you like.' His amplified voice reverberates round the room: 'Millwork and Massfund . . .'

My hands are shaking but I can't run. This is a nightmare and I have to react. People must not see that there's something wrong!

My heart rate's gone through the roof and I have to do something. Tap the microphone. Clear the throat.

Miscreant eyes snap back towards the podium.

'As my colleague Jason Fairacre stated, all material relevant to the offer is contained in the revised offer document, copies of which may be obtained at the door. Once you have had the opportunity to examine it, please feel free to contact me or any member of my team if you require further information or clarification. Our direct lines, together with those of our advisers, are set out at the foot of the press release.'

Will that do? He's smiling at me. I think he's going to ask another question. What does he know? He's trapped me with his eyes – with that evil smile that tells me he knows our secret. I'm finding it hard to move now. *Quick, Simon! Talk. Clear your throat at least.* 'I . . .'

Saved! Out of nowhere one of Dreyfuss's men appears, waving several offering circulars. He gives a copy to the obese accomplice and another to the journalist, makes him take it in both hands and opens it at some page – God knows which one: there's no information about Millwork or Massfund in there. It's a Stock Exchange document – hardly the place to announce you've been engaged in insider trading. There's nothing on paper about those two companies anywhere – outside a safe in Liechtenstein, that is.

Dreyfuss materialises by my shoulder. He spreads a few papers on the podium and takes the microphone. 'Well, ladies and gentlemen, that just about wraps things up. On behalf of the representatives of Mardon Packaging, I'd like to thank you all for your time.'

He smiles at the audience as if they were his dearest friends, walks around the podium until he's in front of me, then turns his back to the hall. There's a mass rustle in the background as they leave their seats. 'I thought I'd step in and cut things short before we were bombarded with abstracts.'

I'm still in shock. Why are they going? These people are meant to be sharp-nosed analysts – dab hands at digging out company secrets. Is no one curious? Did no one even notice?

Dreyfuss is hanging by my shoulder, anticipating praise.

'You did well. I thought things went very smoothly. Your team did an excellent job.'

The tribute is received with a smile. Dreyfuss digs his hands into his pockets and shrugs his shoulders, as if to say: 'It was nothing.' He looks pleased with himself. 'You must be looking forward to some sleep.'

I grin like an idiot and nod my head. Sleep. Of course! He thinks I'm exhausted; that's why he stepped in. Good! I hope the camouflage lasts. I hope I look like a corpse who's been exhumed for a lecture on decay! Anything to escape this hall! There's been a leak, a bad leak, and I have to get back to the office to cover our tracks. I'm feeling shell-shocked. My shirt's soaked. My skin is turning cold where it sticks to my back above the belt. I can't hang around. I must speak to Donald. How did that journalist find those names? This part of the takeover is designed to be double-proof safe.

Fortunately, our limousine is waiting in the cobbled court-yard. The driver's standing on the porch, holding up a golf umbrella in Mardon colours. All five of us huddle in together, as though we were a group of clerks dashing for a bus. Serge gets in last, grinding out a cigarette with his heel before he closes the car door. Disgusting habit. If only

153

France had a level playing field, we wouldn't need their bloody nationals on our team.

We drive down through the City to the Strand. The sky is dark, the streets empty, but rows of lights shine out from the buildings – as if the workers I can see inside are the generators, the actual source of power for the illumination. I don't particularly feel like talking. There's only one person I want to speak to right now: Donald. Happily, we have an American in the car – Arnold Eaglebaum – so an uncomfortable silence is impossible.

'We've put the ball into play,' he starts, 'and this little gut feeling tells me we've got the winning team.'

Unless we're disqualified for cheating. But Arnie doesn't know that. To him, this is some wholesome, all-American game where you play fair and shake hands with the losers before throwing them out on their arses into the streets.

It's time to take this conversation on. 'You handled the projections well,' I tell Jason.

His face lights up with gratitude. 'I tried to focus on the synergies. After all, they're very evident.' He looks around, sees we're all listening, and continues: 'Darlington is such a dinosaur! The management have got their heads in the sand.'

Serge smiles as he fiddles with his Armani tie. He probably wants another cigarette.

'I'd expected some questions about the rationalisations, though.'

'It's only a thousand jobs in the UK – all low-caste industrial dross. And everyone expects us to shed some weight.'

Arnie could do with shedding more than an ounce or two himself. There's something slightly ethereal – unreal – about high finance. I can never quite get used to all the war talk from fat-cat executives. They take themselves so seriously. But in truth they're paper tigers – or something more substantial: lard tigers, butter sculptures.

At last! The telephone rings in the console by my right arm. I pick it up and switch to talk.

'Fill me in.' It's Donald Fletcher – the ringmaster.

'It went well, Donald. Things were very smooth.' I say his name aloud so that everyone knows who I'm talking to. All four shift in their seats, snap to and look attentive, as if the great man had materialised in the car.

'Many questions?'

'Only one – on write-downs. Jason dealt with it.' I pause for a moment . . . We have a code for trouble: golf. Everyone plays it, so no one suspects if you use a golfing phrase. I need to indicate to Donald that we have to speak in private. 'We'll have to reduce Mr Fairacre's handicap. If he continues improving at this rate, soon he'll be playing to scratch.'

Jason blushes and beams and looks as if he's about to kiss me.

'I'll call you at eleven. I'll be on the B line. Make sure you're alone. Now put Arnold on.'

I give everyone a broad stage smile and pass the receiver to Arnie. The coiled wire just stretches across my chest, but I fold my arms and look flattered by the inconvenience: after all, it's no mere cable but the precious vessel blessed with the task of conveying our dear leader's voice.

Arnie utters a succession of 'yups', then kills the line and hands back the receiver. 'He's pleased,' he tells us, aware that we will hang on his every word. 'He thinks he's got the home – I mean the US – side tied up and . . .'

And so on. Rabbit, rabbit. If only they knew. Games, games, games.

'High finance is the great game of the twentieth century.'

It would be if we stuck by the rules. But we haven't. In the City you make your own rules. We've taken a big risk and I'll go to prison if we're caught. Right now Millwork and Massfund, the two shell companies, are in the market acquiring shares. They had nearly ten per cent by last night's close. Five or six more will see us through. This train left the station a long time ago. Operation Rollover is rolling on. We set up two captive companies to buy the shares the stock market wouldn't sell to Mardon through its own free will. And why not? Because it's illegal. Because directors and insiders have duties to their shareholders. Because I occupy a position of trust.

Arnie falls silent. He, Serge and Jason examine my face. All are smiling. What did he say? Fortunately, he repeats himself: 'There'll be less time for dreaming, Simon, when you're running your own show.'

'I'll expect no less than an ordeal when you're in charge of strategy.'

Arnie laughs and extends his hand. I can't refuse it and am pleased to discover my palm is the drier of the two. We've already carved up Darlington, even though the bid is yet to be won. Everyone in this limousine will be promoted. Even Jason, only five years out of Oxford, will earn more than a hundred thousand when this ship comes in.

The car draws up outside our headquarters. This morning's rain has melted the snow that fell over the weekend. One after another, we step across a gutter flooded with slush. We separate in the foyer and I take the lift to my office.

It's good to be behind my desk once more. When I plonk my elbows down on the blond wood it feels like sanctuary: here I am in control. I was panicking a bit out there and that won't do. But then again, when someone throws that sort of question into the ring you begin to wonder how much he might know. Should you try to gag him, or just carry on playing with a straight face and call his bluff? That scruffy little journalist must know something – after all, the Section 147 Discovery Notices only got as far as the Luxembourg trusts. As far as the DTI are concerned, Millwork and Massfund are financed by Belgian dentists. Why should he think any different? I don't like it, but until I speak to Donald there's nothing that can be done.

There's a list of calls on my desk – syndicate banks, rating agencies, assorted journalists. I divide them up – some for Jason to deal with, others for Dreyfuss. And one surprise: a Miss Younghusband, who's apparently phoned three times. The name rings a bell . . . I remember, she's Sir Charles Barrington's assistant. How odd! The police told me he was in a bad way. Perhaps he's recovered and wants to finish his examination? He'll have to wait. I'll give Wendy a shout on the intercom.

'Yes, Mr Norton?'

'Arrange a meeting with Moody's, will you? I'm free for breakfast this Thursday. And call this Younghusband woman and find out what she wants. We sent flowers, didn't we?'

'Yes, Mr Norton.'

'Well, if she wants to arrange another examination, tell her I won't be free until this bid's finished.'

Better have a look at the market. The FTSE's off ten points. Our shares are down 13p. Not too bad. Darlington's down as well, in heavy volume. Excellent: plenty of buying opportunities for those of us with cash. Perhaps we should hold back for a few days? Forget it. *You're too nervous, Simon.* Donald will know what to do. He'll be on the line in less than an hour.

'Mr Norton?'

'Yes, Wendy.'

'I've very sorry, Mr Norton, but it's Miss Younghusband again.'

'Put her through, Wendy. She's obviously giving you problems.'

I pick up the extension on the first ring. It's charm time, I suppose. 'Simon Norton speaking.'

'Mr Norton? This is Eleanor Younghusband. I realise you are a very busy man; therefore I shall be brief. We will be able to discuss what I have to say at greater length when we meet.'

'I'm pleased to hear Sir Charles is evidently recovering, but, as my secretary has already told you, it will be some weeks before I have the time for another appointment—'

'Mr Norton,' she interrupts in a cold voice, 'you have mistaken the purpose of my call. Sir Charles remains in a coma. The hospital advise me that his death is a foregone conclusion. The police are convinced they have caught his assailant – news which, I imagine, you will receive with relief.'

'What on earth do you mean?'

'Simply that from time to time the police make mistakes – arrest the wrong man, who, in the absence of certain evidence, Mr Norton, may appear to be the perfect suspect.'

What is she on about? I don't need another nightmare on my hands. This call has gone on too long.

'Miss Younghusband, I fail to see why you're confiding in me. If you know something that may assist the police, then call them. I enjoyed my meetings with Sir Charles, sincerely regret his accident, and hope to have the opportunity to visit him again. Please feel free to call my secretary when you have any news . . .'

'Be quiet, Mr Norton! I did not think you would be so cavalier with your future. And silence is not expensive.'

She pauses and then, suddenly, it clicks. She wants to blackmail me! Incredible. She must be out of her mind. What can she think I've got to do with whatever it was that happened to Sir Charles? I have to kill this at once.

'Younghusband, I am at a loss to see the purpose of this conversation. I am a busy man. All calls on this telephone line are recorded, and should it be your intention to harass me I will have no alternative but to pass a copy to the police.'

She isn't listening to me; she's talking too, her voice reduced to an acid hiss. 'You know it was no accident and you will meet me to arrange a settlement. I will be at Kettners in Old Compton Street this Thursday at eight p.m. Goodbye, Mr Norton, and don't forget to bring your chequebook. It is you who will be paying for the drinks.'

How dare she! I'm not just amazed, I'm furious! To be threatened by a middle-aged spinster is bad enough; it's worse when I haven't got the faintest idea what she's talking about. Unless she knows about our share dealings . . . No – she can't. Unless she's got a cousin or something in Liechtenstein. Impossible. Another call and I'll send the tape straight over to the police. Blackmail is a serious crime. This is no time to be pestered by lunatics.

Shall I tell Donald? I think I'll have to. No, wait: on second thoughts, it's better I deal with it myself. There's already enough bad news for one day. I'll let it rest for the moment, but if she calls again . . .

There are far more pressing matters to attend to. First, I need a strategy ready for sorting out this journalist. I'm at a disadvantage – I don't know how much he knows about Operation Rollover. All right: assume the worst. He's found out about Rollover – that we're buying shares in Darlington illegally. He's faced then with two choices: to make it public, or remain silent. We need to force him to follow the second option.

How? Legally, of course. We'll get an injunction under the defamation laws. *No, Simon, no good* – first he has to make an assertion that's libellous. Mentioning Millwork and Massfund by name isn't quite enough. And issuing a writ is tantamount to admitting we've something to hide.

What about providing incentives? We could promise exclusive access to new stories, grant interviews, guarantee advertising, that sort of thing. We could even try some leverage higher up. I think Donald knows the editor – we could see if this Hayes man prefers his job to disclosure. I'm going to run a check on him in any event. Anything we can find out about him can only be to our advantage. I'll have his credit-card accounts examined – see if he's exceeded limits. I think we'll look into his private life as well. A divorce or some long-forgotten criminal record would make very useful ammunition.

Telephone. The B line. It's eleven already.

'Are you alone?'

'Yes, Donald.'

'Good. Something happened this morning. What?'

'Bernie Hayes, a journalist on the *Chronicle*, asked a question about the shell companies.'

'What did he say?'

159

' "Will the management of Mardon Packaging please comment on the involvement in the offer of Millwork Limited and Massfund." '

'That's all?'

'Yes.'

'What did you tell him?'

'To read the offer document. Then I closed the meeting.'

'Did anyone else pick up on it? Did any of the directors make any comments?'

'No. They seemed to have forgotten. Everyone was pleased with how well the conference had gone.'

'Right. Listen to me. Phone Martin Palmer at Lister's. He's a solicitor we've got in our pocket. Call him on his direct line. We'll apply for an interlocutory injunction. He'll need you to sign an affidavit. Make sure you do it after hours and off the premises. Understand?'

'Yes, Donald.'

'You sound edgy.'

'It's been a long week.'

'Don't think about it. I'm catching the Red Eye from La Guardia. I'll be in London by eight tomorrow morning. And don't worry about this Hayes character. We already have three writs out against him. He won't get any sympathy in the courts. The injunction will be a formality. Now listen, Simon: I need you to stay on your feet. We're nearly there. Understand?'

'I hear you.'

'Good. I'll see you in my office first thing.'

The welcome voice of authority.

13 Vauxhall, Queenstown Road, Clapham Junction, followed by Wandsworth Town, Putney, Barnes and so on until Teddington. The stations roll by – little islands of light as the train sways along through the night. Going home – home at last! Almost forty-eight hours later to the minute. My bio-clock's gone haywire. I feel wide awake for the first time today. Lunch was a nightmare. Imagine trying to stay on your toes and sound alert when all you really need is sleep. My condition was far too fragile for all that backslapping and wine-guzzling in celebration of our conference's success. Then there was the business with Palmer in those dingy Fleet Street offices. I should have taken more care with the affidavit, but, frankly, I was too tired. Didn't want to be there at all. Just signed the damn thing and left.

The grinding sound of steel on steel as the wheels lock and the train halts. A pneumatic sigh and the door button lights up. I grab my case, coat and scarf and step into the cold night air. There's a flash of headlights from beyond the barrier. Viv's waiting for me. Treasure! She must have telephoned ahead to check the train was on time – no need for a taxi tonight. She starts the car at once.

'Darling!' Viv squints through the door in mock confusion – do I recognise this stranger? – then smiles her wonderful sweet smile when I climb in beside her and kiss her cheek. We're quiet during the drive home – it's only ten minutes to Pine Tree Lane – a short period of suspended animation until we arrive and I can, at last, unwind. Viv is a source of perpetual wonder to me. She's so stable – always straight-forward, pleasant, everything and more I could want as a

161

wife and companion. She's even good at the company functions. She listens to the small talk forced upon her by other directors' dreary consorts, which must be a nightmare – you'd be amazed at the sort of baggage successful men tow in their wake. I think she's found the last six months very hard – having to act as two parents to the girls – but I've promised her a long holiday once the Darlington bid's through.

The headlights pick out white gateposts and Viv swings smoothly into the drive. Home! We've been here nearly a year but the time I've spent in the house can't amount to more than a couple of months at most. Still, somehow it feels like home, which is the most important thing. Viv did the decorating. She's quite artistic, and we share the same tastes. Neither of us likes clutter, so we've kept furniture to a minimum – some modern pieces; others with a more traditional feel. The house was built in the 1930s and is Grade Two listed, which limited the amount of exterior changes we could carry out. We put picture windows in the back extension, so that it feels as if it's part of the countryside in the summer. All the walls are painted in pastel colours, except the kitchen, which is now French farmhouse-style. It was expensive to make it truly authentic but the result is great; we find it very cosy.

The kids are in bed. We tiptoe upstairs together, and Viv holds a finger to her lips as she turns the handle on their bedroom door. They like to share a room, even though they're three years apart in age and the house is large enough for them to have two each of their own. Children are incredible – they sleep so deeply, sweetly, soundly. Hannah has her thumb in her mouth, and Viv removes it, stroking her forehead with her other hand as she bends over the bed. We creep out together and close the door. I know I'll see them in the morning – by six they'll be bouncing round our bedroom – but I couldn't resist a quick glimpse.

'I hope you're hungry, darling?'

'Famished!'

'Why don't you change while I lay the table?'

I loosen my tie and kick off my shoes. 'Ready already! Let's eat in here.'

She smiles and hastens off to the kitchen. On the way, she picks up my shoes and rests them by the staircase.

'There's a bottle of wine open. Shall we have a glass?'

'Perfect!'

I'm about to ask if anything's on the box – habit, really – then think better of it: I've been away nearly two days. Whatever channel we turn to, there's bound to be some news and I've got news coming out my ears – reporters and their oh-so-earnest questions.

Viv returns from the kitchen with a tray. 'Pleased to be back?'

All I can do is nod and smile in reply. It feels great – even if I have to be out the door again by seven tomorrow morning.

'Jenny's losing her milk teeth. One came out today. I told her to save it for the tooth fairy.'

'How much do they pay these days?'

'Fifty pence?' Viv shrugs her shoulders.

'Done!'

She kisses me as she puts down the tray. Viv is an excellent cook. She's prepared salmon *en croûte*, with a Greek salad. The taste and texture are so appealing I forget myself and eat in silence. When I'm finished, she picks up a pad she keeps by the telephone.

'Darling, you had some calls. I wrote them down for you – here: Mr Lightfoot, from the car-leasing company, confirming your test drive this Saturday. The golf club to remind you of the AGM and dinner. Miss Younghusband – she said it's urgent. We had quite a chat; she asked after the girls – sounded very interested in their progress. In fact, I asked her advice about schools – she seemed to be quite a mine of information. Hannah's ten next May, and sooner or later we'll have to decide . . . Darling? I'm sorry. I know you're tired and now's perhaps not the right time . . .'

Viv looks into my eyes, trying to read – God knows what – fear? Then that kind, sweet smile spreads over her face – just like it does when she gazes at our sleeping children.

'I'm sorry, darling; I know you've had a hard few days. You must be dying for some rest.'

I nod my head. I don't yet trust my voice. I reach up, take Viv's hand and pull her close. She hugs me tight and rests her head on my shoulder. Her warmth, the smell of her hair, are a source of comfort.

I can't tell her. I can't get her or the children involved. This is home – sanctuary – nothing to do with the big bad world outside.

Younghusband. That name itself sounds sour. How dare she! This is more than blackmail, it's intrusion – a violation! I'm seldom moved to anger, but by God I'm angry now. It's fortunate that creature is well out of reach or I'd be straight out the door, drag her by the hair into my car and throw her over the counter at the police station.

Viv hugs me tighter and tighter; then, very gently, she breaks away. 'There's a pudding too, darling, but leave it if you can't bear it and get some sleep.'

'I'm sorry, darling. It's been a tough week. It can't be any fun for you, I know. Must be like being married to a robot. But I'll have some time this weekend. And April, come what may, we'll go away together. It won't be this bad in the future. It's just, well, being new, and then this bid comes up . . . it's the largest the company's ever done and I'm right in the thick of it.'

Viv nods as I speak: she sympathises and wants to show it. She takes my hand in both of hers and rubs it softly. I can't tell her; she wouldn't understand. I could never explain the games we play out there in the City. To an outsider's ear, the only way to succeed sounds wrong. As for Younghusband, I can't see why that bloody woman has chosen to invade my life. At any other time she'd be sitting in a cell by now, regretting she ever made the call, but what can I do? There's no way I can attempt anything that might jeopardise this takeover. I think I'll have to tell Donald; there's no getting round that. He'll be furious. In my mind's eye I can see him now. He goes so pale when he loses his temper – falls silent for a few seconds, then begins to shout. All the directors steer clear when he's in that mood, but I, unfortunately, have nowhere to run. We're the only two involved in Operation Rollover, though I suppose Palmer, that lawyer, knows something. I wish I had more control. Donald told me we'd be equals – as if! Still, it's too late to go back. The upside is financial security for life; a house in France, public schools for the kids, the antiques Viv wants to buy . . .

No, it's more – more than that: it's certainty; comfort and respect until I die. I'll have hauled myself and my own above the high-water mark. I'll have put us all beyond the reach of poverty. No one need count. None of my successors will have to waste hours working for strangers. They won't need personal sacrifice in order to be accepted by society.

What about the downside? There isn't one. I haven't been proved wrong yet, and in this deal no one loses. Darlington gets the management it needs and the shareholders get value. The only ones who don't get what they want are the DTI and their precious little rules committee.

By the time I reach my bed I'm at that halfway stage between consciousness and dreams where everything seems to be happening at a great distance. Viv helps me out of my clothes and under the duvet. I lie on my side and she snuggles up, wraps an arm over me and weaves her fingers into mine. Treasure! This is peace, real peace – a safe haven far away from the City of turmoil. The two must always be kept far apart. I'm the gatekeeper – the only connection between these separate worlds – the guardian, the Grail knight, the key-bearer . . .

14   Five to nine on Tuesday morning. Sipping coffee, leaning over Wendy's desk, waiting for Donald to finish his conference with Arnie. Apparently there was a thunderstorm last night that kept half of London awake. I didn't see it, didn't even hear it – slept right through it and didn't know the first thing about it until I saw the flooding on the morning roads. Wendy, it seems, is afraid of storms and chatters on about the mighty thunder blasts that detonated over Hackney.

At last! The handle turns and Arnie emerges, blinking, as if he's just walked from darkness into light. He smiles at me without looking happy, gives me a friendly pat on the shoulder, but with a straight arm – as if to keep me at a distance. '*Cave canem*,' he says. Then his white-shirted bulk vanishes into the open-plan section of the office.

Donald is waiting for me by the door. His jacket is off, shirtsleeves rolled up, short red hair standing slightly on end.

'We'll take breakfast at half past, Wendy. Please bring it straight through.' He holds the door open and summons me in. 'Did you get some sleep?'

'I was out for the count by eleven.'

'Good. Listen, Simon, things have moved on since we last spoke. The bid is like a ship, remember? We've got to keep her sealed tight against any leaks. I've decided to put Rollover on hold. We're going to open up another line of attack. I've instructed Arnie to step in through Puerto Rico.'

'I didn't . . .'

'I know. I told you no one else was involved. But plans have changed. Don't worry – Arnie's got a very safe pair of hands. *Vis-à-vis* Rollover, our defence is in place. The *Chronicle* has been silenced. Palmer got an interlocutory injunction

166

last night. Now it's time to go on the offensive. We'll start by digging over this journalist's past. We need an investigator on board. How good are your contacts in the security market?'

'Not brilliant. I know someone at Kroll Associates. We used them for the Breweries bid at Pendle's. I think I've got a card somewhere.'

'No; no good. They're too upmarket. This has to come from you, Simon – it has to be dressed up as a treasury affair. Give Palmer a call. Explain you need to run a security check. Ask him to recommend a firm with discretion. Stress that – discretion. He'll understand. This is the story: the *Chronicle* have got a contact somewhere in our team, who's receiving unpublished, price-sensitive information. We know they're trying to use it to smear the bid. Cite this as evidence.' Donald throws me a copy of Saturday's *Chronicle*, open at the leader page.

'GUINNESS SHADOW ADDS TO MARKET GLOOM' and 'Fraud Trail Exposes Directors' Greed' run the headlines. The adjacent column in the Arts and Leisure section carries a picture of Donald, with the caption 'Donald Fletcher, CEO of Mardon Packaging, announces new scholarships for the Mardon Foundation.'

'It's the same old trick – guilt by association. They juxtapose a photograph and an accusation and leave the reader to make the connection. There's fuck-all we can do about it, unless we can trip up this Hayes character – which I'm leaving to you, Simon. Cost is discretionary. I want a first report by the weekend, understand?'

'Absolutely.'

'Excellent. It's good to see someone else with a clear head. Now, what else has been going on? Any other signs of trouble?'

I shake my head. It's no use telling him about Younghusband. I thought about it on the train as I came in to work today. She can't know anything about Operation Rollover. She probably thinks insider trading is another name for rigging a flower show. She's obviously got her hands on Sir Charles's files and is fishing. Sooner or later someone else will call her bluff. 'Things are quiet. The conference went well,' I say.

'Arnie told me.'

Arnie again. I'm not pleased he's been brought into the game. When it was just the two of us, Donald and me, I felt safe. We're the only signatories for the Liechtenstein trust. Involving anyone else puts confidentiality at risk.

'If you're worrying about Arnie, don't. He knows nothing about Rollover. His operation is separate – he even thinks it's his idea. There's nothing on paper. If it blows up, he'll hang alone.'

'What exactly is he doing?'

Donald stares at me. 'You don't need to know.'

'I'd like to know.' I'm not afraid to stand up to Donald. 'I mean, if you're taking risks for both of us I think I should be told.'

I might have gone too far. Donald's face is very, very pale. He radiates violence when he's in this mood – like a dog that's about to attack. I'm beginning to wish I was somewhere else.

'All right, I'll tell you. Though I warn you, it's against your interests. Mardon Industries Inc. manages part of its pension fund portfolio out of Puerto Rico. It's incorporated as a bank. Arnie and some half-baked union official are the sole trustees. They own a Cayman Islands shell which started buying last night.'

'And this union official – does he know?'

'Don't push me, Simon. I've told you more than I intended.'

'It's my future, Donald. I have a right to know.'

'A right? Did you say a right!' A knotted fist shoots across the table. Its fingers burn into my throat. 'This is no fucking game, Norton. You're the new boy, so fucking well sit tight and do as you're told!'

The air goes out of me. I'm drowning in slow motion.

God, he's strong! When he lets go I slump forwards, against my will. My elbow knocks on the desk, bone against wood. The pain numbs my arm and for an instant I'm lost. I feel inexpressibly vulnerable – as if I had fallen into a dream.

Donald steps away from the desk. He sways from side to side, just like a predator measuring the distance to its victim. He clenches both fists until the knuckles turn white . . .

Suddenly, the cloud passes. Donald walks to the window and stares at the street. He puts his hands in his pockets and his shoulders relax. When he turns round, the fury in his expression has vanished. He rejoins me at the desk.

'Listen, Simon – we're nearly there. I've got a fuck sight more than you to lose. I'm the CEO, remember? There's fifty million of my money tied up in Rollover. Sit tight. The risk is small. As we agreed, this is a one-off. In two months the whole thing will be wound up and buried. Understand? Buried. Gone.'

'Yes.'

'Understand?'

'Yes, Donald.'

He's right. There's no room for regret. I made my decision six months ago – the short cut that would take me well ahead of all my unimaginative contemporaries. As Donald says, we're nearly there. I'll be the managing director of a major company before the age of thirty-six. From then on, it's plain sailing. A few years' generosity to the Conservative party and I might even have a knighthood by forty. 'Arise, Sir Simon!' Sounds unreal, doesn't it?

A knock. The door edges open and Wendy backs in with the breakfast tray. Croissants, jam, honey, black coffee, freshly squeezed orange juice. We eat in silence. I can still feel Donald's fingerprints, as if some demon had lately touched me. I'd like to rub my neck – soften the flesh – but I don't dare.

Then a curious elation arrives. I've walked the fire! He's right. Donald is right. This is no time to run away and lose it all. So: to business! I'm smiling now and Donald manages one in return. When I stand up he puts an arm around my shoulders and walks me to the door. His touch is gentle, friendly.

'Keep up the good work,' he calls after me, and I can feel eyes turning towards me as I walk away. The door to my office has been propped open. The cleaners came last night and dusted down the tombstones, emptied my litter bin, even changed the plants. A little tree has been substituted for those bushes with waxy white flowers that have occupied the trough between my desk and coffee table for the past month. All the files on my desk have been arranged into neat, rectangular piles. A yellow row of Post-it notes recording incoming calls is by my phone.

First things first: contact Martin Palmer at Lister's. He has a suggestion to hand, as if he'd been waiting for my call. There's something about him I don't like – something oily and insincere. He suggests we have lunch 'sometime', but I ignore the overture. He's not the sort to associate with. At eleven o'clock, Jason comes in and briefs me on sentiment among the banks. They're going through primary syndication right now and the poor bloke's besieged with calls. Banks are such sheep! They rush into, or away from, deals in one great big flock. Fortunately, Mardon's name is in favour. They hope we'll give them treasury business, so I'm inundated with invitations to Henley, Wimbledon, Ascot, the Open – you name it, every sporting event worth seeing. To the victor belong the spoils. If I had time I'd take them all, but you have to be sparing with your favours. Besides, I can't handle too many treasury salesmen at once. The Americans, in particular, are incredible! So pushy! And primed full of technical jargon, which I'm sure they don't really understand. It's as if they expect us to punt all our money on the markets instead of investing it in our businesses. They don't seem interested in Industry with a capital I.

By midday I'm feeling a little tired and rather stale. When I'm in this mood, I make a point of escaping the office for some fresh air. There are five or six sandwich shops in the vicinity, which, depending on the weather and the time I can afford to be away from my desk, give me between two and twenty minutes' worth of freedom. Today, I'll use Alfredo's, the furthest in distance and the slowest in service.

I always find the world outside our headquarters a surprise. The journey through the revolving door catapults me into a different environment. Here, rainfall is more than a decoration for the landscape beyond a windowpane – it's a real inconvenience. Fortunately, I seem to have stepped out in between showers. As I walk, I keep my eyes on my feet. The paving stones are poorly laid and liable to tip dirty water into my shoes. I halt at the kerb and raise my head.

'Simon! What a wonderful surprise!' A familiar voice is shouting at my left ear.

Younghusband! I can't believe it! But it is, it's that dreadful woman. That unmistakable horse face and manure-coloured twinset. She's made up in the most horrible manner, with smeared scarlet lipstick and whorls of pearls. Ten feet away, on the edge of the pavement! Shouting and waving!

I can't avoid her. She dashes up, seizes my wrist, then plants a kiss on both my cheeks. Incredible! I'd like to shake her off but I don't dare – I'm still in sight, and very conscious, of the office.

All right, then! I lock her arm in mine and march her round the corner, heart hammering, breathing heavily. What can she want, the mad old bitch? She grabs on to a railing and forces me to stop.

'Well!' Her voice is shrill.

'Be quiet! We're going straight to the police and you can explain yourself to them.'

'Let go this instant. Mr Norton. Let go, I tell you,' she's still holding the railing, 'or I'll call Rape!'

'Go ahead.'

At last! I've got her loose. She turns to face me, draws breath and opens her mouth. I slam a hand over her lips and force her back into the railings. I can feel her jaw working against my palm. This won't do. A better plan: I'll lead her gently round towards Albemarle Street, then dash into the police station. I'm banking that she doesn't know the area. But first I have to calm her down.

'All right. All right: I'll let you go. But no shouting.'

She nods her head. I take my hand away and step back. I'm panting now too.

'Mr Norton, I'm pleased you seem to have come to your senses. I suggest we go somewhere quiet for a drink.'

'All right.' We're about fifty yards from the Red Lion, so I take her arm again and start to walk. 'How about just there?'

'Not so fast, Mr Norton. Do I look the sort of woman who patronises public houses?'

'There's a wine bar round the corner – what about that?'

'Hmm,' she sniffs, 'not quite what I had in mind. Brown's Hotel is very close. They are famous for their luncheon table.' She tucks her arm through mine in a more conventional fashion and leads off. 'Not far, Mr Norton, not far,' she tells me, and locks on tighter in case I try to break away.

'You have a lot of explaining to do, Younghusband. And it had better be convincing.'

She tosses her head and momentarily adopts a peeved expression, but clearly she is enjoying this whole episode – like a child who's being taken out of school for a day. She certainly knows her way round Mayfair – diving into alleys and marching me through an arcade, maintaining a commentary all the time.

'The fifties! Mr Norton, the fifties! You're too young to know what glamour looked like. Your parents were accountants too, weren't they, so they can hardly be expected to have given you any idea. I came out in nineteen fifty-six. We were still presented to the Queen then, you know, and Mayfair – Mayfair! The very word had a thrill to it, a stateliness, a magnificence, which now, I'm afraid, is sadly tarnished. The Arabs, you see, the Arabs, Mr Norton. They bought the place out and turned it into the cheap little bazaar it is

172

today. The Arabs and taxes . . . death duties . . . those horrible politicians with their provincial accents . . .'

And so on. I'm convinced, now, that she's mad. I don't think she's dangerous, but definitely insane. My mind is busy working on a thousand methods of escape. Damn it! – at any other time this would all be over long ago: she'd be inside – locked in a prison cell or tied to a hospital bed. But for the moment at least I have to humour her – listen to the reminiscences of Debutante of the Year, 1956, which frankly, I can't believe.

'. . . And boys, Mr Norton, the boys! So wild and romantic! I could have chosen from four titles. For nearly a decade, I was danced off my feet. There were fisticuffs over which admirer would take me home. But one grows old, Mr Norton, and a single woman cannot live off her memories, golden though they may be . . .'

I recognise Brown's as we turn into Dover Street – I came here once for an Investor presentation, in '85 or '86, I think, when the Eurobond houses were at their height and roadshows were really five-star caravans, eating and drinking their way round Europe. The staff here appear to know the woman. She gets a bow or two, a friendly nod, and it's a matter of seconds until we're facing each other across a tablecloth.

'Sit down, Mr Norton, please do.' She ushers me into the chair which is against the the wall, then positions herself between me and the exit. A waiter materialises by her shoulder and she orders two gin and tonics without glancing backwards.

'You look like a gin-and-tonic man to me, Mr Norton.'

'I seldom drink at lunchtime. I find it incompatible with my responsibilities.'

'Well, keep it by you when it comes. You may find some need for it yet.'

'Miss Younghusband, I'm giving you exactly five minutes to explain the reason behind all this, and if it's not satisfactory, I shall—'

'Mr Norton, if you attempt to move, I will throw this drink over your rather vulgar suit and set up such a hue and cry that I doubt you will reach your office again this afternoon. I hoped we might conduct this discussion in an atmosphere of cordiality. Now I see that this is not to be the case. Very well, to business. I believe that is the phrase you tradesmen use. You know exactly the reason behind this encounter. No, do not speak, let me finish – I am disappointed by your repeated and rather childish denials. It seems, therefore, that I shall be forced to open the bargaining. I suggest the sum of eighty thousand pounds, to be paid by the end of this month. I believe the best method to be a transfer of bearer bonds. That's right, Mr Norton; no need to look surprised – I have done my homework. Besides, it is a reasonable sum. I am not a greedy woman. However, the sensitive nature of this transaction does not allow for horse trading. I'm sure you would prefer that your family – your delightful wife, those charming daughters – should know as little as possible of what passes between us. The girls are at that delicate age when they still revere their parents. I feel it would not be wise to hasten disillusionment. A father in prison is a poor sort of role model. I am reminded of a contemporary of mine – Amanda Hastings – a beautiful girl, Mr Norton, if somewhat wild. Her father was caught up in some insurance fraud a matter of weeks before the Rose Ball. The poor creature never recovered. She made a bad marriage and took to gin . . .'

The room is spinning. She's staring at me, an inquisitive expression spread over her horse face. She's mad. Completely mad. No, worse than that, *evil*.

'Come, come, Mr Norton. You're allowed to speak, you know.' She taps my knuckles, playfully. 'You're not being very gallant. It's considered ill manners to make a lady work so hard at conversation.'

Right now I have a vision of hitting her, of beating that arch face opposite, mashing it like a fruit until the skin bursts. I'll kick over the table and thump my chair into her ribs, stamp the teeth into her mouth with my heel. I'll grind some reason into her!

The wind changes. Alarm tugs at the corners of her mouth. She twitches back in her chair. The schoolgirl-on-exeat expression vanishes.

'I'm here to talk to you, Mr Norton; I'm relying on you to speak too. If the figure I mentioned seems unreasonable – I mean, if you have a cleaner alternative – I'd be delighted to hear it. I promise to consider it. After all, I came with an open mind, to negotiate, not to demand. I honestly believed my proposal would be the easiest for both of us. If you have something else in mind – an annuity, perhaps – then please tell me. All I ask is that you consider the delicacy of my position. A woman is privy to certain facts in a crime . . . What should she do? Go to the police? Or try to see things from another's point of view – reach an understanding that compensates her for the risk she takes? And as you well know, Mr Norton, I have already taken a risk, by providing the police with an incomplete report. Next month I will be in the witness box, and will be faced again with a choice: to tell all, or merely to repeat my prior statement. What would you do, Mr Norton, if our roles were reversed? Look at it from that perspective, and you may understand my position. The choice is simple: either we can work together and come to an agreement, or my conscience may force me to work against you. You businessmen are not the only ones to tape calls, Mr Norton. Should I choose to make allegations about the assault on Sir Charles, I would be able to substantiate them . . . Mr Norton?'

I realise I'm smiling and quickly correct the expression. She doesn't know! She hasn't the faintest idea about Roll-over, and whatever the true story about Sir Charles may be I don't have the least care. So the police arrested the wrong man? Good for them! Whatever they've done, it has nothing to do with me. At last I'm on top of this whole affair and it's time to put the boot in.

'Miss Younghusband, if you choose to lie to the police,

175

that's your business. Why you then tell me as much, I cannot imagine. It's sheer madness. However, I'm prepared to let it rest, on condition that I never hear from you again. If you make any – I mean *any* – attempt to contact me, I will speak to the officer in charge of the case without hesitation. I will repeat the details of this conversation to him, and suggest he re-examines your evidence. I am prepared to testify to the same effect – namely that you admitted you had perjured yourself, and sought to blackmail me. Prison is a world apart from Mayfair, and I tell you, with absolute certainty, that custody would be the reward for today's admissions. Goodbye, Miss Younghusband. I have a feeling we won't be seeing each other again. I leave the bill in your capable hands.'

And I roll up my napkin, toss it into her lap, slide back the chair and walk straight out through the double glass doors, eyes ahead, dodging the nods and stares of the staff, feet quick over the crested hall carpet, down two steps and into Albemarle Street.

15 What's the difference between a city and its suburbs? Let me tell you: the city has a soul, a spirit, if you like. A city never sleeps. You can feel its presence around you every hour of the day. There's no such unity in the suburbs. I drive through them into London for every shift. It's houses all the way – fifteen miles of terraces, grey from the stale air rolling out of the capital. If you take a look at a map, it's hard to see where London starts. The borough names on the street signs will tell you, agreed, that half one slum is London and the other isn't, but there's a better way: ignore the roads, the shops and houses, and concentrate on the people. Look at the way they walk, how they face up to one another in bus queues and on street corners. Londoners do it differently from anyone else. That's because they can feel the city, feel its spirit: it's the people who make a city and the real shape of London is not as it's marked on the map. For instance, Putney, with its pretty-pretty houses and riverbank life, is London. It's a long way from the centre, that's true, but London none the less. Clapham, however, for all its housing estates and Labour council and tube and rail connections, just isn't London. It's got a different spirit – and not a very pleasant one at that.

I'm not a London man myself. I was brought up near Harwich and I've always tried to live outside of town. Wallington is about as far away as I can get and still keep my shifts. It's worth it, though – London just means work to me and it's hard enough as it is in my trade to have a life outside. Most of the boys socialise together – play rugby, even marry into one another's families. I try to keep away from that. I sail most weekends, but never on a police-crewed boat. Fortunately, at my level, which is serious racing, you get all

177

sorts on board – doctors, bankers, professional crews, the kids with long hair who do nothing else but sail – and I've been round long enough for them to forget I'm a policeman, which makes it that bit easier for me to do the same. They know I won't come down on them like a ton of bricks if they pull out a bit of puff or boast about driving from Portsmouth to Plymouth in under two hours. Besides, I like the sea. When you leave the mooring you leave your background behind as well as the land.

I've had to miss a race this Sunday. During the rugby season there's always trouble filling the roster. Still, if you have to work, it's not a bad day to be out and about. The villains are at home, sleeping off their weekend mischief, and as for the general public, well, the short drinking hours and bad transport keep people indoors, where they're less likely to cause trouble. All this makes it a good day to get about town.

Today I've got an appointment with a victim. Page Ward, St Thomas's Hospital, 10.00 hours. It should all be over in fifteen minutes. As far as I know, he's been in a coma since the assault. He's not a pleasant man, but you can't let that affect you.

I never wear uniform for hospital trips. Some of the boys claim it's the best way to get respect from the doctors and administration, but I think otherwise. Besides, people are nervous at the sight of a copper in the wards. And once the staff come to know you they trust you not to pull the drip from one of their charges or sweat them for a confession. In fact, they understand you can be part of the cure – which makes sense: it's usually victims that we go to visit and the presence of a policeman shows that something's being done.

They've brightened up Thomas's in the last few years. The foyer used to look like a British Rail waiting room and I don't need to tell you how depressing that is, especially in a hospital. I check in at the desk, discover Page Ward's on the twelfth floor, then a specialist, Mr Leonard, arrives to lead the way. Like me, he's dressed in mufti – dark suit and tie; wouldn't take him for a doctor. We bypass the lifts and take the paternoster. It's a funny way to travel – like climbing into a bucket on a vertical conveyor belt. It's sited next to the backstairs, off a service corridor. This part of the hospital, away from the patients' eyes, reminds me of the station. It's got the same paint: battleship-grey to waist height up the hall, to hide the scuffs, then dirty white above that. It's got the same worn lino, the same institutional fittings, only the smell is different – sweat and antiseptic, instead of sweat and feet. Must be a superior air-conditioning system. I can hear it now, feel fresh air, from somewhere, on my face. The whole building hums, as if it were alive. The white-coated staff walking round remind me of technicians – building doctors who keep the whole place in shape and carry out repairs.

There are no doors on the paternoster. You step into a compartment when it is passing by and step out when you reach your floor. In between the floors all there is to see is a number painted on the concrete passing in front of your face, then for a few seconds you get a view on to a white landing, then wall once again. It's an old-fashioned machine. I think it's chain-link driven. I can feel the floor rattling through the soles of my shoes. The journey takes a couple of minutes. I daresay the staircase would be a quicker way to travel. Leonard and I count off the numbers in silence. We'll talk when we get there. At times it feels as though the paternoster is motionless and, instead of going up, the building itself is sliding into the earth around us.

Here we are. A strip of light unrolls like a blind as we rise past number twelve. Leonard and I dismount together. He leads the way towards the ward. All the orderlies stop what they're doing, pause in their conversations and look up and nod as he passes. The ward doors swing both ways on light hinges. They're scuffed at about knee height: wear and tear from rolling the casualties through. We have to make way as two black assistants wheel a white-sheeted bed past. The patient is old, pale and motionless. His eyes are closed.

Charcoal-grey and purple shadows decorate their sockets. A drip is fixed to the bed by a stand like a masthead light. The whole contraption squeaks and rattles as they roll it by.

Leonard takes me to a side room in the centre of the ward. One wall is glass, facing on to a pebbled courtyard – a little roof garden where the patients can get some sunshine when it's fine.

'Coffee?' he asks, then goes off to fetch it. The room's full of ashtrays, just like the station, so I light up a fag and watch the rain fall into the plant pots outside. This ward, Page Ward, is for serious cases. Cancer, mostly, and critical road accidents. You don't need to see the patients to work this out – just take a look at the bedside tables: there are no cut flowers and chocolates and cards like in the maternity wards. Here they have long-term trappings – plants, books, kettles and clocks. They know it's kill or cure.

'It was two sugars, wasn't it?' Leonard is back with a pair of plastic cups. He hands me one and sits on the edge of the desk. 'We'll take a look at him in a minute.'

'Has he spoken?'

'No. No signs of consciousness at all.'

'I hear you've had to operate.'

'That's right. I diagnosed myeloma.'

'Which is?'

'Cancer. Bone cancer.'

'Did you know about this before?'

Leonard hesitates. 'He did. Almost certainly. He'd been prescribing himself morphine for nearly a year.'

'Morphine?'

'Forty micrograms per day. The pain must have been extreme.'

'Surely that . . .'

'Might have affected his judgment?' Leonard pauses, stares. 'In Sir Charles Barrington's case, no. He was not an ordinary man.'

'*Was?*'

Leonard walks round the desk and sits down. He opens

his briefcase, extracts a folder and hands it to me. 'This is an X-ray of his spine. Hold it towards the light. You see those grey areas? Those were vertebrae. The twelfth, thirteenth and fourteenth to be precise. They appear cloudy because they have disintegrated.'

'Was that the spot where he received the blow?'

'Possibly. His ribs and pelvis are now in a similar condition.'

'So the force of the blow was significant?'

'It need not have been. You see, Inspector Evans, his skeleton was, literally, falling apart. In a matter of time it would have collapsed under his own weight. The disease had even started on his skull . . . eating into the bone around his brain.'

'So there's no chance?'

'He may come to before he dies. If he does, I do not think he will be able to help you. He probably will have lost all motor skills, including speech, and the pain will be such that he will require sedation to make consciousness bearable.'

I shake my head. What can you say? He was one of us – working for good.

'Shall we go and see him?'

I nod and Leonard leads the way. Sir Charles is in a small room on the edge of the ward, with a view over the river towards Parliament. It's empty save for the bed, a nasal drip, and a plastic tube leading to the figure beneath the sheets. No flowers, fruit or cards, no personal possessions; just a book marked 'Visitors' on a stool by the door.

'We've stabilised him,' Leonard tells me. He speaks quietly. He's honouring the presence of a great man.

I pick up the visitors' book, turn it over in my hands and flick through the pages. There must be over a hundred signatures, including some very well-known names. I'd have to win a special conduct medal to meet just one of them.

'An eminent man, Inspector Evans.' A stranger is at the door. He's mid-fifties in age, with sharp blue eyes and wiry, iron-grey hair. Like Leonard, he's dressed in a suit. He holds himself with confidence, as if he's used to respect.

'As you can see, many have come to pay tribute. They consider it an honour to have made his acquaintance. You are not alone in wishing that Sir Charles Barrington could speak.' The newcomer smiles at me and extends his hand. 'When you're through, Inspector, and if you can spare the time, I'd be grateful for a word. My name is Miller, James Miller. I'm a specialist at the topobiology department.'

'I've seen what I need.'

'In which case, I suggest we repair to my office. If you've nothing pressing, Richard, why don't you come as well?'

This man's presence has brought Leonard to attention. He mumbles thanks, and follows us out of the room.

Miller's office is in a separate building. No government-issue furniture here – it's the private study of an academic. Miller waves a hand and the three of us draw up leather armchairs. He starts to speak straightaway in a dry, calm voice.

'Thank you for sparing me a few minutes, Inspector. I know you are a busy man, and it is my own and my staff's most earnest wish that your investigations bear fruit. After a fashion, each individual in my department is indebted to Sir Charles. Indeed, we owe him our existence – his discoveries form our *raison d'être*. As a consequence, we have an interest in your progress. I understand you have a suspect of sorts?'

'An arrest has been made.'

A shake of the head. 'Most unfortunate, and, in my opinion, highly unlikely.'

'Mr Miller . . .'

'I'm sorry, Inspector. I realise I spoke out of turn. This is police business, and therefore none of mine. I merely meant to say that Charles chose his friends carefully. The nature of his occupation exposed him to a number of potentially dangerous people, and he was a cautious man . . . I see from your face that once again I am trespassing, so I will come to the point of our meeting, which is: can I be of assistance in

182

any way? Sir Charles and I knew each other professionally for nearly thirty years.'

'Two things are bothering me, Mr Miller. The first is that visitors' book. When Sir Charles kept better health, he was a lonely man. A lot of people seem to be waiting to bury him.'

'That I can explain, at least in part. Charles made formidable discoveries four decades ago. In a few years of research he produced the first anatomical explanation of thought, and his theories on identity resulting from his studies in neurone groupings grow in stature every year. However . . . how shall I put this? . . . Well, nowadays much of his research is considered to be unsound, or, rather, impossible to verify. You see, Charles was working in unusual circumstances. No one has repeated his experiments, and, frankly, no one will.'

'Why?'

'Ethics, Inspector Evans. The world has changed. No political party in Europe has genocide on its agenda and no civilised country in the world is at war. As a result, life in the 1990s is precious. Death is regarded quite differently these days. People die of old age in hospital beds. In 1945, when Charles began his work, public sentiment was radically different. Suffering had been so commonplace that society was careless as to the fate of a few war criminals. If they were condemned to death, what did it matter if someone played around with their brains before execution? Consent was not an issue.'

I'm beginning to catch his drift. 'You mean that Barrington experimented on live patients?'

'Exactly. But remember, Inspector, he was working in an unusual age. To his credit he made the most of the opportunity to conduct research. In a scientist's eyes, this is something to be celebrated. Besides, Charles effected many remarkable cures. In addition to his research on war criminals, he treated children who had suffered in the Holocaust. He returned people to a society they had never believed they could trust. However, the very nature of Charles's research

183

is unpalatable to the modern mind. And since his conclusions could not be substantiated, they began to be doubted. This has not, needless to say, inhibited others from reworking his theories into more acceptable models. To my knowledge, three Nobel prizes, including my own, have been awarded for what, in essence, was Sir Charles Barrington's work.'

'Yesterday's man?'

'Not quite, Inspector. But it is true to say that Charles will be more respectable once he's dead. Then, like many others of his generation, he can be consigned to the safety of the past. It will be easier to recognise his achievements. Indeed, I suspect there will be some distinctly unethical behaviour as various institutions fight for the custody of his records. Yesterday's maverick can become tomorrow's saint . . . Now, Inspector, you told me you had two questions?'

'Would any of his patients bear a grudge?'

'Definitely. The majority, if they had known what he was doing. Executives are perfectly happy to be examined for a disease they know they don't have; less so to be subjected to fundamental character analysis. But, as a rule they are not violent. Businessmen find their revenge in blacklists and so forth. Money is what counts, and if they can ruin a man, then they are satisfied. But Charles was most diligent in maintaining confidentiality. As for his criminal subjects, I think he will be protected by the passage of time. He was close to retirement. He carried out few examinations for the penal system in the last fifteen years. There was a time, however, in the 1950s, when the risk was grave. Fortunately the hangman accounted for a reasonable proportion of likely suspects. Besides, Charles is an unusual first choice for a sustained campaign of hate against the apparatus for the administration of justice. I would imagine the police are in the front line.'

'We look after our own.'

'And I would hope you include Sir Charles Barrington within that category?'

It so happens I do. This world works in a simple enough way: only one man in ten does a job that helps society. Most of the rest are like children. They have no concept of good or evil. They think only of themselves and get pleasure from petty offences. They drive too fast, drink too much, avoid their taxes. They all move in their own little worlds, never poking their noses outside their class or wondering how they must appear to the rest of society. Until one day they go too far and discover what it's like to be in trouble. This usually comes as a shock – they find out about themselves as well as the real world. Look at them in this case: Barrington was an addict, Bruton is a violent neurotic – no one is innocent. But we like to protect the ones who try. As a result, and rightly too, a greater evil surrounds the murder of a police-man, fireman or doctor than a waiter or an accountant.

I've already run a check on Sir Charles's last ten patients. All of them are clean. One, an actuary, had been caught with some puff in the seventies. Otherwise, nothing.

I give Miller and Leonard my salaams and walk back over Westminster Bridge towards New Scotland Yard. I'll have a chat with the boys, then off up to Notting Hill.

The tide's out on the Thames. A grey mud bank stretches from the House of Commons to the centre of the river. It needs dredging badly – it's hardly navigable. It must have been deeper in the past, otherwise how could the trading barges have made their way? They must've stepped their masts for all the bridges. I sailed on one once – in Suffolk, near Levington. They're quite handy, considering their bulk, but hard work in a good breeze. They carry a lot of string and that hemp rope must have made mincemeat of the sailors' hands.

I liked Miller. He told the truth and told it plainly. A lot of people find it difficult to talk straight to a policeman. If they're experts, they condescend – never look you in the eye, just blink away and flap their hands and try to make you feel you're an idiot. Which is wrong. After twenty years in the force, you develop an eye for a lie. You don't have to be bright; you just need to be shrewd – you can soon tell if something's untrue. As it happens, Miller was wasting his time. I know I've got the right man. Our Mr Andrew Bruton has a violent nature. Probably doesn't – didn't – even know it himself. He's the quickest-thinking person I've ever met, but intelligence alone won't keep a man stable. He had no motive, unless you count anger. The man lost his rag; there's no more to it than that. If it weren't for his wife, I reckon Bruton would confess. But she doesn't know, he hasn't told her, and now he's caught up in the lies, which is a grievous mistake. There's a better-than-evens chance of conviction for Section 20 – GBH. Section 18 won't stick – it's too hard to prove the intent. But now it looks worse: manslaughter at least. It's only a shame that Miller and his kind won't believe the simple option. They think Sir Charles was too distinguished to be turned over by a close friend. 'It couldn't happen to me,' they tell themselves, 'so it didn't happen to him.'

Scotland Yard is quiet. None of my mates are around. The weather's clearing up – looks like a nice day after all. I think I'll look over Sir Charles's residence in Elgin Crescent. I'll drop by Ladbroke Grove station and pick up his keys.

By the time I've reached Notting Hill the sun is out and the pavements have dried. In this part of town, London nearly looks like a decent place to live. Mind you, the change in twenty years is amazing. If you crossed north of Holland Park in the 1960s, you stepped straight into an immigrant slum. The brothers were losing the jobs promised to them by Mother England and had plenty of time on their hands to make mischief. It was a lively place, though. They knocked down the walls between neighbouring gardens and every night in the summer there was a cook-up round the fire in one street or another. It wasn't till the 1970s that we found out what it was they were all smoking. In those days the Ladbroke Grove station seemed right in the thick of it.

We were firebombed every carnival. But that was years ago. The front line's retreated way beyond the All Saints Road. Soon that'll be lined with cafés and antique shops, like the rest of the neighbourhood. All the villains are long gone. If they changed the drug laws, it'd be the quietest place in London.

A smile and a wink from the front desk when I arrive at the station. Charlesworth, a beat copper, is on sentry duty.

'Anything up?'

Charlesworth shakes his head. 'Quiet times,' he tells me, 'quiet times.' Then he brightens up. 'Had some fireworks on Friday,' he says. 'You missed the fun.'

'Shame. What was it?'

'Section twenty-three. Possession. Involving a certain Edward Fenton Whitmore of—'

'Number 12, Powis Square. How's his memory coming on?'

'Improving. He sends his salaams. We offered him the chance to deliver them in person, but he declined. Claimed he was still painful from your last chat.'

'Where is he?'

'On transfer to Vine Street. By coincidence, they picked up one of his friends at the same time, so we thought they could keep each other company for the weekend.'

'Who'd they get?'

'Dexter.'

'Blimey! I don't envy either of them. One or other's going to need some sewing done before Monday. Anything else?'

Charlesworth shakes his head. 'It's dead quiet. Must be the season.'

'Agreed.'

'What are you up to, then?'

'I've just been to visit Barrington.'

'Barrington?'

'The Assessor.'

'How's he coming along, then? Recovering?'

'Dying. Where are his keys?'

Charlesworth disappears for a minute, then returns with a bunch on a ring. 'You use this Yale and these two deadlocks on the front door.'

'Cheers.'

'Sign here.'

I scratch my mark and pocket the keys. Before I leave, Charlesworth chucks me a tape measure.

'What for?'

'Alibi.'

Outside the station, it's turned into a pleasant day. There's even a bit of blossom visible on one or two trees. Another month and we'll have spring on our hands. Season of car thefts and insurance fraud – don't ask me why. You could hardly tell it was pouring with rain two hours ago, if it weren't for the dog turds on the pavement. That's the surest sign of poor weather – Rover gets a turn round the block on his lead instead of a run in the park. A quick pause on the corner of Elgin Crescent. The Lonsdale, a hundred yards or so up the Grove, can be a trouble pub and it's a sure way to gauge the mood of the neighbourhood. The pool-room windows are misted up and the doors are closed – a good sign. There are a couple of kids chatting on the pavement outside in their shell suits and trainers. They look relaxed, easy, shifting from foot to foot to keep out the cold.

Number 23's on the south side of the street. It's a three-storey, detached house. The sun is just about high enough in the winter sky to peer over its shoulder. It looks less lived-in than its neighbours – a bit more businesslike: gravel drive and flat, empty plant beds. Three cars are parked behind the gates. Interesting. I'll ring before I use the keys.

Footsteps in the hall to the sound of the bell. The security camera is still missing from its mount above the porch. The door is opened by Sir Charles's assistant. She's about the size and shape of an ideal policeman. Her name's in my notebook, so I pull it out with my ID.

'Inspector Evans!'

'Miss Younghusband. I'm pleased to find you in. I'm here to clear up a few things for my report.'

She stands across the doorway, on guard. Seems on edge as well. 'If you need more details from me, Inspector, I'll be happy to make an appointment to see you at your station.' She closes the door a little as she speaks. She's nervous. She's got company too: I can hear voices behind her.

'If there's anything you forgot to tell us, then the desk sergeant can take your statement at any time. I'm here to measure up – confirm the dimensions of Sir Charles's study. I'll be out of your way in fifteen minutes.'

I push gently past her. For an instant, her hand rests on my arm, as if to restrain, but she doesn't have the weight and falls into line behind me as I cross the hall.

The door to the reception room on my right is open. A quick once-over as I pass: there's a vase of fresh daffodils on the mantelpiece and six people reflected in its mirror. They are holding glasses, smoking cigarettes and chatting as they wait for their hostess. The dining room comes next, at the base of the staircase. Here the door opens on to the middle of the room and I observe its table laid for lunch. I'd estimate upwards of ten places – some guests must be late. The smell of cooking reminds me of my empty stomach and I resolve to pick up a pie on my way back to the station. I wave my measuring tape at Younghusband and set off up the stairs. She fidgets, but manages a grin in return and a nervous flick of the hand. In the background, a curious face peers out of the reception room and looks sideways until its eyes meet mine. They belong to a bloke about my age in tie and blazer. His hair has been slicked back to hide a bald patch. County sort – used to see them at the Cheltenham races.

The cleaners have been in upstairs. The bloodstains have been scrubbed from the carpet and someone's tidied up the books. I select a leather-bound volume from a pile – *The Voyage of the Beagle* by Charles Darwin. I rest this on the floor by the wall, trap the end of the tape measure, then lead it across the room. I take a perch on the edge of the desk, open my notebook, rest a biro across the pages, and wait.

Strange place, this. It looks like a cross between a museum and a space station. It's quiet too. I can hear only the ticking of a clock somewhere. There it is, by the cabinet. I gaze about me. It's surprising what you find behind closed doors in London. Drug dealers do up their council houses like palaces inside – it's the only way they can spend the cash. The prostitutes are the same, though in their case it's usually business first – torture chambers in leather and velvet, often no more than a few feet and a cardboard wall away from Mrs Smith and her cat. You'd have to be on the game for a century to afford a place like this. The insurance company tell me the electronic kit alone is valued at a hundred thousand. And judging by what Miller had to say, the files and computer records are worth plenty more.

A knock.

'Miss Younghusband?'

Her horse face peers round the door. She seems to be grinding her teeth. She's probably working out what to say. I could save her the trouble and tell her the first line – I hear it every day – *I suppose you're wondering, officer . . .*

'I expect that you may be curious, Inspector Evans, as to the presence of these people, and I thought I'd set your mind at rest.'

I let the silence hang.

She clears her throat. 'As you may be aware, my responsibilities as employee include the security of this house. On the advice of the insurance company, I have moved in while Sir Charles is convalescing. I had organised this gathering some months back, and had no alternative but to hold it here.'

I don't know why she bothers. It's never been a crime to eat. We often have this effect on people – send them straight back to the classroom as if an invisible teacher had bidden them 'Explain yourself!' Which is no bad thing: an open mouth keeps few secrets.

190

'Don't mind me, Miss Younghusband. I'll soon be on my way.'

'Perhaps I could get you a cup of coffee or something, Inspector?'

'Some tea would be nice.'

She smiles and scuttles off.

Better measure up. Fourteen feet by twenty – a bigger room than it looks. Security is good: reinforced grilles on the windows, infrared beams in diagonal corners, internal and external locks on the doors. Sir Charles liked his privacy. It's cold in here. That's unusual. Invalids prefer to keep themselves warm. Perhaps it was the morphine? Junkies don't feel the chill.

Younghusband returns in double-quick time with two cups, cream jug, sugar bowl with lumps, all laid out neatly on a tray.

'Have you found what you wanted, Inspector?' She hands me a china cup on a saucer.

I stir in sugar and take a sip. 'Nice cup of tea.'

'Thank you.'

Silence falls. Suits me. I've no time for small talk. The woman keeps fidgeting – she's the type who's never happy unless her mouth's open. Probably talks to herself when there's no one else around. I'd hate to see her phone bill. Each time I look her way she twitches, snaps her head forward like a hen to corn. When she sees I'm not going to speak, she herself starts.

'I'm so pleased to see you, Inspector. It makes me sure that something's being done. I know it's been over a week now, but I still find it hard to think about. Everyone tells me to be brave, but I'll never forget finding poor Sir Charles lying there. The shock was terrible. And, as they've pointed out, it could just as easily have been me.'

Younghusband sits herself down on a chair, crosses her legs, straightens her skirt over her knees, then leans towards me to continue. 'You see, Inspector, I knew something like this might happen. I've always prided myself on being practical. But Sir Charles – poor Sir Charles! – was getting old. He just didn't seem to care so much. I think that's very sad. You know, six years ago, when we were still in Harley Street, we had security guards – everything. But people never listen to advice. Perhaps, and I hate to say it, he couldn't look after himself any more. He was a stubborn man – very proud. He didn't believe anything like this could ever happen to him. I brought it up with him several times. I pointed out that the two of us – an old man and a single woman – were sitting here unguarded with a fortune's worth of art. And you know, Inspector, his job was dangerous. He dealt with criminals all the time. It must have seemed like an invitation to them to help themselves. And then, after all that, after the trauma of the burglary, he was attacked by a close friend. Isn't that terrible? I never liked that boy.'

'And how well did you get on with Sir Charles, Miss Younghusband?'

Her face rocks back – no bad thing: she's one of those women who can't understand you're listening to them unless you're staring them in the eye from a distance of six inches and matching them expression for expression.

'I worked for Sir Charles Barrington for ten years, Inspector. There's such a thing as loyalty, you know. Sometimes I think I was the only one who really understood him. He always asked my opinion when he had a difficult case. "Younghusband," he would say, "if I possessed your extraordinary judgment I could dispense with method." He was very intelligent, you see. He had no time for fools.'

Everything but an answer. I pick up the tape measure and pocket my notebook. 'Don't let me keep you from your friends, Miss Younghusband – I've had too much of your time.'

'Not at all, Inspector. It's always gratifying to know one's been of use. And it's comforting to realise there's someone else who cares.' She walks, still talking, by my shoulder to the door. 'Please keep me informed, Inspector. I feel as if I'm almost family, and, few though we are, all of us have to rally round till Sir Charles is back to health and out of plaster and all the rest and that man is put away where he belongs.'

The front door snaps shut behind me. Sometimes, as an exercise, I pretend I'm in court – in the witness box, answering questions from some hostile lawyer – so as to try to view what I've just seen objectively. I'm not pleased with this Younghusband woman, so in my mind's eye I step up and take the oath. I concentrate as I walk and the defence barrister materialises inside my head: a cocksure twenty-five-year-old, with spots on his face and a red patch on his neck where his new stiff collar rubs him raw.

'So, Inspector Evans [he begins], what did the late Sir Charles Barrington's devoted assistant have to tell you when you chose to pay an impromptu and, may I add, unauthorised, visit to the premises?'

'That she hated her employer and didn't know or care if he was alive or dead.'

'In so many words?'

'No.'

'Then how, Inspector, how? If she failed to communicate using the conventional medium of speech, in what manner were you apprised of the witness's thoughts? Did she jot them down in your notebook? The jury are normal, sensible people, capable of greater deductive powers than you would give them credit, so I leave it to you to explain to them how, if not verbally, this ideal witness managed to express her antipathy, her purported indifference.'

'It was clear she had no idea what sort of condition he was in. She hadn't been to visit him. She was holding a party in a dying man's house.'

'These, you would have us believe, Inspector, are clear demonstrations of "hatred" (to use your own word), actions so unusual as to fill your mind with conjecture, which you now choose to present before this court as evidence, when it is clear to everyone present who possesses an iota of compassion that this poor woman was distressed, in need of consolation, indeed was looking for assurance that the system of justice, of which this country is rightly proud, was, albeit belatedly, quite probably ineptly, seeking to ensure that the perpetrators of this evil crime were identified correctly and prosecuted. Is that not so?'

At this point, my mental identity has no reply. As usual I've argued myself into a corner. This case is nearly two weeks old and already it's being smothered in words. It'll be months before it reaches court; then we'll spend days disputing the actions that were executed in less than a minute. I think I'll round off the shift by playing over some of the interview tapes while my mind's still on Barrington. Tapes are so much better than transcriptions – speech carries feelings which typed words can't. I'll start with Younghusband – close my eyes and picture her as her voice plays.

When I return to the station, Charlesworth is still at his post. He's holding the hands of a middle-aged woman, who leans towards him over the front desk. She's nondescript to the extent that she is faceless: a building block for a crowd. Her short, broad body is covered by a grey polyester mac. Her red plastic handbag rests on the counter beside her. One of its straps is broken. She's crying quietly. Her body trembles in a series of quivers, followed by a single, painful sob.

I catch Charlesworth's eye. He shakes his head, so I let myself in through the security doors. I find a cassette player in the equipment room, dig Younghusband's tape from the files, make some tea, put my feet up in a quiet corner and listen. I interviewed Younghusband with a policewoman, Dudley, who gives the preamble – name, address, date, and so on. She was going to take the statement, but sometimes you get a woman who prefers to talk to a man, so it's me who asks the questions. That makes a change. Usually they only let me loose on suspects or hostile witnesses – the ones who need to learn respect. Younghusband dithers before she catches her stride and starts to rabbit on. I fast-forward past the initial tears.

'When I arrived, Inspector, there were two men standing

194

on the porch with a ladder. They said they were from the security firm and couldn't get in, which made me very nervous – you know, that awful feeling when one feels something terrible might have happened. It was horrible – I was fumbling with the house keys, then one of them took them from me and let us all in. Well! I knew about the burglary, of course, but I suppose I just wasn't ready for the mess! And that terrible smell of burning! My heart sank. I was feeling rather shaken and the security men kept asking questions – Where's the alarm console? Where's this? Where's that? . . . Anyway, I pulled myself together and walked straight into my office. I suppose I should have gone upstairs at once, but I can't tell you how upset I was by the mess. I had to calm down. Just then I felt like a robot – going around and doing my duties as if everything was normal, when in fact, deep down, I could feel that it wasn't. It was like a premonition, Inspector – do you ever get premonitions? Anyway, I tried to fight it off. I even opened the mail! Can you believe that? As if it was an ordinary day. I played the answerphone messages and took notes. There were only two: one from that Lydia girl (who sounded quite drunk), the other from the cleaners, who are usually so reliable, apologising and saying that they couldn't come in . . .'

'We have the tape, Miss Younghusband. We'll want you to identify it later.'

'I'm sorry, Inspector – it's just . . . Oh! I can't get it out of my mind. Anyway, one of the security men came in to ask me for the code – the alarm code, you know – and, to my shame, I couldn't remember it, so I walked upstairs to find Sir Charles and ask him. I noticed his study door was open and knew right away something was wrong. You see, Inspector, Sir Charles was such a careful man. He never lets anyone in there, even me, and he always locks himself in when he's working . . . I called out his name twice, "Sir Charles! Sir Charles!" but no one answered, so I pushed back the door and there he was . . .'

At this point Younghusband grabbed my arm and held it

while she wept. Her face was plastered with make-up: I've still got the mascara stains on one of my cuffs. There was no real sadness in her tears – I'm sure of that now. The woman wanted sympathy for what she thought she'd been through, bugger the fact that her employer was half dead.

'The first thing I saw was the blood. I couldn't bring myself . . . I mean, I knew one shouldn't touch him. That's right, isn't it? That's what the ambulance crew told me: "You did the right thing, otherwise you could have aggravated his injuries." I remember feeling very weak, my legs were giving way beneath me, but somehow, and from where, I don't know, I found the strength to make it to the top of the stairs and cry out for help . . .'

The tape continues, then something catches my attention.

'So, Sir Charles is currently examining only one patient?' I hear myself ask.

A sigh. 'Client, Inspector – please! He wasn't just a common doctor. And, I'm afraid to say, I'm not sure quite how much I can tell you about that. It's confidential, you know – we were very careful with our clients.'

'Miss Younghusband, please keep your mind on recent events . . .'

'I'm sorry: you're right. Perhaps I'm being just that bit overprotective. He was examining Mr Norton, of whom he seemed very fond. Poor Mr Norton! It will all come as a terrible shock, I'm sure. A very pleasant young man, Inspector. It's quite impossible that he could have anything to do with this. In my opinion, if poor Sir Charles had only kept up with the right sort of people – his own type, if you know what I mean – then this could never have happened to him. But you know how stubborn old people can get. They start strange, quite unsuitable friendships, as if their best years are yet to come, and never seem to realise that the other party may have something altogether different on their mind. In short, Inspector, they don't realise when they're being used . . .'

And so on. I'm disappointed. I don't like Younghusband,

she didn't like Sir Charles, but in all those thousands of words I can't seem to find anything new. She could just as well be giving me a list of her likes and dislikes. But her voice sounds unconvincing. Something's not right. She didn't want to tell me what had happened; instead she concentrated on how she had felt. I suppose there's nothing new there. Nevertheless, I'm going to have another listen.

'When I arrived, Inspector, there were two men standing on the porch with a ladder. They said they were from the security firm and couldn't get in, which made me very nervous – you know, that awful feeling when one feels something terrible might have happened. It was horrible – I was fumbling with the house keys, then one of them took them from me and let us all in. Well! I knew about the burglary, of course, but I suppose I just wasn't ready for the mess!'

Stop. Rewind. Play.

'I knew about the burglary, of course—'

Stop.

Did she? Bruton told me she didn't. He said he stopped Barrington from calling her.

One of them is lying. If Barrington didn't call her, how did she find out? Only twelve hours passed between the attack and her arrival at work, and she was sick the day before. She didn't have flu when I interviewed her. Could she be involved? She knew the house, had copies of all the keys, knew Barrington's habits and his weaknesses. But why would she do it? I don't believe she'd act alone, so who would she have worked with? She's very protective of Norton – fair enough, I suppose. He seemed a pleasant young chap – not the sort who'll ever trouble us. He's what they used to call officer material. It's a shame there's no opportunity to call him as a witness. I think I believe her story. It's not all true, but the important parts are, and I'm convinced Bruton is lying. Besides, Younghusband will go down well in court. She looks and sounds respectable enough and she'll paint up Bruton as black as she can. Poor bastard – he could do with a friend. I feel sorry for him. If he confessed, he'd get three years maximum; he'd be out in eighteen months. I know his wife would wait. As it is, he'll get seven and she won't forgive him so easily for lying to her.

Four o'clock. Time to knock off. I drop the recorder and tapes at the desk, wave at Charlesworth and am halfway out the door when he shouts: 'You've got a call.'

'Can't it wait? Who is it?'

'Don't know. Some bloke. He says it's very urgent.'

'All right, then. Give it here.'

He hands me the receiver over the desk.

'Inspector Evans.'

'Patrick, it's Roy Samuels at the *Chronicle*. I thought I'd see how you are faring.'

'Not so bad, Roy. What can I do for you?'

'Patience, Patrick, patience. In a few minutes' time you'll be very pleased I made this call. Tell me now, what do you know about takeovers?'

16 I hate old people. I hate decrepitude. Decay is worse than death. I don't want to grow old. This, among other reasons, is why I hate my office staff. The young ones are the worst. They imitate geriatrics in behaviour and physique. They speak too slowly. They cultivate their jowls. They ache to be old, respectable and rich. They putrefy before my eyes. They're in love with the City and its seething, stinking, sewer masses. I hate cities. The endless walls crowd my movements. I hate the barren landscape. I'll always be an alien inside it. I feel like a desert prophet in search of his God, a bearded wanderer, with blood crusting on thorn-torn, sand-worn feet, his wild voice hoarse through calling, 'Where are you?' and hearing no reply, not even an echo in the sterile air.

I hate London. I was born too close to the Equator to endure six damp months of darkness in every twelve. The child remains master of the man and I was a vicious child. I spent too many of my learning years alone to love my fellow citizens. Our farm was thirty miles from the road – thirty red-hot, dust-covered miles, lurching and choking in the back of a Land Rover with two Ridgeback dogs as companions. They were my friends. I controlled them. With a word I could send them racing off in tandem to hunt young buck. I'd sprint after them, barefoot over the veldt. From time to time I arrived for the kill. That was sweet. The buck would writhe and roll – terror sent spasms through its muscles – until the teeth of my dogs found an artery and surprisingly bright blood squirted over the sand.

That much of my childhood I miss. When I think back, my collar itches. I hate my tailor in Savile Row. I enjoy baiting him at fittings. He hates me too. He'd rather dress high-class filth, but they can't afford his bills. He needs me for my credit cards.

I hate February. My childhood clock tells me it should be late summer, six months after the rains. The veldt will be loaded with fat, sleepy animals and their careless off-spring. The rivers over there are drying up right now and you can wade in to catch fish with your bare hands. I counted my freckles at the end of each summer until I turned eight. By then there were too many. The African sun had changed me. He didn't need more than eight years to mark me as his own. I made myself a promise then, the day before I boarded the *Lusitania* for England, that I'd never live any other way. A promise I betrayed. Children should wait until their balls drop before they try to think. They sell themselves to an ideal, then stagnate. What if I had stayed on? I'd be cele-brating thirty years of marriage and infidelity to some bush pig. I'd have set up a safari park to sell the carcass of that once wild world to tourists. Tourists! With their shopping-trolley minds and lazy flesh. They can't exist without drag-ging a baggage train of possessions in their wake. They'll need generators and porcelain toilets to venture into the veldt.

I could return. I could buy a farm. I could buy half the country and build a chain-link fence round it to keep the animals in and the people out.

No. Thirty years is too long to take to draw a circle. I can't go home. The bets are still on the table. I want to see this one out. I like gambling. It's the purest form of mental stimulation. It's a predator's adventure. The real pleasure of flesh consuming flesh is otherwise hard to find in cities, so I survive by taking risks. Danger is all that stands between me and self-destruction. I was like that by the age of five. It was the summer my mother lost her authority. I climbed the acacia tree by our porch.

'Come down, Donald – you're too high.'

'No.'

'Come down now.'

She threatened and she promised. When she began to despair, I jumped. I broke both legs, of course, but I didn't cry. Victory is never celebrated with tears. I learned then that age is irrelevant to authority. People are born weak or strong. I'm strong. After that incident, I hated my mother. When she died two years later I forgot her. She was the first in a long line of frightened faces. Now I don't need to look. I can smell fear. London reeks of it. Its population live on top of each other and from the penthouses to the tube trains passing underneath the pavements the stench of cowardice pervades.

For most of the last twenty years I've enjoyed this poison atmosphere. It's a predator's heaven. I am a creature created to consume other creatures and the temptation to stay on has been irresistible. It's a noble obsession. Every time I buy another company I feel like a young boy dancing out a herd animal's death song, alone with his dogs in the heart of the veldt.

It may be possible to go too far. A prudent gamester would have walked away from my current position long ago. In fact, anyone with a passing interest in odds would never have taken the bet. It looks outrageous in perspective:

Donald Fletcher, CEO, managing director, and as many other titles as my accountants suggest I should add to my name, has staked a reputable manufacturing company to satisfy his perverse desire to take risks. Not content with the vagaries of the stock market, he has added savour to this venture through insider dealing on both sides, buying shares of the target company with his own company's money, and selling his own company's shares short with money raised through a ring of private Indian investors, some of whom will be present for a dinner this evening at the company flat. Its ostensible purpose is the commemoration of Mardon Packaging Corporation's first capital investment in the sub-continent. We're building a pulp mill in India, right on the edge of a national park. A thousand-acre site has been cleared of virgin forest, flattened, fenced, and plugged into the national electricity grid. Among other feats of engineering, three separate tributaries of the sacred River Ganges have been dammed at distances ranging from fifty to one hundred miles to ensure constant supplies of feedwater to the pulp mill. Bamboo groves have been cleared to make way for the chlorination plant. Some 10,000 people were employed in the construction phase and 2,000 semi-skilled workers of the Brahmin class have been trained for the mill's operation. A new shantytown has been born and named. The Indian ambassador will attend my dinner in gratitude.

It's a busy day today. In addition to dinner, I have a signing ceremony at Credit Suisse scheduled for twelve noon. It will grant Mardon Packaging drawing rights over another £300 million. Good. I can go and buy more companies. I also have to wear my art lover's mask. I bought another Impressionist painting last month for the Mardon Arts Foundation and it's being delivered to my flat at four. That's eight hours away. Will I be there to see it hang? I think so – I rate the odds ten to one on. I'm sure the DTI are on my tail, but the first sign of trouble will be a Section 2 notice: the Government equivalent of 'own up'. If the newspapers know what's going on behind the scenes in this takeover, the police will soon find out. I reckon I've got twenty-four hours' grace. Twenty-four hours, then a Section 2. Shame. Bureaucrats are too predictable. I wish they could work themselves up into spontaneous violent action every now and then. It's not impossible that they have. It could be that now, right now, at a minute before eight on a Monday morning, two or three Government inspectors are watching themselves in the lift mirrors on their way to the fifth floor. Will they knock, or barge right in, slap the Section 2 on my desk like the ace of spades and start preaching: 'Come clean now, Mr Fletcher, and you'll get a fair trial'? I wish they would. I'd be delighted if they broke down the teak doors with fire axes and sent in starving Rottweilers as the first wave. It would really please me if they stamped over the threshold waving firearms and shouted, 'Dead or alive!'

They won't. The forces of light have lost their heroes. No more heroes. The people don't want to be saints. Corner-shop mystics, perhaps, neighbourhood martyrs, certainly, but they're too frightened to stand out in a wider world.

Well, it's eight o'clock and the champions of law and order have yet to appear. Perhaps, at heart, they'd like to encourage me into further excess? Anything to brighten up the hours they'd otherwise spend filing paperclips. Company takeovers in general are routine: ranks of overfed grey-haired fools ranged against one another, shouting out the rudest names they dare. This time I've succeeded in creating a few interest-ing diversions: corruption of the innocent, needless bor-rowing in a high-interest-rate environment, senseless redund-ancies. So far so good. I take pride in my achievements. I've managed to contaminate a number of my staff – irretriev-ably, I hope. The outstanding triumph to date has been that little pussy Simon Norton. I played to his greed and made him a criminal. He was easy. He was so greedy, so desperate for success, he mauled me with eagerness when I gave him the chance to deal on the inside track. This is normal: mankind is naturally obsessive. Leave a child alone in a room with a butcher's knife and sooner or later it will start to bleed. The key to power rests in discovering each man's obsession and pandering to it. The usual wish list is pleasingly short: money, titles, that sort of thing, but it's important to get the right one. For every fish that swims there is only a single, irresistible bait. Find that lure and own the man. Morals are abandoned with splendid ease – offer your target the one thing that he covets and he'll renounce his identity for its possession – there's a Mephis-topheles for every little Faust.

I'm musing on the prospect of Norton in prison when the phone rings. It's Palmer.

'Where are you?'

'In a call box. Outside the RCJ. Listen, Donald, there's been an unfortunate reversal. The judge looks like he'll overturn last Tuesday's interlocutory injunction against the *Chronicle*.'

'Can you play for time?'

'I've set up an adjournment.'

'For how long?'

'Twenty-four hours. It was the best I could do.'

'And after that they're free to publish?'

'I'm afraid that's correct.'

'What's their evidence?'

'Documentary. I'm sorting through it now.'

'Where from?'

'Luxembourg. We won the adjournment on grounds of admissibility.'

'Meet me at seven. At 6 Embankment Gardens.'

Excellent! It's happening at last! The bets are placed and the game begins. The *Chronicle* must have some real evidence. I wonder how much they paid for it – and who they bribed. They've certainly got us in their sights. They must have a dozen leader pieces on file already, waiting to be delivered into circulation at the twitch of a typesetter's finger. I can picture the headlines: **'Fletcher Fraud Trail Exposed!'** *Olé!*

'South African Recluse Gambles Company Millions!' *Olé!*

I love newspaper sensationalism. I love the way they get their noses right up the skirt of any tragedy. I love all the pictures of burned flesh, screaming women, bleeding babies. I adore the principle of overfed drunken newsmen reporting tearfully from the scene of the latest famine. I love their disregard for privacy and sentiment. If I wanted friends, I'd find many in the fourth estate. I'm convinced they hate slovenly mankind as much as I do.

I'm going to call the *Chronicle*'s hand. As far as I know, one man is doing all their digging: Bernie Hayes. And who is Bernie Hayes? Hardly a man at all – a shabby little journalist in a rented flat, a village Hampden, a bedsit crusader who thinks he's being brave, standing up and throwing stones from the safety of his publishers' offices. It's time to immunise him. He can't afford a place at this table. The stakes are too high. He can watch or fetch drinks, but he can't play. If the *Chronicle* want a part in this hand, they'll need to be reminded of the risks. Perhaps they've forgotten who pays their bills? Mardon gives them close to a million dollars in annual advertising revenue. How much is that worth in news? I'll give their lard-arse proprietor a call in his Winnipeg hideaway. What time is it in Canada? Too early for a surprise. I'll sort out matters at this end instead. I'll take the stick to his poodle. He employs an Old Etonian with a pulpit voice to look after his UK affairs – a certain Christopher Smith-Codrington, who hates me for my wealth and power. I can feel the envy in his fingertips every time we shake hands. 'It should be me,' he tells himself.

I'll invite him to dinner this evening. He'll go down well with the Indian ambassador. They can discuss tennis and society balls. Between them they'll talk up a thirst. I'll load their glasses and put the boot in after port is served. I'll rest my arm over Smith-Codrington's sloping shoulders and say, 'My dear chap! I'm being persecuted. Isn't that too frightful? Why does your newspaper portray me as the villain? After all, I'm doing my bit for exports. I'm helping you buy circulation.' And so on.

I'll concentrate on the journalist Hayes. I'll isolate the man. I'll break him away from the safety of his herd, then deal with him beyond the protection of his employers. That's always the way. A man as employee is part of the corporate body: attack him and you're taking on the entire collective. But if you can turn his employers against him, they'll do the job for you. Self-cleansing is preferable to war. Good! Another refinement added to the wager.

Where's this evening's seating plan? I'll have Wendy call Smith-Codrington at six, which leaves him no time to ponder. He'll come, of course. A privilege of power is the certainty of command. I'd be pleased with the invention behind the invitation if it didn't represent a compromise. I hate compromising. You can't qualify success. A man either gets what he wants or fails.

If I'm going to win, I need to make some time. I'll go straight to the company flat after lunch. That leaves me three hours to spare before Christie's deliver my new painting. This daubing is the latest addition to my company's collection of Impressionists. If I remember correctly, it's a dainty portrait of an orphan, playing with a kitten. It would be cheaper to wallpaper the entire flat with bank notes – but then, the display of taste and wealth is a necessary part of the tycoon illusion. You need to throw a bit of bread on the water to bring in the fishes. Besides, all the world loves an art lover . . .

The company flat in Embankment Gardens is the perfect tax-deductible playground – the way I like things best: possession without ownership. I use it as a throne room. I do more business there than in my executive suite. People enjoy the personal touch. They feel especially favoured if invited to a great man's home. I thrive through encouraging expectations. I use houses in New York, Geneva, Hawaii and Paris without owning a single one. Mardon pays for them all and everything inside them – right down to the suits in the wardrobe, the cars parked outside. No one except the accountants knows – every visitor assumes use equates to possession. That's the common way, obsession to possess – married with kids, single with toys – a man is defined by what he controls.

My private line rings again.

'Donald, it's Martin Palmer. I think we need to meet at once. They swore in two new affidavits, and I've just this minute got discovery on the documents.'

The man sounds frightened. He's probably wishing he stuck to country conveyancing.

'Can it wait?'

'No. I mean, not really . . .'

'All right. Meet me at eleven. Same place.'

Bloody hell! Is there no one under fifty with any balls? To

listen to the man you'd think the sky had fallen in on his head. He's not going to get arrested, whatever happens. He won't even get a reprimand – the Law Society are easy on their beloved members and though some of the senior solicitors may try to shun him on the golf course I dare say he won't miss the company. I learnt very quickly what it's like to be in trouble – I was barely nineteen when they overran our position on the Imjin River. If you've had to stick a bayonet in a man before your twentieth birthday it's hard to feel threatened again.

Still – this time it's not Koreans but the Establishment who are about to appear over the top. Fuck it! I need another twelve hours to make things safe. My own signature's on nothing, but if they catch up with young Norton I may be in trouble. Time, I think, to cut him adrift. I wonder if they'd dare arrest me. I don't think they'd try tonight. Diplomats are coming to dinner. It looks bad for the country if their host is handcuffed before he dishes up the soup. That aside, I don't think they'd have too many qualms. It's not as if I'm the darling of the Establishment, some rosebud Old Etonian with chums in the Cabinet who merits special treatment. In truth, I'm a bit of an aberration. I know they'd be pleased to see my back, despite the fact that on paper I'm a model capitalist, waving the Union Jack for industry. They'll never see me as more than a jumped-up colonial. It took me years to find that out. When I went into business back in the 1950s there was still an Empire of sorts and if you came from Rhodesia your operations were valued as much as if your assets were concentrated in Dorking. Then territory after territory was given away and fortress Britain set in. All the investors had seen one too many independence ceremonies. They became wary of anyone outside the home counties – considered us high risk, even when we took over their pet businesses and ran them better. It's ridiculous: the British Establishment sat at home, happy to preside over a slow descent into the third world – 'assisted decline', I think that's what they called their policy – and made pariahs of those who could have saved them.

There's a timid knock at my office door.

'Yes?'

It opens to reveal one of our younger executives. Can't remember his name, but I know he works for Norton. He blushes as he summons up the courage to speak.

'Mr Fletcher? It's the gardener, sir . . . on the telephone. I'd have transferred it, but I don't know how.'

'Which line's he on?'

'I've got him on my desk.'

'I'll take him there.'

He opens the door into his face to let me through, then stumbles along behind me. I scan the room and see a desk where there's a telephone with its receiver off the cradle. I lean over the partition and pick it up.

'What is it, Thomas?'

'It's the new window boxes, sir. I'm not sure they're taking.'

'Call me at the flat at eleven.'

The line dies. I hand the receiver to the junior. At the same time, a nameplate on his desk catches my eye.

'Thank you, Jason.'

He blushes at my back as I return to my office.

So, something's up. Window boxes represent tape recorders. If a man is going to function without an entourage, he needs a powerful information-gathering system. Thomas, the gardener, is the nerve centre controlling mine. He's a curious chap. You can still just about hear the Rhodesian accent behind the Somerset vowels. He was a killer, a real killer, in his time. He had a reputation in the Selouse scouts, where, believe me, you needed to be a systematic savage to stand out at all. On the surface he's a reformed man. Lives in a cottage on the company's country estate, where his nominal duties include supervising the upkeep of the park. He married a local girl and became a father for the first time at fifty. He's a small man, not the sort you'd notice in a crowd; the only thing remarkable about his appearance are his huge hands, which look as though they were grafted on by some scientist for a joke. He's aware of this, I think: he keeps them behind his back or in his pockets when he talks; if he didn't smoke, you'd never see them. But if you want to define loyalty, no need for a dictionary, no need to keep a dog – Thomas is your man.

I have half a dozen or so tape recorders in place at any one time, monitoring various people who need to be kept under observation. If I had an entourage – the usual flea circus of hangers-on who surround a great man – I'd get my information from their gossip, but as I prefer to operate alone I rely instead on a more impartial system of information-gathering. Thomas has a network of old African hands, most of them ex-services, who couldn't face life under the corrupt governance of some black politician who in all likelihood used to be their cook so upped sticks to the old country, where they soldier on in menial jobs, their CVs tainted through association with the last form of good government Africa ever had. Together, they make a surprisingly effective information service. No one needs to teach them the value of confidentiality, and in return for planting and picking up the odd microphone Thomas acts as their counsellor – helps them out if they need a job, a reference, somewhere to stay, some cash to tide them over, that sort of thing. Collectively they constitute my Gardening Club – a security guard here, a wine waiter there, all placed in unskilled jobs with access, and all trusted.

Who are we observing at present? The list lives on my pocket computer. It's an excellent machine – no need for paper trails. Its only flaw is keyboard size. You'd need a child to operate it efficiently. Here's the list:

Andrew Jenkins, the Minister for Trade, courtesy of the Rhodesian farm manager he employs.
Kevin Felch, Secretary, Paper Makers' Trade Union.
Hans Kultz, the German ambassador, if he travels. Their

last chauffeur, Fritz Squarehead, became confused while driving on the left, with the result that they hired a local – unfortunately for them, a man with an interest in horticulture.

Simon Norton.

Arnie Eaglebaum.

Perhaps it's one of the latter two? All senior executives are subject to routine monitoring. This guards against them building factions. I've only got 20 per cent of Mardon's equity – not enough to be absolute ruler. I take a great deal of care when selecting executives. I look for loners. Like me, they need a veneer of acceptability, but no more. If they're too far into the system, their loyalties may lie elsewhere – with the old school, clubland, with whichever tribe they can claim membership. That's another reason why I never employ Jews, nor anyone from a family that's had more than two generations at public school.

A light flashes on the intercom.

'Mr Fletcher? Elizabeth Anderson, Lord Keldon's PA, just called.'

'What was her message?'

'That Lord Keldon apologises for not calling you directly in person, but he's gone down with food poisoning. He hopes you'll accept his regrets for this evening and asked to arrange another mutually convenient date.'

'I see. Call her, pass on my consolations and say that I look forward to his company when he's recovered.'

'Thank you, Mr Fletcher. I'll pass that message on.'

Bloody hell! Something is very wrong. Keldon has got the most sensitive political antennae in town. And the constitution of a shantytown pig.

If Keldon knows, so do the police . . . They may be here already.

I'll check the security monitors. I keep two by my desk, buried in decorative mahogany cases. Number 1 relays pictures from the conference room. Number 2 connects to twelve other cameras scattered through the building. It's got a split screen and I can call up each view on command. I'll start by checking the front desk. Waves of speckled grey dance across the monitor's face and resolve into still life. Five floors below my feet, three men are standing at the reception counter; three tall men with short hair and badly made two-piece, two-button suits. One sticks a sheet of paper on the desk top and jabs a thick forefinger at the print. At the same moment, his accomplices separate. One goes to the right. The other heads towards the camera. He looks up and points straight at me. A scowl spreads across his black-and-white face, shaking shadows into the jowls. He turns his head to shout something at the receptionist. In the last week, I've pictured this scene an unimaginable number of times. Sometimes the forces of light arrive with violence. More often they steal up on me in my sleep. I wake up bound and surrounded, then they throw over my head a coarse blanket, which stinks of cellars, stagnation and decay. I fight back in vain. Whatever I try to strike absorbs the force and sucks me in.

This is it! This is the truth! This is the real thing! Here are the DTI, waving their credentials to the doormen, their pockets loaded with indictments and handcuffs, and I feel so adrenaline-charged I have to grab the desk before I lose control and tear down the office! Excellent! Alive again!

Intercom to the car pool: 'Get me Van Huul.'

'Here, sir.'

'Is the Bentley ready?'

'She's just been topped up, sir.'

'Meet me at the Curzon Street entrance at once.'

'Very good, sir.'

My office suite has an emergency exit that leads to the lifts and fire-escape stairs. How long do I have before the DTI reach the fifth floor? Ten seconds to cross the marble foyer. Fifteen more minimum, a minute maximum, until a lift opens its doors. Thirty seconds to ascend. Another thirty to get clear and orientate themselves towards my office.

What do I need to take? Briefcase, air tickets, cash from the safe? No time. I'll leave it.

Here we go! One, two, three . . . Out the door, over the corridor; the lift lights are blinking – third floor, fourth, fifth – and as I bang the fire-door bar with my forearm I can hear the whisper of the lift doors.

I grab the banister and jump the first two flights of stairs. I collide with the wall on the landing and the impact drives me onwards. After another floor I stop accelerating. I need to control the force. I'll use a hunter's stealth . . . No, why bother? No one else takes the stairs. My employees are so lazy they'll wait half an hour for a lift to the first floor.

The double fire doors open with a crash into the basement. It's a half world down here: everything is raw – a contrast to the automated luxury of the offices stacked above my head. I've only been here a couple of times. It's a part of his palace the king rarely sees. The low sodium lights mute colours and I strain before I can pick out the fire-red Bentley. It's posted at the base of the ramp, engine running. I chuck my case on to the front seat and climb in.

'Where to, sir?'

'Embankment Gardens.'

Van Huul slips the machine into gear and we roll away. He can sense what's going on. His shaven head is locked straight ahead on his bull-terrier neck. Not even a curious glance in the mirror. I know he's smiling. He loves this sort of work. Rivulets of water stream down the ramp as we spiral towards daylight. Bloody country. I've been here 90 per cent of my adult life and I still can't get used to the rain. The people born here don't notice it – at least, it seldom attracts comment. Perhaps the population is immune to precipitation – great and small, they stand around getting wet while the world wonders at their complacency.

I need a plan. My adventures will fill this evening's news.

I think I have three options: stay and bluff, stay and pay the tariff, or run. I'll examine them in turn:

What will happen if I stand and fight? Will they prosecute? Definitely. Entrepreneurs are hate figures. We ruined too many lives in the 1980s. This Conservative Government needs to demonstrate success in the boardroom wars. They'd be delighted to discover a plump director to display in the stocks to their disenchanted voters. I've planned for that: Mardon's made donations to the main political parties – Labour, Liberal and Conservative – so none will be too eager to raise the matter in the House. It won't be a case of another Tory flagship sacking workers and robbing its pension funds. That won't save me. They'll reach a gentlemen's accord and prosecute. I've committed too many crimes: theft, fraud, insider trading, false accounting, offences against a dozen different sections of the Companies' Act. My trial will last for years. I can't face that. I need to be free.

What about option two: paying the tariff? I wonder what prison's like. Curiously, the prospect doesn't frighten me. It's not as if I'd re-enter society at the bottom. Van Huul would be waiting for me in the Bentley at the prison gates. I'd be barred from my directorships. I'd have to move my operations abroad. Still, a cell can't be any worse than some of the accommodation we used to suffer in the army. And whoever they give me for company will be considerably more genial than the South Korean troops who shared our mess. I doubt Her Majesty's Government will serve up boiled dog for the Sunday roast.

Which leaves option three: running. I'll think about that when I reach the flat. Too many ifs confuse the brain. Speculation is a game for academics and fools. They'll be too busy catching the bodies I'm throwing overboard to get their hands on me.

To business. The Bentley's a mobile conference centre: telephones, data screens, a cocktail cabinet. First call, Luxembourg. Let's get Raymond busy with his shredder. I wonder if the Stock Exchange has heard anything? Key up the FTSE page on the Reuters. Mardon's off twenty, the index ten – that's about right. The City's uncertain, and we've never been a popular holding. We often get the sell pressure first. Any rumours would have taken us down at least forty pence – ten per cent. I'll keep an eye on matters – see what happens after lunch, when New York opens. We've quite a few holders over there. Which reminds me, I have to speak to Arnie soonest. He can deputise at the signing. I'd better get a call in and warn him to hold back on the drinks front. I'll need him to have his wits about him. No, on second thoughts, I need to know what the Gardening Club's come up with before we speak. He could be the source of the trouble.

The Bentley spins round the corner and glides to a halt in Embankment Gardens. Van Huul opens the door and hands me my case as I climb out. The company flat is on the first floor – the *piano nobile*. Floor-to-ceiling windows provide a view of the sunset over the Thames. Hardly a spectacular event, but the best London can offer.

Mrs Dawkins, the housekeeper, is waiting for me by the door. Her wrinkled face quivers, the veins stand out like seams on her shaking hands and a trace of spit appears on her lower lip when she sees me. I make her nervous. She enquires after my health and follows me into the library. This woman can only function in a specific order – as if she's learnt to live by rote. Dawkins delights in establishing little rituals, in which she expects me to play a part. She uses these charades as reference points, from which she can proceed to the next stage of the formula. The instant I place my case on the table, Dawkins steps back, coughs, composes herself, then sidles towards me, the housekeeping book in both hands. Every month she presents me with accounts to inspect and sign. This is the preliminary to a tea ceremony and chat about the royal family, for whom she possesses an unusual obsession. Her own story is a sad one. She married late and her husband was a sergeant in one of the Border regiments who beat her and converted her savings into

214

whisky. They had no children, so she transferred her maternal longings to some niece whom she adored, who then died in a fire some years ago. I like misfortune. It's nature's revenge for complacency.

'I'll look at them tomorrow, Mrs Dawkins.'

She's disappointed. She purses her lips and her withered arms drop to her sides. I wonder, could she be the source of the leak? She's low enough in the hierarchy to have had her head turned, and sufficiently feeble-minded to believe bringing criminals to justice serves the common good.

'Could I fetch you a cup of tea, Mr Fletcher?'

She's reached the next part of her programme. The flat contains a special Wedgwood tea service, each piece of which bears my initials. Every fitting in this flat has the same decoration – DF – stamped, gold-blocked, embroidered, carved: ownership demonstrated wherever possible. It's a necessary part of the illusion – identify the chattels with the man.

'No. I'll speak to you this afternoon. Mr Palmer, of Lister's, will be here for a conference in a few minutes. Show him straight in when he arrives.'

'Very good, Mr Fletcher.'

She turns and leaves, looking weak, frail – deflated. For some strange reason she's developed a liking for me. Perhaps her position gives her confidence, identity. By using me, her employer, as a boundary post she can establish her own position in the world.

Palmer had better be prompt. I hate waiting. What's the time? New York opens in three hours. I don't think the Yanks will be the first to sell. You never can tell, though. Decay doesn't always begin at the weakest point. If the whole structure is rotten, every part is vulnerable. But I'm banking on ignorance. They don't really understand our market, in the same way that we can't comprehend theirs. The States has been a graveyard for a thousand British endeavours. It's not a certain disaster area like Canada is, but it pays to be circumspect when dealing there.

215

I fail to notice Palmer's arrival. He's quiet, even for a lawyer on the prowl, and he's standing in front of my desk before I realised he'd entered the room. I have trouble working out Palmer's age. I perceive him as younger, junior, of course, but it's quite possible we could be of equal years. He's lost a lot of hair, but what remains retains its colour and body. His face has lines but no wrinkles and he stands proud and straight. When I speak to him on the phone I conceive a very different individual. His voice is slightly too highly pitched – prone to whining, as if its owner lived in constant fear of a beating. He's been on the payroll for nearly five years. He functions in a similar manner to my Gardening Club – forms part of the protective cordon I've developed to guard my back. His firm, Lister's, is respectable in a quiet way. Their financial partners do a lot of work for the Arab community.

'Fill me in.'

'Take a look at these.' He pushes a bundle of documents over the desk. On top is a single, handwritten page, set out in point format. I gesture with my hand for him to pick them up. I pay him to brief me, not to recommend reading material.

'The *Chronicle* have alleged that two Luxembourg shell companies, namely Millwork and Massfund, are owned or controlled by directors of Mardon Packaging. They further allege that these two companies have been acquiring shares in Darlington Card PLC, thus committing the crime of Insider Trading. This morning they swore in two affidavits to support their claims.'

'Is my name on anything?'

'No.'

'Is Mardon's name on anything?'

A shake of the head.

'Then where's the link?'

Palmer extracts a photocopy from the bundle, spins it so it's the right way up and pushes it over. 'This is the problem. As you see, it's signed by Simon Norton.'

216

'Is that enough?'

'Possibly. It's the sort of document that'll set alarm bells ringing at the DTI. Does Norton have any stock options?'

'A few.'

'That may help. The Liechtenstein trust could be explained as a tax-efficient vehicle to enable him to realise his holding. But, I'm afraid, the first conclusion they're likely to reach is that Norton's involved in insider dealing.'

'And if he is?'

'They'll start searching out collaborators.'

'For which they'll need more evidence.'

'Which they might try to get from Norton, unless, of course, it can be demonstrated that he cooked this thing up himself. If he were the sole trustee, for example.'

'He is.'

Palmer smiles. I think he gets pleasure from this game. He knows all about the trust, of course – it was he who designed the whole buying structure for Operation Rollover. But even now, in a safe room in a private apartment, he pretends ignorance. I think he's trying to show me an escape route.

'Go on,' I say. 'Tell me more.'

'You understand I'm speaking hypothetically?' I nod. 'Good. Now, say the DTI were to receive information proving Norton's link to Millwork and Massfund. Say also that they received this information from Mardon Packaging itself, coupled with a press release stating that Norton had been relieved of his duties, pending an internal investigation into the matter. Assume, finally, an announcement was made which declared that Mardon was withdrawing its bid for Darlington Card. In such circumstances, the DTI may be satisfied with a single, successful prosecution. It is even possible that, in return for co-operation, Norton could expect clemency during sentencing. This assumes, of course, that Norton did not attempt to fabricate evidence, by, say, pointing to the involvement of other directors of Mardon in his share-buying operation . . .'

'Surely it won't end there?'

'The consequences for Mardon would be grave in any event. Darlington has a very strong prima-facie case against the company. I understand Norton has been bonded?'

'All of my senior employees carry Professional Indemnity insurance.'

Palmer frowns. 'That may not be enough – the policy is likely to exclude fraud. And if a claim were made, insurance companies often pursue their interests with greater diligence than the DTI.'

'How long before the DTI start on the trail?' I wonder if Palmer knows I had visitors.

'It is likely that they've already started. Teams are assigned to monitor companies involved in takeovers as a matter of course. Further attempts to hinder the *Chronicle*'s investigations will be taken as evidence of Mardon's involvement.'

'Unless we can show an internal investigation was already underway which may have been prejudiced by premature publication.'

Palmer nods. He looks at me, searching, trying to read which way I'll jump. Winter sunlight breaks through and sweeps the room, causing a squint to distort his face, picking out colours on the oil painting behind his head. It's Celestial, my first horse. She never won. She was a useless beast who looked the part but lacked the blood. I sold her for dog meat after her first season.

'So you'd recommend immediate action?' I say, holding his gaze.

'If Mardon wishes to retain any sort of reputation, it will be best if it is seen to be taking exhaustive measures to remedy the situation . . .'

Palmer is about to continue when the telephone rings. It's Thomas.

'We picked up Norton's call record yesterday,' he reports. 'It appears he's being blackmailed. We monitored the following conversation last Monday.' While the tape plays through the receiver into my ear I watch Palmer's face. The line dies when the recording ends. Thomas knows me well enough not to bother with analysis.

Good! This little blackmail is a fortunate diversion. It's most pleasing to see the bit-part players starting up a game of their own. I'd forgotten the Assessor. I'd forgotten the break-in I arranged at his house. How amusing that his assistant has decided to exploit her employer's demise. It's better still that my arrangements with her were carried out in Norton's name.

I hate Barrington. I hated him for living in a wheelchair and exercising power over me. We first met in 1955. I'd shot a Hussar captain in the back at the retreat from the Imjin River and the army court-martialled me. I was nearly a hero – I'd been mentioned in despatches and they had no proof, so they turned me over to the Assessor. Barrington knew what I was at once. I admired and hated him for that. When Mardon's lenders insisted Norton be assessed I saw an opportunity for revenge. His house was the last of his territory so I sent round some South African pen pals to remind him he was old and weak. They were instructed to break things up, hold a fire ceremony, but leave the man alone in fear. I'm surprised they went further and took out the old man as well. Perhaps they were eager to please and exceeded orders? Excellent! I admire that sort of enthusiasm. I suppose it was predictable. I gave no explicit directions for what to do with Barrington and it seems they presumed the usual.

This is a double happiness – Norton is implicated in a further crime, and an old debt is settled. Total satisfaction for a mere £5,000. I'll have to use them again one day.

Solicitor's fingernails tap my desk. Palmer is growing impatient.

'What needs to be done?'

Palmer tilts his head clear of the sunlight, nods a couple of times, then reaches quickly into his briefcase and pulls out a folder. 'You'll need to make all the announcements today, but I advise you to wait until the stock market closes.

Three documents must be prepared at once – Norton's suspension notice, the Stock Exchange announcement, and a press release. You'll need to retain advisers . . .'

'You do it.'

'In which case, I need access to certain internal corporate documents.'

'Granted. I'm hosting a dinner here this evening. Shall I cancel?'

'What's its purpose?'

'Trade relations.'

'I advise cancellation. It may be best that you make yourself unavailable for the next twenty-four hours – overseas, if possible . . .'

Palmer continues, running through his list. For an instant I feel weary and study the knots of wood in the walnut surface of my desk while he covers contingencies. Thirty years ago I wouldn't have stayed to listen. I'd be sitting in the airport, waiting for a flight. But this time I've had such a long run of luck that it's difficult to walk away – just say fuck it, slide back my chair and leave the room. It's as if I've become attached to Mardon. I used to be so hard-edged – immune to misfortune – but age erodes desire and reduces ambition to a sand-worn skeleton of what might have been. I'm nearly sixty: I don't have time to rebuild another capitalist folly. If I run this time, I won't come back. I couldn't face months, years perhaps, of questions from some committee trying to pin the fraud on to me. Better to be rich and far away – notorious but beyond their reach. They can discover the crime without the satisfaction of imprisoning the criminal. They'll have to take out their malice on Norton. Which is a pleasing prospect – hand them their best beloved for punishment. How will they treat him? A family man, ideal product of their vaunted winner-picking system – head boy, golf-club captain, ex-accountant and banker with the blue chips. Pure officer material, the sort of man the system believes incapable of doing wrong, deposited trussed on their doorstep, with evidence of his greed and folly stuffed into his mouth. While the *provocateur* who tempted this adolescent paragon into crime builds a villa in the tropics and buys himself a harem of virgins.

I've always existed on the edge, so the outlaw life is no more than a change in status. Norton won't find it so easy. His problem. In my eyes, he's a single item of a valueless commodity – other people. Some are born to build, others to store, and a very few, like me, to destroy. Everything I make that seems constructive to the material-obsessed world is nothing of the sort – it's a trap, baited with the promise of treasures, but spike-loaded so that the individuals and organisations it attracts inevitably impale themselves through their own folly. There were sufficient institutions in the City eager to profit from my operations that the Establishment overlooked their instincts and gave me my chance. When Mardon goes they'll fill the papers, flood Parliament with their tears, disclaim responsibility for the monster their collective greed created. They'll play the part of innocent lenders – sheep who've been fleeced – damn the fact it was their money that made my success possible.

Nothing would give me more pleasure than exposing them all – standing up in court and explaining how I deceived the nation's great and good. I doubt my testimony would be received with gasps of admiration. Instead, I'm going to walk away and leave them to unravel the mess – tie them together by the tails and enjoy the fight from a great, safe distance.

'It will be necessary, in addition, to hold an extraordinary general meeting. You must be seen to have the shareholders' interests at heart. Again, the sooner the better . . .'

Palmer drones on, piecing together his complex scheme to keep me from disgrace and prison, meticulous in his role as the architect of a social salvation I don't want and won't get. I'm almost tempted to hang on, to play things out. I might carry it off, after all. It would be Norton's testimony against mine in the first instance and this happy little blackmail would discredit him. I might even gain status from the affair – be acknowledged as the injured party, the altruistic

221

magnate whose kindness blinded him to the machinations of an ambitious executive. One should never underestimate the incompetence of the DTI – it's quite possible they may be satisfied with Norton's scalp. After all, he has a clear motive – instant wealth – something the whole country shares. No court in the developed world would recognise my reasons. I did it for fun. I did it for the risk. I did it because I could.

No. I need more than Norton's silence. I can trust the Continentals not to break ranks. Their livelihood depends on secrecy: a thousand dictators would withdraw their deposits if they suspected their identity might be revealed. But there are other threads of evidence – and Arnie, of course. He'd do anything to save himself; a pre-emptive strike is the first thing I'd expect from him. Norton knows he's involved – unless he hasn't acted yet, in which case any accusation would further undermine Norton's own evidence.

No, a fresh start beckons. They might not look too hard or far – I haven't had my hand in the till: there are no missing millions. Just an overvalued listed company and a lot of angry institutions who'll be wishing they took more notice of the oldest maxim in the book: *caveat emptor*. I think I'm going to enjoy the privacy. Besides, if I cut and run it will send them absolutely fucking mad. In their strange way, they somehow expect the outcast to sit around and face the music – to brazen it out to the last moment, when, in best chivalric tradition, St George will arrive, lance at the ready, and slay the beast. Fuck it. Let them sort out the mess. With no single figure to unite against they'll have to fight among themselves. I won't give them the satisfaction of a scapegoat – they can have one another for revenge. St George will go empty-handed. Norton is a poor consolation prize, though I've no doubt they'll tear him apart. Imagine their fury when they find I'm out of reach. If I'm truly lucky, I might keep some status abroad. Britain has plenty of enemies who provide sanctuary to its fugitives. If I can bribe the right dictator I might yet be reincarnated as an altruist.

'You'll need either to sign in advance, or to authorise another representative of the executive to carry out the actions I've advised. We can communicate by fax, of course, but it looks best to show that some forward planning has gone into the operation – that there's a system in place to filter out fraud . . .'

Palmer halts, a troubled expression on his face. The intercom has interrupted.

'Mr Fletcher? I've Simon Norton on the telephone.'

'What shall I tell him?' I asked Palmer.

'Nothing. I advise against taking the call.'

'Tell Mr Norton I'll be in conference till five o'clock, when I expect to see him here. Understand?'

'Yes, Mr Fletcher . . . Oh, and another thing, Mr Fletcher, I've just received a call from the Indian consulate. They regret, but Mr Singh will be unable to fulfil his commitment this evening.'

'I see. Dawkins, please cancel the other dinner guests.'

'Cancel, sir?'

'That's right. But wait; don't make any calls till four-thirty. Explain that urgent business in the States has forced me to alter my schedule, and . . . Dawkins?'

'Yes, sir?'

'Send them out the gifts in any event. By courier.'

'Yes, sir.'

Palmer smiles at me with appreciation, gratified that I appear to be following his contemptible master plan. I smile in return. For some reason I feel ridiculously pleased with myself. I'll be a sadhu figure – one of those venerable Indians who renounce all things material to wander through the subcontinent – with the important distinction that I won't be abandoning possessions – merely responsibility. How the English Establishment will hate me! What's better, they'll never understand.

17 Judgment Day. I awoke this morning drenched in cold, oily sweat. My clothes were saturated and clung to my body like a membrane. I was disorientated. I'd been dreaming of the ocean, and these drab green walls matched the sea theme still running through my head. I propped myself up on an elbow and measured my surroundings: a steel cabin door, complete with porthole, and, beneath that, a letter-box serving hatch. Overhead, a single bulb caged in steel hoops and frosted glass. The air was thick and rancid, a coastal fog which carried the salt tang of urine. An iron bell sounded – once, twice! – a dissonant note. Before its reverberations died, a face appeared at the porthole, curiously distorted by the fish-eye shape of the plate glass and its cataract sheen of surface dust. For the instant of time that lies between sleep and consciousness, I believed the door and circular window belonged to the face of an inhuman watchman – a leviathan.

That was enough to snap me into the present. I'm in a police cell, two floors beneath the pavement, about to start the third day of incarceration. Slave-ship calls emerge from other cells nearby. I hear a ring and slam! as bolts are withdrawn one by one to allow each inmate his regulation minute to stand by the single washbasin in the corridor and shave. I'm beginning to pick up the routine. I'm learning to live without time. They removed my wristwatch as 'evidence' and the hours flow past in an even stream. Events such as feeding occur in changeless sequence, punctuated by occasional clamour when a prisoner arrives or is released. Last night, they captured the Moroccan. I remember his proud voice rising, in fierce contest with the sergeant's watchdog growl. Their exchange was mundane:

224

'Name?'

'Ali bin Dara.'

'So! You're the Moroccan!'

'And what if I am?'

But in the confined twilight of my cell it acquired a seedy magnificence. The Moroccan's image materialised beside me – slight, strong, vain, complete with a villain's curling moustache, a dagger concealed in his tones as he shouted back his challenge. In the absence of real food for the senses my brain seems capable of the most fantastic invention.

The letter box in my cell door opens to reveal a nose, lips and chin – a slice of a human face.

'Mr Bruton! There's breakfast here, sir, if you want it.'

Judgment Day has arrived. The penitent will meet his confessor. I sit up and my head spins. When I lean back there are brown eyes watching me through the slot.

'No breakfast, thanks.'

'Some tea, then, sir?'

'Please.'

Back goes the hatch. A white plastic cup, two-thirds filled with grey liquid, appears through the aperture. No spoon, lest I try to fashion it into a weapon. The same reasoning has stripped me of belt and shoelaces. Precaution is taken to bizarre excess in these cells. It is accepted wisdom that a prisoner alone with an implement will set about himself with the fury of an onanistic serial killer. Why do they bother? Why not leave us to it? After all, a suicidal zealot deprived of his belt could finish himself off with his teeth. But, question: where to bite? Perhaps mother nature constructed the anatomy so as to render this escape route impossible – you can't reach anywhere vital on your own body with your own teeth; at least, not without years of yoga in preparation for that moment of release. Far better to wait for a blade . . . Aha! I have it! The wrists. I could tear out my veins with two quick bites . . .

'The basin's free, if you'd like a turn at shaving, sir.'

I shake my head at the porthole. My face needs it, but I

can't face it – scraping away with a single blade set in plastic while a policeman watches by my side, poised to intercept a lateral slash at the jugular. Two faces appearing in the same mirror would confuse. I'd inevitably cut myself, which they'd interpret as a well-intended, but poorly aimed, quest for freedom – evidence of suicidal tendencies. A strange phrase, that. It would be astonishing if such tendencies could survive untested for any period of time. Imagine waiting for a train. How could one resist the happy combination of steel wheels and track? Come to think of it, any moving vehicle, high-up open window or electrical device with accessible live wire represent an opportunity for release. A suicidal tendency must be deeply latent to persist.

'Would you like a look at the papers, sir? Inspector Evans will be in to see you at nine, or thereabouts.'

'At nine? What time is it now?'

'Just gone seven, sir.'

'I'd love the papers. Which ones have you got?'

'*Sun* or *Mirror*.'

'*Sun*, please.'

It appears with a rustle at the hatch, small enough to fit through unfolded – an absurd token of the sane world beyond this cell, its brightly coloured pages redolent of the deceitful abstracts employed to keep the honest halfwits at their workbenches and desks. From the perspective of a prison cell, its daily parade of lies seems pathetically transparent: feed the workers trivia to contain their anger, so that, distracted, they can carry themselves unquestioning through the futility of another week. Every page reeks of bogus temptation: Look: here's Jackie, 63, likeable widow from Surbiton, who won £10,000 in last Friday's bingo. What will she spend it on? Toy boys? Timeshare? Embalming fluid? A perspex pyramid to mark her mortal remains?

Even this comic book, this apple-cheeked vision of New England is enough to drag me out of limbo. Before it intruded I was protected by the simple timelessness of these four walls. Now, the printed folly has thrust the whole world, or, rather, realisation of its absence, into my cell. Up there – out there – the rooms have doors that lead to streets and fields; there are rivers that run into seas which swell between the continents. Metropolis, ocean, wilderness – it's all out there – a million playgrounds for all mankind. Except me. Except murderers. Prison is my place. I hated it outside. I was carrying a secret in my head which altered my perception of the world: a simple, horrible filter that divested life of meaning. I have killed a man, and now I must carry the burden until I die and the debt is paid.

I became a murderer two nights ago. They rearrested me at Ifield Road at three in the morning – the spirit's weakest hour. The police announced their presence with crowbars at the door, cracking splinters from its frame. Sudden light tore a white phosphene hole in my vision as I struggled to find my clothes. Every childhood nightmare of impotence and shame was enacted as they banged my face against the wall and slammed handcuffs round my wrists while my body was still limp with sleep. By the time I could register events in sequence I had been dragged downstairs and out into the street. I fought to spin sense out of the poison string of words poured into my ear as I was pushed from hand to hand, squashed into the transit van and finally suffocated by the warm sour odour of a policeman on either side. Murder. The word sounds too melodramatic to sustain the horror it conveys. So Charles was dead – extinguished by the arresting officer in a sentence.

The journey was completed in silence. It seemed as if we were enveloped in fatigue. We shared a sense of loss. We were all ashamed – they, the police, who spent each day shoring up defensive walls around society had failed, their protective efforts been demonstrated contemptible, and I because I was the only one who knew that what had taken place was simultaneously accidental and inevitable. I had a vision of morticians stretching out Charles's crippled limbs once the vital tension had departed – correcting his posture on a steel bed. Was it easy? Did they lay him out like a saint, a sleeping marble crusader with hands crossed over his chest?

I remember the journey with the detachment of a third party. In spirit I was there as an observer, watching the prisoner and his captors seated side by side on the transit bench, like worshippers in a church pew, whose silent faces are fixed in contemplation of the eternal. The roads were all but empty at that hour and we rocketed through the night in near silence, from time to time strobed in orange from the sodium glow of the street lights. Occasional traffic sounds penetrated the interior, but it seemed they came from far away. I felt I had been locked in a ship's cabin far below the water line and we were passing the coast of an unknown continent by night, where sensations of smell and sight and sound arrived abstracted from their physical source – separated by the wind and tide and moonless night.

When they booked me in I was beyond sleep. I telephoned Travers, then sat in the cell, this cell, and resurrected Charles in my mind – ran a picture show of memories here on the bare wall. It was easy, with concentration, to reconstruct his library around me – expand and panel the concrete walls, knock out an aperture for the window over the square, glaze it, then slide up the frame to admit scent and warmth from the garden beneath. I watched Charles sitting in his wheelchair, sometimes turning my head to contemplate the leaf-shadow tapestries on the far wall as his mechanical voice rolled on.

For the remainder of the night I spoke with the shadows, questioning Charles's spirit before I allowed it to leave. My powers of recollection were already altered by the knowledge of death and I knew I had to grasp my last opportunity to study Charles as he was before, but, as our conversation progressed, the illusion began to fail. I could see for the first time the astonishing optimism that had enabled him to prolong his struggle, which had struck a contract of pain with his body. It was an agreement signed in blood, which allowed him life while perpetually teasing him with the pros-

228

pect of relief from its torment. His self-control was awesome. He had to summon every nerve in sequence to produce a sentence, bend and twist his body to create the sounding box, the echo chamber for communication. He persisted, even though his personal creed did not admit salvation – that this life's work might win him merit in the next, ensure a crowd of expectant angels at the foot of his hospital bed, waiting to sing him to his rest.

At dawn I could detain his spirit no more, and slept until they brought Travers at ten.

The duty sergeant knocked, explained that the meeting rooms were full, then his squat black form withdrew and Travers stepped into my cell. I was on my feet, ready to shake his hand, but his face drove me back against the concrete wall. Its soft white flesh was composed into an expression of loathing and disdain. He stood by the open door while the sergeant fetched a chair, then he sat and examined his cuffs, waiting with hostile impatience for me to speak. I had given no consideration to what I'd say to him – my mind was still with Charles – but his forbidding appearance smothered my will and I confessed.

'Why did you hit him?' He asked me that twice. 'Why did you hit him?'

I wanted to explain the provocations: Charles could flay a man with words. Ultimately, I acted in self-defence. Charles exposed the instinct – he cut through my soul, as surely as if he'd taken a scalpel to my flesh.

In the event, Travers didn't wait for a reply. He addressed me in his best clipped courtroom tones. 'No jury in the world will listen to a plea of self-defence from the lips of an able-bodied man who struck an elderly cripple in a wheel-chair. Furthermore, the law does not make allowances for an unusually frail victim. It was cancer that killed Charles, but the aggressor must take his victim as he finds him. Do you wish to change your plea of "not guilty"?'

'No.'

'Very well. You have a right to silence. I advise you to

229

employ it. I am going to arrange for a barrister who will represent you in court. The preparation of your defence will be in his hands. I want no further involvement in this sordid matter. If it were not for . . .' He halted and looked me in the eyes for the first time. 'Does Lydia know?'

'No.'

His eyes narrowed, scrutinising my face. He had the air of a man performing an odious, if necessary, task.

'She doesn't know. I haven't told her.'

Travers rose, turned his back and knocked hard on the iron door. After the sergeant had released him, I heard water running in the basin outside. He was washing his hands. I imagined him flicking water from those plump fingers, purging himself of contamination.

I can't think about Lydia. I tried to tell her on my first day of bail. We were lying together on the sofa and I was composing words as she watched my face, but before I could speak she covered my mouth and said: 'I don't care.'

Lydia belongs to a future I won't share. At heart, I never understood her love. When I met her I was in awe. She was more than human. She had been invested with spirit powers to care for sordid, trivial mankind. She had a healing presence – not enough to raise from the dead, but some elemental faculty none the less. She held the power to ease fears. She could absorb other people's pain. I found it impossible that she could love me. How could such a spirit be moved by flesh? The only manner in which I could interpret this love, this gift, was as a natural phenomenon – like sunshine.

I won't think of Lydia now. Time has passed. The remainder of my tea has long been cold. Evans will be here soon. I feel a sudden need for company. I need to build some confidence before the interrogation. Even Malcolm, that sad little rent boy who shared my cell the last time, would do. He told me that sometimes they fit four people in each cell: evidently I should feel privileged in my solitude. Malcolm was a strange creature – two distinct, if incomplete, characters within one head: a cocksure sodomite who offered me a blow job on credit – 'help take your mind off things' – and an ardent romantic, yearning for chivalrous love with some housewife he'd met at the Harrods sale . . .

No, solitude is best. I need to learn to be alone. Even if I'm acquitted I'll be shunned. Words have an unnatural longevity: they linger after the actions that prompted them have passed. The whispers that have gone round since my first arrest will survive in the memories of friends as an indelible record, making absolution impossible: the accused becomes outcast before the verdict is pronounced. It is impossible to conceive how tightly society swaddles its subjects until one is forced outside its bounds . . .

The bolts ring back with a *clang!* that resonates in this enclosed space. Two policemen, both young, in shirtsleeves, materialise in the doorway. They wear friendly, slightly nervous smiles and their attitude is in curious contrast to that adopted during the recent leper treatment. What is this, tactical psychology? They've worked out I'm about to confess and are aiming to make me garrulous through hospitality? No – I couldn't suspect them of such a complex strategy.

'Inspector Evans is ready to see you, sir.'

Absent-mindedly, I extend my wrists.

'No need, Mr Bruton,' says one. 'Not this time, sir,' adds the other. They beckon me to cross the threshold. 'Follow us.'

I feel strangely insecure when I step outside my cell. There's nothing in the corridor that sings of freedom – simply a lino floor, scuffed with black marks from rubber heels, a lingering stench of disinfectant, the distress buzz of fluorescent strip lighting. The corridor leads to an anteroom with low-standing, heavy pieces of furniture – rectangles and squares with not a hint of ornamentation – no concession to the decorative superfluous. Bic biros; a black telephone with a circular dial – it must be the last in London. The duty sergeant is interviewing a dark-haired suspect at the desk. They pause and watch me as I pass, measuring me up, both asking themselves the same primal question: 'Is he one of us?'

We climb two flights of stairs and push through the security door on each landing. The light increases as I ascend, until the synthetic glow of the ceiling tubes is drowned by sunlight pouring in through a barred window on the stairwell. Another corridor, several more closed doors, then a final, heavy door, with an empty slot where a nameplate should sit. One of my escorts knocks hard – a sharp knuckle rap, whose sound dies instantly, absorbed in the thick grained wood.

'Come in.'

The policeman pushes open the door and waves me forward. This is it – the end of the line. I want to hesitate, but, without thinking, I find myself inside the room and it is as though I have been pushed there by destiny – that any resistance would have been impossible. Evans is waiting, leaning against the front of a desk, arms folded, talking to a stranger in a cheap fawn suit who has the waxy complexion of the office worker. There's always a desk – turns any room into a workplace; it's the modern altar, a symbolic prop for interaction with abstracted man. The door closes behind me – the escort have completed their task: delivered the penitent to his confessor.

'Sit down, Bruton.' Direct as ever. When Evans speaks, the aggression is so evident that the brain receives the words as a bite. His presence is simple and brutal. His face reminds me of the station furniture – functional and no more. Eyebrows, eyes, nose, lips, chin: all present and correct, that's true – the right number of crude organs have been added to his face: good enough, no doubt, to carry out their sensory roles, but otherwise graceless flesh appendages. 'This is Inspector Hatton, Mr Bruton.'

'Of the Serious Fraud Office.' A hand extends across the table and reveals the policeman beneath the suit – a hard palm and strong grip, button cuffs which ride up to his wrist. 'Cigarette, Mr Bruton?'

'No, thanks.'

Hatton pulls out a box of Embassy, lights up, then waves a hand at Evans, who starts to speak. 'First things first, Mr Bruton: all charges against you have been dropped.'

'I see.' I don't.

Evans gives me a soulless stare, a tight-lipped attempt at a smile, then continues. 'The police, however, feel you could still be of some assistance in this case. Inspector Hatton has some questions for you.'

'Go on.' I walked into this room with the certain knowledge of my own guilt. I came looking for the hangman, but something in his words has stirred the impossible yet astonishing hope of freedom.

Their eyes meet, then Hatton clears his throat and rests his cigarette in the ashtray. Its blue smoke curls between us in the sunlight. 'I'm going to start by saying we owe you an apology.'

Evans twists away and exhales sharply. 'An explanation.'

'An apology.' Hatton is firm. 'We have infringed your rights, for what we now know to be the wrong reasons.'

'Go ahead.'

'I know that it's difficult for someone who's always believed in his own innocence to have to face others who assert the opposite, and that it may be even more difficult to adjust when your accusers suddenly agree with you, tell you you were right all along. It must seem hard to trust them, but I'm going to ask you to do just that. You see, Mr Bruton, at the time of your arrest the case against you was clear cut. All the available evidence pointed in the same direction – indicated that someone close to Sir Charles had tried to rob him. Because he was a solitary type, we were left with a limited pool of suspects, among whom you were the most likely. When other evidence emerged to corroborate this possibility, a warrant was granted for your arrest. I know you must resent the way it was carried out, but, remember, we had no idea what sort of man you were.'

Hatton pauses and looks anxiously at my face. I'm not sure

how I should appear. Aggrieved? Vengeful? The adrenaline's been firing round my body at such a speed I can barely stay seated, let alone compose my features. I came here to hear the executioner's song. Clasping my fingers to keep them still, I nod gently – which seems an acceptable response.

'Anyway, fresh evidence has emerged in the last twenty-four hours that not only exonerates you, Mr Bruton, but shows this case to be far more complicated than it first seemed. This new evidence also explains the involvement of my department, the Serious Fraud Office. We were contacted by Inspector Evans here when his investigations lighted on some discrepancies among the witness statements that pointed to the involvement of other individuals.'

'I'm very grateful.'

'Don't push it, Bruton.' Evans spits out the words.

Hatton glares at us in turn, then turns to me again. 'I don't expect you to become friends, but I hope you will understand how much Evans has done for you. Without his work, you would still be facing charges, Mr Bruton, with a better than evens chance of conviction.'

'As the wrong man?'

Evans shrugs his shoulders. He earns a look of reproach from Hatton and a finger raised in warning.

'Whatever the rights and wrongs of your treatment, remember it's now in the past. You're a free man. We know you were a close friend of Sir Charles, and as a gesture of good will, and in the hope you may come to see our side of the story, I'm to tell you what we know came about on the day of the assault. Some of the things I'm going to say are still subject to investigation, and I hope you will keep them confidential.'

I nod my head. *Free!* I'd like a cigarette but I can't trust my hands. I'm burning up with impatience. I want to get up and walk – no, run – run out through the streets, keep going until I'm clear of the city, clear of the suburbs, among fields and streams, then swim, sleep and dream – wake up in another year, a better time.

'At the time of the assault, Sir Charles had been examining a certain Mr Simon Norton. Does that name mean anything to you?'

Is this a trick? They're both watching me, waiting for speech.

'We met professionally.'

'How?'

I can feel their curiosity.

'He made me redundant about eight months ago. I was working for Constants, the technical writers, and we were taken over by Mardon Packaging. They instituted a cost-saving programme. I was part of it.'

'Did you see much of him?'

'No. He read me my notice – and that was it.'

'Did Sir Charles ever mention him to you?'

'No. He never spoke to me about his patients.'

'He didn't give any hint of the progress of his work on Norton?'

'No, none. Why? Is he involved?'

This time Evans replies. '*Was* involved, Mr Bruton.'

'I'm not sure I understand.'

Hatton glances at Evans, then resumes. 'Mr Norton attempted to kill himself last night. He was found in his car just off Berkeley Square. The park attendant noticed a pipe running from the exhaust to a window. The car's engine was running, but its doors were locked. Mr Norton was seen lying motionless across the rear seat. Fortunately, the man who discovered him had the nous to break the windscreen.'

'So he survived?'

'After a fashion. His car was fitted with a catalytic converter, which reduced the levels of toxin emission. However, his brain had been starved of oxygen for some time, and it seems that the damage suffered is irreversible.'

'In plain English, Bruton, Norton's a vegetable.'

'I'm sorry to hear it.'

Evans sniffs loudly.

'I understand you must be feeling impatient, Mr Bruton,'

235

Hatton continues swiftly. 'I would not be surprised if you also feel aggrieved. Please bear with me for a few more minutes and I'll explain our interest in Mr Norton and his connection with this affair. As it happens, my colleagues in the City of London Fraud Investigation Department have had an eye on Norton for some time. His association with a certain Donald Fletcher prompted our interest. We suspected the pair of running a share-rigging operation, but unfortunately much of the evidence lay outside the jurisdiction. Last week we believed we were close enough to issue a Section 2 notice – that's a legal way of calling them to account. On the same day, I received a call from Inspector Evans. He told me about Sir Charles, and that he believed Norton might have something to do with it. He'd just been interviewing a Miss Younghusband, and had found discrepancies in her statement. His suspicions were further roused when he received a tip-off from a source.'

Evans grunts and a slight smile is discernible – at least, the corners of his mouth twitch and he mutters something about persuading her to see the light.

'Inspector Evans then confronted her with these contradictions and she decided to come clean. She told us she'd been paid to immunise the alarms on the day of Sir Charles's assault. She implicated Norton in the arrangements. She confessed she'd been contacted on the telephone by an individual purporting to represent Mr Norton's interests. When we played her a recording of Norton's voice she identified it at once as the same man. She had agreed to feign illness and to keep out of the house. She was paid two thousand pounds in cash – an envelope was dropped through the letter box. I know this is painful for you, Mr Bruton – she gave us a less than flattering account of you when you were under suspicion.'

'I'm sure Evans taught her the error of her ways.'

Evans spins round, knocking over his coffee mug. He's clumsy, but very quick. Veins bulge on his wrestler's neck as he stares at me, striving for restraint. 'That was out of order, Bruton.'

'Leave it! For God's sake, leave it! Let it rest.' Hatton looks at us both, sees we seem settled, then continues. 'Anyway, this piece of evidence enabled us to tie our two investigations together. Norton had a motive for the attack: Sir Charles's assessment was vital to the success of his share-rigging ploy. He needed a positive result to get financing so the takeover could proceed: Mardon had to borrow money; the lenders demanded insurance. We believe that either singly, or in concert with others, he carried out the attack on Sir Charles. It was intended to appear as a break-in, and when that went wrong he came back to finish off the job. This put the banks on the spot, and, as he had calculated, they went ahead without the insurance. He confessed as much on his suicide tape.'

'He left a tape?'

Hatton looks at Evans, who shakes his head – doesn't want me to know any more. I can see Hatton measuring – how much is my good will worth? He's ticking off the causes of action in his head: wrongful arrest, false imprisonment – ten thousand pounds for the pair. Assault, myriad breaches of procedure – worth another ten. The cost of placating me could be very high. 'That's right. He dictated a suicide note before he attempted to kill himself. It's not a very pleasant record.'

'I would like to hear it,' I say.

Instantly, they turn to each other. If it were a battle of wills, I'd back Evans, but Hatton has the rank.

He faces me and snaps his fingers. 'Why?'

'Sir Charles Barrington was my closest friend. I feel I have a right to know.'

That seems to be the correct formula. Evans walks to the door, brushing against me as he passes. Voices in the corridor. Footsteps leave, hurry back, then Evans closes the door and crosses to the desk. A dictaphone emerges from his fist.

'He left two messages. I'll play you the second – the other

was for his family.' Hatton rests the machine on the desk top, winds forward and presses PLAY. All three of us hunch towards it, waiting for a voice to emerge.

'This is Simon Norton, financial director, Mardon Packaging Corporation. The following message must be passed to the . City of London Police. If possible, it should be copied to the Department of Trade and Industry. I have evidence as to the involvement of Donald Fletcher, chairman and chief executive officer, Mardon Packaging Corporation, in certain criminal activities. As I myself am also involved, I would ask that, in return for this testimony, all possible efforts are made to protect my wife and family from the unpleasantness that will emerge from these matters . . .' He pauses. The voice is surreal, totally surreal, as if he was already spirit. It exercises fascination beyond anything that a fictional representation could generate – all three of us know it's true – voyeurism, as opposed to fantasy. In the background there's a steady engine hum: the clock has started. 'I feel that I have betrayed the trust invested in me by my colleagues and contemporaries. I have behaved in a manner that is quite unacceptable, and wish to ensure that no one follows my example . . .'

'Like the true gentleman he is.' A stage whisper from Evans.

'On the tenth of December last year, I was approached by Donald Fletcher regarding the incorporation of some off-shore trusts. At first, he did not reveal their true purpose. We met at the company flat in Embankment Gardens, and I began to realise he was planning a fraud. I was flattered to be working so closely with him, and thought it was a sort of loyalty test. I suppose, in a way, I was in it even then . . .'

Norton's words are beginning to distort. Strange pauses appear mid-sentence. The confident, close-to-casual tone is melting into despair.

'That's the carbon monoxide,' says Evans.

Hatton leans across and whispers. 'He didn't allow for the effect it would have on his brain. I think he thought he'd

238

have time to say what he had to, then five minutes later it would all be over.'

'We put two shells in place to buy shares in Darlington Card. Their names, places of business and so on are set out in the memo I sent dated July the fourth to . . . I forget . . . the man black . . . Anyway, that year – no, this year . . . That's it . . . Younghusband!' He shouts out her name. It emerges, hard, complete, fired with hate from the increasingly slurred voice. He cries out accusations – she deceived, she betrayed – but his consonants are dissolving. He loses mastery of them one by one, and the words drift away. '. . . She was the ones, the one . . . she told them all the lies . . . and Hayessssssh!'

'Journalist at the *Chronicle*. Gave us our first lead.'

'Hayesssh!'

Inhuman. Hatton switches off the tape. I can feel the sweat trickle down my flank under my shirt. Hatton extends a cigarette across the desk. There's a tremor in his fingers. 'He finishes speaking shortly afterwards,' he says.

'I see.'

Hatton looks at his watch. 'That's about as far as we can help you, Mr Bruton.' For some reason, I'm loath to let it end like that. They're both watching me, waiting for me to stir. 'No doubt you'll follow this case with interest. I'm very sorry for what you've been through, and would hope you don't think too harshly of the force, or of my colleagues. We have a hard job to do, but we like to think we get it right in the end. You're a free man, Mr Bruton. Inspector Evans will take you to get your things.'

He stands up and sticks out his hand. I take it, hold it, feeling slightly numb. Free. Restored to the citizens' list. An individual again, free to mill around with all the million others in the city streets – to drift, unrecognised, in the uniform shoal: there we all are with our fish eyes and school instinct, our accumulated centuries of taboos against independence. It somehow makes me feel less of a man – resurrected, yet no longer human.

Evans is holding open the door. I cast a backward glance at Hatton, who smiles reassurance, then follow Evans along the corridor, back downstairs to the basement registration room where my belongings are waiting in sealed plastic bags. I sign for my possessions as each one is handed over. Last is the IWC watch – Lydia's anniversary gift. It's engraved on the reverse – our initials intertwined within a ring of hearts. The hands have stopped at ten to two. Has Travers told her? I can't stop staring at the stationary hands. They look like dark fingers on a pale face. The silent instrument accuses. Where will I go when they let me out?

A constable stamps downstairs, claps an arm round Evans's shoulder and whispers.

Evans nods his head in thanks and turns. 'We'll leave by the back entrance, Mr Bruton. There's someone waiting for you.'

I pick up my shoelaces and rethread them slowly. Evans is getting impatient. I straighten up and he takes me by the arm and propels me through a side door into a new corridor – a final entrance to the mausoleum. Our shadows dance together around its narrow walls as we proceed in single file under dim unglazed electric bulbs. Of course! Another cell. We're going nowhere. But Evans plods on ahead, reaches a staircase, rises tread by tread, pushes down the crossbar on a fire door and daylight floods in.

I rub my eyes more through reflex than need. I want to bolt, but I steady myself and instead slip a foot through the door – the swimmer who dips his toe before he dives.

'Very dainty, Bruton. Now fuck off.'

Power returns. I slam a fist into Evans's face. His head snaps back, surprised, but not hurt. A thin red serpent uncoils at the point of impact above his eyebrow. His face contorts and his body seems to swell. But he folds his arms and speaks softly, in not much more than a whisper. 'Goodbye, Bruton. Don't let me see you again. Leave London. Soon. Don't even get a parking ticket.' A push forward and the door slams.

The yard around me expands in size beyond infinity. I spin on my heels, receiving images of cobbles, vehicles, grey-blue sky, pools of oil-smeared water in the gutters. Then a car rolls into the courtyard, Lydia drops from its door at a run, looking at me with a mixture of hope and wonder and adoration.

18

11 June 1990, 8 a.m. Travelling westward, gathering speed. Clear at last of London, the summer trees flash past the car. Our ferry leaves at noon. A sleeping Lydia lies curled in the seat by my side. She has the enviable ability to compose herself in comfort in any position. She folds her body into the smallest shape, closes her eyes, then speeds away to some silent world. There's a sweet note of disproportion in her belly: four months to go, then Spain can welcome a new citizen. I hope it's a girl. If it's a girl it seems to me she'll have fewer of her father's traits and a better chance of being pure. Corruption too is hereditable. Even now, in the womb, the genes could be building dangerous paths. I wonder what it's like in there, inside Lydia. The unborn exist in a world of unimaginable purity. Their experience of humanity is limited to warm fluid and delicate tissue. It must be wonderful. It must be the most outrageous, dreamtime existence. Everything they touch is softer than the softest skin. Think of her, think of my daughter to be, reaching out a new-made finger to drift across the membranes of Lydia's interior. It will change. One day as she floats on her sunless sea, the waters will part and she'll be ejected, screaming, into a world of hard sensation.

I think it'll be another fine, dry summer. Already the fields are baked hard and dust cloaks the road. The windscreen is smeared in places by insects. Their crushed bodies refract the sunlight, creating diamond sparkles with vital oils. PORTSMOUTH 20, says the road sign. Sunshine and the scent of warm dry earth flood the convertible, while the wind-of-passage blows the baggage labels on our cases into a blur. In the background, soul music plays on the radio. It's interrupted for news on the half-hour. My hand reaches down for the controls and switches channels. It's been two months since I watched television, read a newspaper or listened to anything but music. I've been treated like a laboratory animal by the press: after death comes dissection.

We're far enough from London for the preset buttons to return nothing but static, so I spin the dial across the waveband. I find voices and listen for an instant.

'It must have been quite a trauma for you.'

'It was.'

I recognise that voice! My fingers shake as they try to locate the correct wavelength.

'But, as I understand, you've drawn strength from your charitable work?'

'That's right. The Mardon Foundation has expanded its role to help the underprivileged in all parts of the world.'

'So this morning's decision not to prosecute must have come as a relief?'

'I consider it a vindication. Remember, I, too, suffered in the fraud.'

'You lost a good deal of money.'

'It wasn't the loss that hurt me. It was rather that I'd been betrayed by people I trusted. But, at last, I'll be able to put it all behind me. I've found a new direction for my skills.'

'So from now on, we can associate the name of Donald Fletcher with charity?'

'Exactly.'

The interview ends in applause. I turn off the radio and concentrate on driving, convinced I've just been witness to a further illusion. In the past this might have made me indignant, but today I'm indifferent. We are all dreaming.

The road ahead widens into three lanes and slants downhill. Instinctively, I accelerate. Sometimes, driving in an open car can feel like flying – and that's it: we imagine we can fly away. All city dwellers preserve a dream of freedom, and it seems so real too – they believe, they just *know*, that one day they'll be born again into a second state of innocence, free to wander barefoot through a new Eden. Let them enjoy their delusions of salvation! Let them spill their tears on the feet of their silent hardwood idols, their plaster saints.' They're right to build Paradise conveniently out of reach – make it beautiful, really, truly, achingly so, but a matter for the dead alone to discover. You see, there's no God, no Saviour, whose forgiving hand can wipe clean the past. Life is no proving ground for eternity. A man lives with his actions until he dies and is forgotten. Charles knew that much. Perhaps he knew, too, that I would hit him, or, at least, hoped as much when he provoked me. I think he knew, but at the same time he wanted it, he invited me to act. He was tired and old and dying, waiting for the blade.

A final turn and the horizon opens out in front of me. There's a mass of buildings, threaded with miniature roads, along which vehicles race, windscreens flashing in the morning sun. The structures multiply around the port, an ugly agglomeration of artificial shapes: concrete rectangles, punctured with rows of coloured glass. Beyond them waits the sea.

FREE TO TRADE

Michael Ridpath

Paul Murray is a junior bond trader. New to the job, he's keen to make a good impression – but how far does he have to go?

When the corpse of Debbie Chater, a vivacious colleague, is found floating in the Thames, Paul's world is turned upside down.

And when his crusade for an explanation results in his being framed for murder, accused of insider trading and left to find twenty million dollars by lunchtime, Paul's got to find some answers – fast – before someone else makes a killing.

'This is *Bonfire of the Vanities* with attitude' – *The Times*

'A gripping story of murder, corruption and intrigue . . . the thriller everyone has been waiting for' – *Daily Telegraph*

ARMED AND DANGEROUS

James Kennedy

Superintendent Gilston sighed and shifted noisily in his chair. 'You had better accept it, you know. You have a mole in M15, burrowing away at the foundations of the IRA's peace process.'

But accept it or not, June Maybury has more urgent issues to deal with. Like a violent jail-brake which has left four IRA members on the run, desperate to complete the mission their imprisonment postponed. And rumour has it the plan involves an attack on the Crown.

If they succeed, the fragile peace in Northen Ireland will be shattered – an appalling thought, especially when those who are meant to uphold the peace seem to be implicated at the very heart of the struggle . . .

Gripping fiction meets terrifying fact in James Kennedy's thrilling debut novel of peace, power and the awful politics of fear.

'Fast pace, well maintained tension and the topicality of the theme makes it read like today's headlines' – *Irish Times*

'Kennedy cranks up the suspense in this pacy thriller, leaving a trail of corpses in its wake as it speeds towards a major catastrophe in London . . . *Armed and Dangerous* is a real page-turner' – *Belfast Telegraph*

KOLYMSKY HEIGHTS

Lionel Davidson

Kolymsky Heights. A Siberian permafrost hell lost in endless night, the perfect setting for an underground Russian research station. One so secret it doesn't officially exist. Once there, scientists cannot leave. But someone has got a message out to the West – a message summoning the only man alive capable of achieving the impossible

'A fabulous thriller . . . a red-hot adventure with a stunningly different hero' – *Today*

'Spectacular . . . a breathless story of fear and courage' – *Daily Telegraph*

'A tremendous thriller . . . warmth, love, heartstopping action' – *Observer*

'A sustained cliffhanger – brilliantly imagined, thrilling, painfully plausible' – *Literary Review*

'The book is a triumph' – *Sunday Times*

THE SILENCE OF THE LAMBS

Thomas Harris

The most frightening book you'll ever read.

There's a killer on the loose who knows that beauty is only skin deep, and a trainee investigator who's trying to save her own hide.

The only man who can help is locked in an asylum. But he's willing to put a brave face on – if it will help him escape.

'Thrillers don't come any better than this . . . razor sharp entertainment, beautifully constructed and brilliantly written. It takes us to places in the mind where few writers have the talent or sheer nerve to venture' – Clive Baker

'The best book I've read for a very long time . . . subtle, horrific and splendid' – Roald Dahl

A Selected List of Thrillers available from Mandarin

While every effort is made to keep prices low, it is sometimes necessary to increase prices at short notice. Mandarin Paperbacks reserves the right to show new retail prices on covers which may differ from those previously advertised in the text or elsewhere.

The prices shown below were correct at the time of going to press.

☐ 7493 1972 0	**The Cruelty of Morning**	Hilary Bonner	£4.99
☐ 7493 1528 8	**The Minstrel Boy**	Richard Crawford	£5.99
☐ 7493 1713 2	**Kolymsky Heights**	Lionel Davidson	£5.99
☐ 7493 3665 X	**Primal Fear**	William Diehl	£5.99
☐ 7493 2062 1	**Show of Evil**	William Diehl	£5.99
☐ 7493 2112 1	**Gone Wild**	James Hall	£5.99
☐ 7493 1749 3	**Mean High Tide**	James Hall	£4.99
☐ 7493 0054 X	**The Silence of the Lambs**	Thomas Harris	£5.99
☐ 7493 1400 1	**Carriers**	Patrick Lynch	£5.99
☐ 7493 1964 X	**I'm Coming to Get You**	David Ralph Martin	£5.99
☐ 7493 1905 4	**Free to Trade**	Michael Ridpath	£5.99
☐ 7493 1968 2	**The Tick Tock Man**	Terence Strong	£4.99
☐ 7493 2182 2	**The Mortgage**	Sabin Willett	£5.99

ALL MANDARIN BOOKS ARE AVAILABLE THROUGH MAIL ORDER OR FROM YOUR LOCAL BOOKSHOP AND NEWSAGENT.

PLEASE SEND CHEQUE/EUROCHEQUE/POSTAL ORDER (STERLING ONLY) ACCESS, VISA, DINERS CARD, SWITCH, AMEX OR MASTERCARD.

EXPIRY DATE .... SIGNATURE ....

PLEASE ALLOW 75 PENCE PER BOOK FOR POST AND PACKING U.K.

OVERSEAS CUSTOMERS PLEASE ALLOW £1.00 PER COPY FOR POST AND PACKING.

ALL ORDERS TO:

MANDARIN BOOKS, BOOKS BY POST, TBS LIMITED, THE BOOK SERVICE, COLCHESTER ROAD, FREIGHTING GREEN, COLCHESTER, ESSEX CO7 7DW.

NAME ....

ADDRESS ....

....

Please allow 28 days for delivery. Please tick box if you do not wish to receive any additional information ☐

Prices and availability subject to change without notice.